In My Father's Image

Life in the Shadows of a Local Legend

by
R B Conroy

CCB Publishing
British Columbia, Canada

In My Father's Image: Life in the Shadows of a Local Legend

Copyright ©2009, 2015 by R B Conroy
ISBN-13   978-1-926585-55-0
First Edition, revised (2015)

Library and Archives Canada Cataloguing in Publication
Conroy, R B, 1944-, author
In my father's image : life in the shadows of a local legend /
by R B Conroy. -- First edition.
Issued in print and electronic formats.
ISBN 978-1-926585-55-0 (pbk.).--ISBN 978-1-927360-25-5 (pdf)
I. Title.
PS3603.O57I5 2009   813'.6   C2009-905585-6

Cover illustration by Kim Gause: dklagause@embarqmail.com
Author photo by Julie DuBois: www.sunrisephoto.com

Publisher: CCB Publishing
              British Columbia, Canada
              www.ccbpublishing.com

WITH LOVE TO MY WIFE CHERYL,

Thank you for your unwavering support.

and

TO SUE ELLEN ARBUCKLE,

Your knowledge and expertise were invaluable.

-Letting go lifts the spirit

and restores the soul-

Prologue

It had been a long evening, and yet the black tie only crowd seemed to be coming alive; a sense of excitement filled the air. The lanky master of ceremonies paused and shuffled through some papers on the podium. He cleared his throat and addressed the waiting audience. "Ladies and gentlemen, this evening has gotten away from us, so I will make this as short as possible. Our final inductee into this year's Hall scored 2062 points during his impressive high school career. In his senior year he led his Maple City Giants to a 24-4 record and ended the season with an unforgettable victory over the highly favored and undefeated Indianapolis Tech Titans in the final game of the Indiana High School Basketball Championship. His 32 points in the final game still stands as the record to this day."

The emcee smiles broadly. "I'm sure there are a few in this crowd who remember that game." He paused and listened as applause erupted throughout the room.

"During his phenomenal senior year, he led his Giants to a championship in the always tough North Central Conference, averaging 28.7 points in league play. In his senior year, this versatile athlete was voted First Team Allstate in football and he set a state broad jump record that stood for seventeen years. Members and honored guests, I will waste no time. I give to you our final inductee this evening, Mr. Beau Kinsey. Stand up, Beau! You are now a member of the Indiana High School Basketball Hall of Fame! Stand up!"

A tall handsome man slowly stood up in the back of the large banquet room in the posh Indianapolis Hilton Hotel. The crowd rose to their feet, giving him a standing ovation. The cheers continued as the smiling inductee waved and nodded to his enthusiastic fans. The emcee's hand fell over the mike, he turned to those seated next to him at the head table and exclaimed, "They haven't forgotten!"

Moments later, the gavel slammed ending the lengthy ceremony. The tired crowd wasted no time exiting the room. The last honoree shook hands with a few lingering fans, gulped down the remnants of a martini, loosened his tie, and ducked out a side door into the dark Indianapolis night.

Chapter 1

Stepping out of the rental car parked next to a dense yellowing cornfield, he listened as long leaves rattled in the brisk September breeze. Filled with a rising sense of nostalgia, he stood still for a moment surveying the scene around him. He glanced up at the faded letters on a nearby street sign that read Rolling Acres Road. He looked past the tilted sign and up a winding lane at the red brick farmhouse of a childhood friend. It appeared much smaller than he remembered. Above the weathered garage door stood a graying backboard with a tattered net dangling from a rusty rim. To the west, gray smoke belched from giant chimneys and faded into the afternoon sky. *I'm home—it feels like home.*

"Excuse me." He was brought out of his evocative trance by a lady's soft voice. She smiled and led several people past him on the slanted roadside. The quiet country lane was turning into a parking lot of last resort for the overflow crowd. Straightening his tie, he hurried to blend in with the fast moving latecomers smiling politely and nodding at a few recognizable faces.

He looked both ways and then hustled across the dusty road, the gravel crunching beneath his black wingtips. Once across the well-worn roadway, he turned and ducked away from the pack and darted down a narrow clay pathway that led through a wooded area of white birch, soft maples, and evergreens—a little known shortcut from his childhood days.

He heard voices up ahead. *Someone else knows the shortcut*, he thought. Skirting around the trunk of a large maple, he was surprised to see his younger sister, Maggie, standing and talking to someone on the path ahead. He cleared his throat to get her attention. She glanced back at him. Her pretty face instantly broke into a smile. She excused herself from her companion and walked briskly toward him with her thin arms outstretched. She looked lovely in her pink cotton dress and matching pearl necklace and earrings. They shared a warm embrace.

"Oh, Danny, I'm so glad you're here. How are you?"

"As good as can be expected, and how's Maggie?"

"Under the circumstances, not too bad," she groaned. She gently squeezed his arms and stepped back. "That was Casey Lund I was talking with just now. Remember her, the police chief's daughter?" Maggie was making small talk to avoid getting too emotional. She was always one to hide her feelings. Her reluctance to face her emotions right now was okay with Dan.

"Yes, she was younger, but I remember her. Sorry for interrupting."

"No problem, I think she was ready to get going anyway. So how's the banking business?"

"Fine," he replied.

"Just fine? I hear you're the big boss now!" She flashed that cute little grin he remembered so well.

"I guess so," he said humbly.

"Were you expecting the promotion?" She looked at him inquisitively, begging more information.

"Not really. I think they were desperate and needed somebody for the job. I happened to be standing near the water cooler the day my boss retired. He walked out of his office, looked around, didn't see anyone else, so he gave the job to me," he replied. "What about you? How's teaching going? Still second grade?" Dan was anxious to change the subject.

"Okay. Class sizes are too big and there are never enough hours in the day, but I'm struggling along. And yes, it's still the second grade."

They both turned and continued walking down the well-grooved pathway. Maggie slid her hand under his arm.

"Feeling okay?" Dan looked intently at his sis.

"Yeah, I'm on some new meds—only missed twelve days last year."

"Oh, Maggie, that's great!" Dan patted her hand. She pulled in closer, leaning on his shoulder as they navigated the narrow pathway.

"Know what, Dan?"

"What, Sis?"

"You've been a problem for me all my life, ya know."

"Oh yeah?"

"Yeah, I've been divorced three times, all because I can't find anyone as wonderful as that stupid big brother of mine." She bumped her head against his shoulder playfully.

Dan chuckled nervously, "Better not ask Ann about that one."

"Are you kidding? She'd give me a big thumbs up."

"More likely it would be a thumb in the eye," Dan joked.

Maggie laughed heartily.

The secret passageway suddenly came to an end and the two siblings found themselves merging back with the other folks on the regular sidewalk. Suddenly their discussion was interrupted by a familiar voice.

"Dan! How are you?"

Dan glanced to his left and smiled, "Why, Mr. Pruitt, it's so good to see you! How are you?" Dan vigorously shook the outreached hand of his beloved high school history teacher.

"Fine, thank you. I'm retired and loving every minute of it. Congrats on your promotion; the local paper carried an article."

"Oh, thank you," Dan replied, "You remember Maggie, don't you?" Dan was once again anxious to change the focus.

"Why, of course I do! One of the best students I ever had! Much smarter than you, my boy," he said with a sly grin. He gave Maggie a quick hug.

"You're as pretty as ever."

"Why, thank you, Mr. Pruitt,"

"Glen, please call me Glen."

"Okay, Glen."

"You'll always be Mr. Pruitt to me," Dan chimed in.

"You never were one for change, Dan. I remember I rearranged the seating chart one time and you pouted for two days." The slender teacher laughed enthusiastically.

Dan shook his head and grinned shyly.

"Well, I best be going. The wife's getting away," Mr. Pruitt said quickly. "Please accept my condolences and I hope I see you later!" He nodded and hurried off.

"Thanks, and I hope so too," Dan shouted at the departing educator.

"He's still wearing those baggy suits and ugly ties. I guess some things never change," Maggie grinned.

"Yeah, I guess not."

He and Maggie rounded the final corner next to the wooded area. Dan paused. His pulse quickened as the little church that his family had attended every Sunday as a child suddenly came into full view. Amazingly, it still looked pretty much the same as it had so many years ago. The tiny maple tree that his Sunday school class had planted in the side yard was still there, but now it was very tall and full, and showing its brilliant fall colors. Other than the tree, little had changed. The beautiful high steeple on the church still reached for the sky above a green shingled roof. The freshly painted white wood siding was aglow, and the building's lovely array of stained glass windows continued to present a myriad of dazzling colors to those approaching. The small octagon window, Dan's favorite, was still positioned above the front entry and featured the Lord's hands pushing open and welcoming all.

Inexplicably, Maggie stopped on the path at the exact same moment as Dan. Both were overcome by the strong emotions triggered by the familiar scene. The two of them suddenly turned and fell into each other's arms, sobbing quietly. Just a few seconds into the warm embrace, Dan felt a sharp tap on his shoulder. He turned to see his older brother Mark standing next to them. Without hesitating he threw his arm around the thick neck of his stocky sibling and pulled him into the huddle. Mark gave no resistance as they all stood sobbing unashamedly, while latecomers filed past them mumbling their regrets.

The last to join the tearful embrace, Mark was the first to step back. His square face broke into a rather weak smile, "How's my smart-ass little bro?" he asked.

"I'm hanging in there, and how about you, Mark?"

"I've been better."

"Where's Ellen and the girls?

"They're inside with Ann and your two. Ann asked me to come out and try to find you. She is worried."

"I'll bet, we'd better get in there," Dan replied.

The three offspring of the legendary Beau Kinsey, collected their emotions and hustled toward the church.

On the way to the front door of the church, Dan felt compelled to explain his tardiness. "It was hell waiting in that airport in Paris the past couple days," he said abruptly.

"Ann said something about that. What happened?" Mark asked.

"After I got the call about Dad on Monday, I left my merger meetings and rushed to the airport to grab a flight home, only to find that the airport employees had decided to go on strike. They were able to open a few terminals yesterday, but the only flight I could get was to Cleveland via New York."

"The dreaded layovers," Mark groaned.

"Yeah, and I had to shave and clean up in one of

those tiny restrooms at the Cleveland terminal this morning. After that, I rented a car at the airport and made the long drive home. How do I look?" Dan stopped. He playfully adjusted his tie and smiled at his two siblings.

"Handsome, as usual," Maggie smiled.

"Not too bad for a skinny kid," Mark joked.

"Thanks to both of you for taking care of the arrangements. I'm so sorry I couldn't be here to help."

"No problem," Mark said. "Maggie did most of it. I was along for the ride. And as usual, Ann was a big help. She covered your butt again."

"I really do appreciate it."

Arriving at the front entrance, Dan observed two large tents next to the church that had been constructed to handle the possible overflow from the sanctuary. Long lines were already forming outside the tents.

"He was a popular guy," an observant Maggie said softly. Dan and Mark nodded their head in agreement.

Dan's eyes suddenly widened. "Can you believe it?" he said quietly. "Pastor Jenkins is still up there greeting people!"

"Now that's amazing," Mark exclaimed. "He has to be eighty years old."

"Eighty-three to be exact, and I have exceptionally good hearing for a man my age." Pastor Jenkins grinned mischievously at the now crimson-faced Mark.

"Good to see you again, Mark." The nattily dressed old man stepped toward Mark and reached his bony hand forward for a shake.

"Well, uh, hello again, Pastor Jenkins," Mark murmured sheepishly.

"And how are Danny and Maggie?"

Dan extended his hand, "Fine, sir, and it's so good to see you, Pastor Jenkins."

"Hello, Pastor," Maggie said sincerely.

"Hello to all of you, and I am sorry to hurry you, but we need to get the service started, so please come in. Of course, your family is seated at the front."

The pastor clasped firmly onto Dan's hand, pulling him toward the sanctuary. "I'm so deeply sorry for your loss. Please accept my sincerest condolences."

"Thank you, sir," Dan replied. He hesitated for a moment and then stepped over the threshold into the old church. He took a second to glance down at the bottom of the dark frame of the massive door. He was anxious to see if somehow thirty years later, they were still there.

"Oh my!" he murmured under his breath as he looked down. The old markings had been varnished over several times, but they were still visible. The carved initials "d. k. + a. h." could still be seen. The crude etchings Dan had made with his little pocketknife so many years ago had stood the test of time. *Ann will love this.*

"Hurry up, Dan," Maggie urged.

"Oh yes, sorry," Dan responded, slightly annoyed at her for interrupting his pleasant memory.

Entering the sanctuary, Dan looked around at the standing room only crowd. He spotted Ann and the girls sitting on the front row. His lovely Ann turned toward him and smiled, mouthing the words, "Over here." She pointed to the empty seats next to her. Dan hurried over and sat down, and looked over at his daughters, Ali and Meghan. Their pretty faces were stained with tears, but they smiled bravely at their father. It was obvious their hearts were breaking.

Maggie squeezed into the seat next to Dan, and Mark filled the empty spot next to his family. They all settled in for what they all knew would be a long service with the loquacious Pastor Jenkins at the helm.

Several members of Dan's extended family leaned forward from behind, tapped Dan on the shoulder, and whispered their condolences in his ear. A few seconds later, the familiar sounds of the popular old Christian spiritual, "Back in His Arms Again," came blaring forth from the old wooden pipe organ that occupied a good share of the northeast corner of the spacious sanctuary. Dan watched as the energetic organist swayed from side to side, just as he did so many years ago.

Dan searched the front row. "Where's Grandma?" he asked.

"She's a little under the weather, nothing serious. She said she'll be at the get-together after the funeral," Ann whispered. She lifted her finger to her lips and nodded toward the front. A slightly sheepish Dan nodded in agreement and fell back against the wooden pew.

Pastor Jenkins, his shoulders slumped by his eighty-three years, walked briskly across the stage to the podium. He lifted his shaking hand, and the music abruptly stopped.

Pastor Jenkins began. "In my more than fifty years as pastor of First Christian Church, I have conducted a mountain of services—more than I could ever remember; but my dear friends, this is by far and away one of the most difficult services I will ever perform.

Today we lay to rest a man who has been a beacon of light in our fine community." Many heads in the large crowd nodded in agreement.

"Beau Kinsey was a God-fearing man, a man who was known and loved by every single person in this beautiful sanctuary. A man revered but not defined by his amazing accomplishments in the athletic arena. Who among us will ever forget that State Championship game at Butler Field House? He thrilled us all that day."

Pastor Jenkins continued on with what Dan knew would be a very lengthy speech about his popular father and his athletic accomplishments. The predictable ramblings by the aging cleric began to recede into the background as the middle son soon found himself thinking back to his childhood days when an unexpected tragedy catapulted his legendary father and family into a life-changing crisis, a crisis that would drive their already self-absorbed father deeper into his own troubled world. Powerful feelings were stirring inside Dan and taking him back to those early days when he was a young boy growing up in the basketball-crazy community of Maple City, Indiana.

Chapter 2

"Pass the cereal, dummy," Mark demanded as he reached over and cracked his little brother on the head with his two middle fingers.

"Cut it out, Mark," Danny yelled. He swiped wildly at Mark's hand in a futile gesture.

Little five-year-old Maggie leaned forward on her chair, "Pick on someone your own size, Mark!" Her face was contorted with rage. She yanked her spoon out of the cereal bowl and waved it at her older brother. Beads of milk splattered across the table. "You're fourteen, and Danny's only twelve!"

"Oh, poor little Danny's only twelve," Mark leaned over and ran his fingers through Danny's dark, wavy hair.

Finally Danny had reached his breaking point. Fist doubled, he stood and threw a punch in the direction of his tormenter. Mark ducked just in time, mocking in delight as Danny's fist passed harmlessly over his head.

"Nice try, nimrod. Why don't . . ."

"You boys settle down in there, right now!" Mark

was interrupted by his mother's firm but kind voice.

The always obedient Danny sat down immediately at the sound of his mother's voice. Mark smirked and shot his tongue out at Danny.

The feisty Maggie glared at her insolent big brother.

"I swear, you boys are going to put me in my grave with all of this fighting," she admonished as she entered the kitchen.

Their mom slid a bowl of peaches and bananas on the table and gently patted Maggie on the head. Danny smiled at his pretty mother. He thought she was beautiful. He thought she looked just like a movie star he saw in one of her movie magazines, an actress named Elizabeth somebody. He could never remember her last name.

"Eat up, children. It's seven-thirty and you have to leave to catch the bus in ten minutes." Danny looked starry eyed at his pretty mom, his eyebrows high, chin on hand.

"Did you get your math done last night, Danny?"

Danny's expression changed quickly.

"Not all of it," he whimpered.

"How much is not all of it?" his mother pressed.

Danny stared silently at his plate.

"He didn't do any of it!" Mark gloated in delight. "That's why he's not talking. I got all of mine done!"

"Is that true, Danny?" his mom asked. She walked around the table and laid her hand on his thin shoulders.

Danny's head bobbed up and down.

His mom gently slid her hand off his shoulders. "You're a good boy, Danny, but you have to do better on your homework. You'll have to stay in after school until you get it done."

"Okay," Danny whispered with resignation. Mark giggled with pleasure at his younger sibling's misfortune.

"If you think that's so funny, Mark, you can help me with the canning after school. The garden vegetables are ready for canning and I need help with them, so hurry home after school."

Mark looked at his mother in shocked disbelief. "Canning! I don't wanna do canning! Everybody's going to play basketball after school at Mikey Smith's house!" The wide eyed boy was incredulous. He continued to glare at his mother and then he whispered "I hate you," under his breath.

"Maybe this will teach you to be nice to your little brother." His mom's left eyebrow lifted just a little when she looked over at the defiant boy. "And, I want you to go out right now and put up that extension ladder. I don't know how to work that darn thing and I have to get the stuff for canning down from the loft. I'll prepare the tomatoes while you're at school and you can put the lids on and seal them when you get home."

Danny turned his head slightly and grinned at his big brother. A defiant Mark scowled. He bounced his spoon on the table, got up and stomped out to the garage. He glanced at his mom out of the corner of his eye. "I hate you," he mumbled again. Busy buttering toast for Maggie, his mother didn't hear him.

"Mom?"

"Yes, Maggie."

"Kimberly Cain called me a little stinker yesterday at school."

"Why . . . oh my! That's not nice at all." Her mom

covered her mouth to hide a small grin.

"It's not funny, Mom!" an indignant Maggie shouted at her tickled mom. "I'm not a stinker."

"Oh, I know you certainly aren't, darling. I was smiling because I thought of something funny one of my friends told me yesterday, that's all. Why, that Kimberly should be ashamed of herself!"

Mom walked back toward the kitchen to begin washing the dishes. With narrowed eyes, Maggie watched her mom's face closely for any reaction. Satisfied that her mom wasn't smiling any longer, Maggie went back to eating her cereal.

A short time later, Mark returned from the garage, shoulders slumped, head hanging. He trudged over and dropped in his chair. "Ladder's up," he growled.

"Why, thank you, Mark, I appreciate it. See you after school, dear."

"I hear the bus!" Maggie shouted. "It's over by the Carlton's."

"Finish your breakfast and get going. You've only got a few minutes," Mom yelled. "Don't forget your books!"

After a couple quick bites of cereal, the children jumped up to leave. Snatching their books off the little wood table in the corner of the kitchen, they raced through the living room and out the front door. They blended in with other neighborhood kids running past on the front sidewalk. Approaching the bus, the scrambling horde of kids put their hands over their ears to shield them from the loud air brakes. With ears covered, they stood by the door of the bus waiting, like a herd of wildebeests about to cross a river.

The painstakingly slow accordion-like doors finally opened allowing them to rush up the steps into the bus, screaming and shoving and fighting for the best seat. The Kinsey kids were led by Mark who elbowed his way through the crowded bus to their favorite seats at the back of the bus. Danny and Maggie, with their index fingers hooked in Mark's belt loops, held on for dear life. Nobody messed with Mark. He always got the seat he wanted. Once seated, they all turned to look out the window and wave good-bye to their mom who was standing and waving by the front door of their house.

Danny looked over at Mark, "I heard what you said to Mom."

"I didn't say anything, Danny," Mark stared menacingly at his little brother.

"Yes, you did. You said you hated her two times."

"You better keep your mouth shut, Danny, or you're gonna get it!" Mark doubled his fist and waved it in front of his younger brother's face.

Danny bounced back against the hard seat and stared straight ahead.

"Our mommy's nice! You shouldn't have said that!" Maggie shouted.

Mark showed little Maggie the same fist. "You'd better be quiet, too!"

Maggie stared hard at him for a few seconds and then also fell back against the seat. Neither of them wanted any part of an irritated Mark.

The bus suddenly jerked to a stop and the door slowly opened letting in more boisterous kids. Finally, after several more stops the packed bus arrived at the school. The door banged open for the last time with the kids once again fighting to get out of the bus. Mark jumped over his little brother and sister and led the charge. With the strong Mark leading the way, the Kinsey kids got off the bus first and raced toward the front doors of the old school building.

Shoulder low, Mark pushed through the heavy metal door and rushed into the large brick schoolhouse. His brother and sister were close behind him and scrambling to keep up. The bright green vestibule spread out before them as they joined in with the flood of children pouring in from the other doors. The sounds were deafening. The morning ritual was in full swing with a thunderous herd of clamorous children flowing out of the foyer into the main hall.

Danny patted Maggie on the head, "Bye, Maggie."

"Bye, Danny! Bye, Mark!" little Maggie yelled.

"Bye, Sis," Mark said looking straight ahead.

Mark grabbed Danny's arm and gave him a little shove. "Don't forget what I said, barf-bag."

Glaring defiantly at his big brother, Danny stumbled for a second, righted himself, and then pivoted on the cement floor and rushed to find his locker.

He arrived at his locker, grasped the lock and slowly turned the dial left to nineteen, right to seven, and then left one full turn to fourteen. The lock popped open. He reached in and grabbed his math book, while tossing the other books on the bottom of the locker. Slamming the locker shut, Danny hurriedly locked it and ran toward the south wing, which was located at the far end of the school. It was the same desperate race each day to get to his mathematics class on time.

Striding through the hallway, he glanced down at his

math book to make sure he had his assignment. His eyes widened. The crinkled corners of his math papers were not sticking out from the book. He had left his assignment in his locker. Frightened that he would have to suffer through a chewing out from an angry teacher, he turned around and bolted back to his locker. Getting close, he slid on his knees the last few feet. He grabbed the shiny lock firmly in his sweaty hand. Nineteen, seven, fourteen; he yanked, but the lock didn't open. A bolt of fear shot up his spine; a vision of his teacher's angry face popped into his mind. For some reason, the dial was sticking around the last number, fourteen, causing the dial to jump to fifteen or sixteen. With trembling hands, he grabbed the lock again. His heart was in his throat as he wrapped his fingers securely around the lock and gave it a hard yank. Danny felt a flood of relief when the lock fell open. He quickly reached inside, grabbed his math papers and resumed the daily race to the math wing.

The hall was empty now and was eerily quiet. The only sound was the sound of Danny's heels clicking on the tile floor. The silence was broken when one of the large tardy bells that lined the narrow hall blasted just above his head. *Oh no, I'm dead,* he thought.

With his panic growing, he charged along the darkened hallway to Room 224. Just before entering the room, he slowed to a walk in an effort to avoid attracting attention. Walking nonchalantly down the aisle to his desk, he slid quickly into his seat and casually glanced towards the front of the room. Mr. Bolton was browsing through their textbook. For a glorious moment Danny thought he had escaped the eye of his teacher and would be able to avoid his possible execution. His hopes were soon dashed.

Mr. Bolton slowly closed the book. His small beady eyes peered over the top of dark horn rimmed glasses toward a terrified Danny. He slowly pushed his chair back from behind the large oak desk and stood. With his eyes still locked on Danny, he addressed the class.

"Students, I want you to complete problems one through six at the end of chapter seven. You have twenty minutes to finish the task."

The stern man stepped out from behind his desk and walked directly towards Danny. Beads of perspiration began to pop out on Danny's forehead; a sense of dread filled him.

Twenty minutes—plenty of time to torture me, Danny fantasized as Mr. Bolton drew closer. His black leather shoes made a weird creaking sound on the tile floor with each terrifying step down the aisle. Afraid to look up, Danny's eyes were glued to the scary shoes. Abruptly the shoes stopped. They were side by side directly in front of his desk. Danny slowly lifted his frightened eyes off the shoes and followed the teacher's deeply creased pant leg, past his blood-red tie and up to his narrow devilish face.

"Daniel!"

"Y . . . yes sir." His voice sounded unfamiliar, as if he were in an echo chamber or more appropriately, a terror chamber.

"I do believe you have a little of your father in you. I saw you out of the side door, and the way you flew down the hall just now was quiet impressive. Your father, Beau, was the fastest human being I've ever seen.

He could run like the wind and he was never tardy. You, my friend, have been tardy five times this term alone! I do believe it's time I have a talk with your father about this."

Oh no, not my father. Anyone but my father. Danny's heart was now truly in his throat—a sense of panic surged through him. He had to do something.

"I promise I'll never be late again, I promise!" he pled frantically while looking into Mr. Bolton's dark, penetrating eyes. He was searching for any sign of sympathy or kindness. He found none.

Mr. Bolton hesitated for what seemed an eternity, continuing to rub his bony thumb back and forth across his pointed chin. Finally he spoke; the death sentence was coming.

"I won't tell your father on one condition, Daniel."

For some unknown reason, his life was apparently going to be spared. Danny felt a glimmer of hope. He looked up, eyes wide with anticipation.

"I want you to run the dashes in the sixth grade track meet next week. Mr. Jones' class beat us last year, and I don't want that to happen again. I'm certain that if you can run anywhere near as fast as your father, you will win the dashes hands down." Mr. Bolton's brow furrowed. He made a weird groaning sound, kind of like an angry bear and waited for Danny's reply.

Danny looked up and beamed. "I'll run all the races! You name it and I'll run it. And yes, I am fast, sir, I've never lost a race on the playground!"

"Wonderful! And just the dashes will be fine," Mr. Bolton replied. "Now, you'd better get busy on those math questions. There's only about fifteen minutes of work time left."

Danny reached down and grabbed his math book with all the zest and enthusiasm of a man just spared the guillotine. His textbook flew open, his little hand pushed through the pages to chapter seven. He opened his notebook and began scribbling down the answers with tremendous vigor.

The remainder of the class went by quickly with Danny's arm shooting in the air several times to volunteer an answer.

"Alright students, class is almost over. Do the review questions at the back of chapter eight for tomorrow," Mr. Bolton ordered.

Books closed and desk tops banged shut as the shrill sound of the period ending bell blasted into the room.

With a new lease on life, Danny hurried from the room. Slipping momentarily on the freshly waxed hall floor outside the classroom, he righted himself and then flew full gallop down the hallway to his next class.

Chapter 3

"No running in the hallway, Daniel," the stern hall monitor shouted.

Danny slowed to a walk until he was out of view of the monitor and then he was off to the races again. He didn't want to be late for study hall after the scary run-in he had just had with Mr. Bolton.

"Watch out Danny!" Danny felt a shoe hit his lower leg. He stumbled for a second and then was back to full stride. He turned and waved his fist at his grinning antagonist. "Jam-it, Wilcox!"

The hallway reverberated with the sound of metal locker doors banging shut as Danny raced down the wide hall. He shouted "hi" at several passing friends and fought desperately to keep his books from sliding out from under his arm. Finally, he could see his destination ahead, room number 108. He slowed to a fast walk for the last fifty feet and then ducked through the open doorway. He had made it on time.

He paused and looked around the room. His heartbeat was accelerating, but only partly from running.

There was something else making his heart beat rapidly and it wasn't long before he spotted her sitting at her desk and looking like a million dollars. He looked at the seat next to her and he couldn't believe it—the chair was empty. Grinning broadly, he walked immediately toward the unoccupied seat.

On the way to the seat, he unexpectedly saw something out of the corner of his eye. *Oh no!* he thought, it was his nemeses, Tubby Shelton, charging from the back of the aisle toward the empty seat. Danny knew he had to move quickly. He ran headfirst from the front of the aisle with Tubby coming from the back. The hard charging boys both reached the vacant seat at the same time and dove for the seat. Danny's skinny body crashed hard into Tubby's enormous stomach.

"You're gonna get it, Danny!" Tubby screeched, throwing his bulbous body toward the empty seat.

Danny knifed forward, pushing with all his might. Surprisingly, he was able to squeeze between Tubby's protruding midsection and the corner of the empty seat. With one last monumental effort, he pushed free of Tubby's belly and fell safely into the opening. He quickly turned and smiled at the lovely Ann. Then he winced in pain as an angry Tubby jabbed him hard on the head with his knuckle.

"Hi, Danny," Ann said softly. "I'm glad you got the seat." She smiled warmly.

Danny melted at the very sound of her voice. His head was throbbing from Tubby's knuckle, but he couldn't take his eyes off her. She was so beautiful. Her skin was smooth and creamy, her brown eyes were bright and lovely, and her smile lit up the entire room. She was the most gorgeous girl he had ever seen. *I'm going to marry her someday,* he thought.

All of a sudden, the class got quiet as Miss Fenstermaker entered and gave the class "the look".

"Okay, children, let's get busy and make the most of your study period."

The tall skinny, witch-like Miss Fenstermaker's raspy voice sent a chill down Danny's spine. Everybody, including Danny, threw open their books and got busy. Nobody disobeyed Miss Fenstermaker.

As he busied himself, Danny heard an angry whisper coming from directly behind him.

"You're dead meat, Kinsey. I'll be waiting for you after school." Tubby laughed wickedly. He loved intimidating the much smaller Danny.

Danny quickly scribbled, "Mark will kill you!" on a piece of notebook paper and held it up behind his head so Tubby could see it.

The voice from behind came forth once again, "I was just kidding, Danny. No biggie, gimme five!" A smiling Tubby raised his chubby hand toward Danny.

Now free from Tubby's wrath, Danny ignored the high-five gesture, spun around and grinned at the bulbous tormentor. A subdued Tubby slid down in his seat and Danny once again turned his eyes back on the pretty Ann Harper. The droopy eyed staring session was soon interrupted by a tap on the shoulder.

"Daniel," Miss Fenstermaker said firmly.

"Yes, Miss Fenstermaker?"

"She's pretty, isn't she?"

Hearing several giggles, a crimson-faced Danny slid

slowly down in his seat.

Miss Fenstermaker went on, "I just received a note from the principal's office, and you're to report there right away. The note says that you should bring your books." Surprisingly, she smiled warmly at him.

A confused Danny gathered up his books, smiled at Ann and quietly exited the room.

"Please don't run, Daniel!" cautioned Miss Fenstermaker.

Danny walked steadily from the room, and then once outside and a safe distance from the room, he looked back one last time and sprinted toward the office for his unexpected meeting with the principal, Mr. Bolton. *What'd I do now?"* he thought.

As he approached the office, he could see gray silhouettes through the thick smoked glass windows that surrounded the office, and he could hear voices talking quietly inside the room. The secretary told him he could go in. He approached the door cautiously, carefully pushed it open and peeked inside. He was shocked to see his dad sitting in the principal's office, along with Mark and Maggie. His brother and sister had been crying; their frightened eyes darted toward him.

"Come in, come in, Danny," Mr. Bolton encouraged.

Danny pushed the door all the way open and stepped in. Seeing his brother and sister crying, and his dad obviously distraught, tears welled in his eyes.

His dad rushed over and laid his muscular arm on Danny's shoulder. "It's your mom, Danny. She had a fall, and she's in the hospital. We're going there now to see her."

Danny felt his heart race. This had to be serious.

Why would everyone be here at the same time? Why would they take him, his brother and sister out of class? He was terrified and began to cry. The thought of something happening to his beautiful mother was more than he could bear. His dad held him firmly in his arms trying to console him. Unfortunately, Danny was almost inconsolable. His sudden reaction seemed to only intensify the feelings inside Mark and Maggie, whose wailings suddenly became louder.

"It's okay. It's gonna be okay!" his dad said trying to calm the frightened children. "The doctors are taking good care of your mom. We're going to the hospital right now."

The principal was sitting behind his large mahogany desk watching the emotional scene that was unfolding in front of him. "Is that all you know at this point, Beau?" he asked attempting to deflect some of the attention away from the frightened children.

"Yes, at this point it is." Danny's father stood and gathered the kids together under his arms and prepared to leave for the hospital. He thanked the principal for his help. They shook hands and the four Kinsey's started to leave the office.

"My prayers are with you and your family, Beau," Mr. Bolton offered. Holding tightly to his father, Danny's heart sank even further.

Chapter 4

The three children sat huddled together in the back seat of their dad's custom Chevy.

"The car's bouncing a lot. Daddy's going fast," Maggie whispered.

"Yeah, I know," Danny mumbled.

Mark didn't say anything. He just stared out the window at the telephone poles whizzing past on the dark fall day.

"You go to bed and rest and you'll be all better in the morning," Maggie said softly to her rag doll, Sadie. She pulled the limp doll up to her chest and hugged her tightly.

Danny looked over the green seats at his father's foot lifting off the gas pedal and moving over to the brakes. His father was slowing down to round a corner. After the turn, he watched his dad hit the accelerator again. Looking up at the rearview mirror, Danny could see his father's face and the worry in his eyes. He instinctively reached up and rubbed his dad's shoulder, in an attempt to console him. His dad left the steering wheel for just a second to pat Danny's hand. Feeling only slightly better, Danny fell back against the seat.

Coming up to an intersection and rolling through the stop sign, his father accelerated just briefly and then the car jerked to a stop. The kids lurched forward in the backseat. Their dad quickly opened the front door, jumped out, and opened the back door for the children.

"We're at the hospital. It's a pretty big place, so let's all stay together," he ordered.

Maggie tucked Sadie firmly under her arm, slid off the backseat and followed her dad while holding tightly to his hand. Heads hanging, Mark and Danny exited the car and walked closely behind Maggie and their father.

When they reached the hospital entrance, their dad held the heavy glass door open for the kids. A bright white sign with red letters that read "EMERGENCY ROOM" hung above the door. Maggie didn't know what the sign meant, but she squeezed Sadie a little tighter when saw the concern on her older brothers' faces.

Inside, a nurse in an all white uniform and pointed hat walked quickly toward them. She had a troubled look on her face. "Oh, Beau, how are you doing?"

"We're okay, Nancy, thank you."

"Anita's in room 24, just down the hall," the kindly nurse said, "but right now they're doing a procedure for her breathing. They've been with her about twenty minutes. It shouldn't take much longer. A tracheotomy usually takes about half an hour. Why don't you and the children have a seat? There's a waiting room right across from her room. I'll tell Dr. Browning where you are and to come over when he's finished."

Their dad pulled the nurse aside and Danny heard him say that big word again. His dad didn't seem to like that word. The nurse's hat bobbed as she talked to him. She said a few more words, nodded toward the waiting room and walked away. Their dad's forehead was wrinkled, a sure sign that he was upset.

"Let's go, kids," he ordered. Danny and the others followed their father down the hallway to the waiting room. The frightened boy looked around at the dizzying bright lights and white walls in the corridor. He felt like he was in the middle of a terrible nightmare. Scared and disoriented, he felt like crying, but he knew he had to be brave. He was relieved when his father finally reached the door of the waiting room and pushed it open.

"Oh damn!" their dad mumbled. Almost all the seats were taken. Looking around, he finally spotted three seats right next to the door.

"Let's sit here by the door," he said quietly.

"You can sit on your daddy's lap, Maggie."

Their dad lifted Maggie up and fell into the seat closest to the door. Maggie held tightly to Sadie. Mark fell into the chair next to his dad and slid his head under his dad's arm. Danny sat down dejectedly in the third chair, feeling a little left out. Sensing this, his dad lifted his hand off Mark's shoulder and gently patted Danny's head.

A short time later, a balding man wearing dark-rimmed glasses and a long blue gown walked in and searched the room. He looked right past them as they sat huddled next to the door. Maggie said something to Sadie and he heard her. He glanced down at them and smiled.

"Oh, hello! I'm glad the little one said something. I didn't see you there," the tall doctor sighed. He and Dad shook hands.

"Hello, Beau."

"Hi, Dr. Browning."

"Uh, why don't we step over to Anita's room," he said. "Have the kids stay here."

"The doctor needs to talk to me, kids. I'll be back in a few minutes." Their dad smiled reassuringly at them and left the room with the doctor.

Mark, Danny, and Maggie all piled into the chair next to the door and leaned forward. They watched as their father and the doctor walked across the hall and entered their mom's room.

"Look!" Danny said, "The door didn't close all the way. It's open a little. Maybe we can hear them."

The kids leaned around the corner of the metal door frame and strained mightily trying to hear what the doctor was saying.

They could hear voices, but couldn't understand what was being said. Unexpectedly, the doctor walked closer to the open door to get something from a drawer. His voice was deep and commanding, allowing the kids to hear every word.

"Vertebrae three and four in her lower neck were crushed by the fall from the ladder and they appear to have splintered into the spinal cord. She also hit her head very hard on the garage floor during the fall. There's too much swelling now to determine how much brain damage there is, but . . ."

"Brain damage!" they heard their father exclaim.

The doctor hesitated for a moment and then

continued. "Yes, if Anita pulls through this, there could be paralysis from the shoulders down and I hate to have to be so blunt, but there is a good chance that she will have some brain damage. The amount of swelling indicates that she must have hit the floor awfully hard. We've done what we can to relieve some of the pressure." It was quiet for a minute. "I'm so sorry, Beau, I wish I could be more positive," he said softly.

"Will she, uh, make it?" their dad's voice trailed off.

"It is difficult to determine at this point. With the type of traumatic head injury she has suffered, it could be a matter of months to a few years. I'm not absolutely certain at this point, but I should know more in a day or two."

Paralysis! Brain damage! A few months! The doctor's words exploded inside Danny's head. Fear shot up his spine. *Mom will never be the same again! She'll be in a wheel chair! Mom's going to die!*

"It's okay now, baby. You be a good girl." Maggie talked quietly to her doll, unable to comprehend the horrible tragedy that was unfolding around her.

With tears pouring down his face, Mark stared straight ahead, not saying anything. His ashen face was filled with pain.

The door across the hall swung open and the doctor and their dad walked out. With the door wide open, the kids were able to get a glimpse of their mom. Terrified, they quickly jumped back in their seats.

"Did you see all those tubes sticking out of Mom?" a panic stricken Danny wailed.

"Why were her eyes closed? Was Mommy sleeping?" Maggie asked.

Mark didn't respond, he just leaned back against the chair and continued to stare straight ahead.

"Mommy has a tube in her neck, Sadie," Maggie mumbled.

Their dad and the doctor talked out in the hall. "Come with me for a minute, Beau. We need to go over a few things. The children will be fine here," the doctor said.

Their dad nodded and the two men walked down the hall toward the nurse's station.

All of a sudden, Mark bolted from his chair, his strong legs pushing him towards his mom's room. As he rushed towards her, he stumbled and fell on the well-waxed hall. Sliding out of control, his head slammed into the metal door on the other side of the hall.

"I don't hate you, Mom!" he screamed. "I don't hate you!" He was lying on the tile floor and punching the bottom of the large door. "I want to do the canning, Mom! I don't hate you, Mom!" he kept screaming, sobbing uncontrollably.

Danny began to weep as he listened to the torment in his big brother's voice. He leapt out of his chair and raced across the hall. He fell onto the back of his wailing brother and held on with all his strength.

"I love you, Mark!" Danny shrieked. "And Mom loves you!"

He felt Maggie's little body land on top of them. Sadie came loose from Maggie's grip. The rag doll bounced and then fell still on the shiny floor below. Maggie was screaming and crying, unable to comprehend the reactions of her big brothers.

"What the hell?" Danny could hear footsteps. He

turned his head and saw his father racing down the hall toward them. Soon he felt his dad's strong arms around them, hugging them.

"It's alright, kids, it's alright," he murmured as he tried to reassure the frightened children. His arms formed a canopy over the children.

"I'm sorry, I don't hate you!" Mark continued to moan. His knuckles were bleeding from the pounding on the heavy door.

Their dad gently lifted Maggie and Danny off Mark's back, and then fell on his knee next to him. His arm went under Mark's thick body. He pulled him up to his chest and held him tightly, speaking quietly in his ear.

"It's okay, son. It's okay! No matter what you might have said, your mom loves you very much. You're just a boy. Your mother knows you didn't mean what you said."

Mark continued to sob, squeezing his bloody hands on his dad's shoulder. His legs were dangling in the air, his baggy socks protruded from the bottom of his jeans. The shoulders on his dad's white dress shirt were soon stained with blood.

"Oh, my!" Dr. Browning lamented, hurrying toward them. "They must have overheard what I said." He laid his hand gently on their father's back. "I'm so sorry, Beau."

"It's not your fault," Beau replied. "They would have found out sooner or later."

Three nurses approached the children, talking softly and consoling them. One of the nurses took the opportunity to bandage Mark's hands. Mark was stoic, glancing up occasionally at the door to room 24. Maggie held tightly to Sadie and Danny stood next to his dad, sobbing. The shattered family was attempting to come to grips with the awful tragedy that had been so unexpectedly thrust upon them. What none of them understood that day was that this tragedy would have far reaching effects—effects that would cast a huge shadow over this family for years to come.

Chapter 5

The car rambled down the rutted street. Danny was quiet, too exhausted to cry anymore. He leaned against the soft padding on the door. Maggie's blond curls spread out over his arm as she fell against him and spoke sweet nothings to baby Sadie. On the other side of the seat, Mark just stared out the window, continually squeezing his thumbs inside his bandaged fingers. Danny sensed his tough brother wanted to punch something, but he couldn't, so he just squeezed on those thumbs.

They all bounced violently off the seat when their father drove over the sharp curb at the end of their drive. It seemed he never slowed down for that curb. Dan looked up and saw the house number 822 on their gray mailbox as they continued down the drive. The brakes squeaked and their dad jerked to a stop at the end of the drive behind the house.

Their dad's elbow appeared over the top of the front seat. He turned to look at them and smiled warmly.

"Okay, kids, go in, get your baths and get ready for bed. I have to go pick up Grandma Carrie. She's going to be helping out until your mom gets better."

The saddened children slowly pushed the car doors open and headed for the house. It brought Danny some comfort knowing that Grandma Carrie was coming over. He loved his Grandma Carrie and one of her big hugs would feel real good right now.

"You're in charge, Mark. I'll be right back!" their dad shouted out the window of the car. He backed down the drive and rolled out of sight. Mark usually loved being in charge, but not today.

Mark stood at the backdoor staring blankly down at the tattered door mat. Observing Mark to be sure he wasn't going for the key, Danny quickly reached behind the back of the porch swing and grabbed the hidden key off the rusted little hook. He stuck it in the lock and pushed the door open. Still wanting to be somewhat in charge, Mark folded his arms on his chest and waited for Danny and Maggie to enter before he walked in.

Danny was searching around on the wall for the light switch when Mark pushed him out of the way. "I'll do it," he barked.

Light soon filled the family room and kitchen area. A box of glass jars topped with metal lids sat on the kitchen counter. His mom's delicate gold watch was lying next to them. It was a Christmas gift given to her by his dad and she always took it off when she was working so it wouldn't get scratched. Danny looked over at his mom and dad's picture on the refrigerator and tears began to once again flow down his cheeks. In the picture, his parents were both smiling broadly and were surrounded by friends. It was taken at their high school reunion just last summer.

Danny looked at Mark and shuddered. His older brother saw the glass jars and let loose with an excruciating groan. His face was overcome with grief as he raced from the room. The door to his room slammed hard behind him.

Frightened by her brother's rapid exit, Maggie began to cry. Danny wrapped his arms around her and held her tightly. "It's going to be okay," he whispered. "Everything will be fine."

Danny struggled over to the rocking chair holding Maggie close to him. He pulled mightily on her little body and lifted her up. They both fell into the chair. He reached out and pushed the ground with his foot to get the rocking started.

"Grandma will be here soon," Danny whispered. "Everything will be fine."

....

A short time later, the back door swung open. A tall, pretty gray-haired lady stepped in and searched the room with worried eyes. "Oh my dear, dear children," she cried. She rushed over, her eyes glistening with tears, her arms outstretched.

"Grandma! Grandma!" Both children cried out with relief. They jumped up from the rocker and fell into her waiting arms, hugging and sobbing once again.

"I love you so, my children! I love you more than anything."

Danny glanced over at the dark silhouette of his father who was standing motionless in the shadows by the door. He could hear him quietly sobbing.

Chapter 6

After losing a determined battle to regain consciousness, Anita Kinsey died at the Maple City Community Hospital of a massive brain hemorrhage two weeks after the accident. Immediately after her death, Grandma Carrie left her beloved farm and moved into town to help care for the Kinsey children. Anita was only thirty-four years old.

Chapter 7

Immersed in his emotional reverie, Dan gets a bump to the arm from his lovely Ann. With scolding eyes, she nodded toward the preacher. Dan smiled, patted her forearm and mouthed the word "Sorry." With his attention now focused on the pulpit, Dan listened as Pastor Jenkins continued his talk.

"Friends, at this point in our celebration of Beau Kinsey's life, it's time to let some others have the opportunity to express their feelings." He glanced down at the shocked Kinsey family, who were surprised and taken aback by the unexpected pronouncement. "I believe it only appropriate that we hear from some members of his devoted family."

The pastor's eyes searched the family for the most likely candidate. The family of Beau Kinsey sat motionless, staring straight ahead, hoping he wouldn't pick them—all of them, that is, except Mark. The attention loving Mark lifted his hand just a smidgen off his leg, but high enough for the observant clergyman to pick up on the modest signal.

The anxious pastor smiled broadly, "Why, I do believe Beau's son Mark would like to say a few words. Please come forward, Mark." The Reverend motioned toward the stairs to his left that led up to the podium. "Come right up, my boy," he commanded. Many of those who had gathered for the somber occasion chuckled at the "boy" comment.

Sensing the humor, the aging pastor smiled, "Why, I guess he's hardly a boy anymore." The crowd broke into a more audible laugh at the smiling minister's admission.

As Mark climbed the stairs to the pulpit, he smiled at the pastor's comments. Mark looked very striking in his pinstriped three-piece suit which was accentuated with a beautiful burgundy tie.

"Come forward, son. Come right on up." Pastor Jenkins gave Mark a quick hug, stepped to the side, and waved his hand toward center stage.

Mark cleared his throat, walked over, and wrapped his thick fingers around the podium. He lifted his head and began to speak, sounding very much like the polished businessman he had become since leaving Maple City so many years ago. While upset by his father's passing, it was obvious to Dan that Mark relished the opportunity to be in front of the hometown crowd.

"Thank you all so much for coming today. It means so much to my family and me. We all have such fond memories of our childhood here in Maple City: the ball games on Friday night, the picnics, the Sunday morning services right here in this beautiful church. None of us will ever forget those wonderful days. All of you mean so much to my brother and sister and me. You were such a huge part of our childhood that I . . ."

Relieved that Mark had taken the stage, Dan fell back in his seat and listened as his confident brother spoke of their father's athletic prowess and accomplishments, saying very little about him as a father except to reference the "desire to succeed" he had instilled in his children. The crowd had interrupted the self-assured Mark several times with applause and laughter. Anticipating that he would be taking his turn at the podium, Dan hoped his brother would speak for a while longer and take some of the energy out of the air before he had to get up there. Dan was certain that Maggie was out of the rotation. Her timidity was legendary. Nobody would expect Maggie to take to the stage.

Dan's mind was racing as he tried to figure out what to say that would be fair to his father, yet truthful. Mark was obviously covering most of his father's past athletic accomplishments, leaving him room to speak only of more personal matters. Yet, if Dan told the truth about his complicated father, he would give the impression that he was insensitive or ungrateful. Dan listened with some trepidation as Mark completed his remarks.

"Thank you all for always being so kind to my father and our family. God bless you all." Mark was greeted by warm smiles from the crowd. They all loved him. He had always been a local favorite reminding everyone so much of his iconic father. Lacking the athletic skills of his older brother, Dan wasn't quite as popular. He was hoping against all hope that maybe they had heard enough from Mark and that no further comments from the family would be necessary. His older brother quickly dashed all hopes of such a reprieve. While departing the stage, he shot his index finger toward Danny and then pointed toward the pulpit. There were numerous smiles and nods from the crowd.

Before announcing Dan, Pastor Jenkins out of politeness glanced toward Maggie. Terrified, she quickly looked up shyly at the much-loved preacher, dropped her chin in a submissive fashion, and subtly shook her head no. The gregarious minister turned his attention quickly away from Maggie and onto Dan.

"As we all know, Beau had two outstanding sons."

Dan covered his mouth and whispered to Ann. "Do they need to be reminded that I existed?"

Pastor Jenkins continued. "Why, I've lost count of the number of times I looked out my living room window on Wesley Avenue only to see the two boys running past with little Danny trying like crazy to keep up with his much bigger brother." Chuckles filled the room.

"Much bigger, my foot! I was just as tall as Mark. Skinnier, but just as tall," he whispered to Ann. Slightly annoyed, Ann pushed her finger against her lips.

"My friends, I am hopeful we can now have a few words from Beau's younger son Dan, or Danny, as we all called him back then." The smiling pastor pointed toward the stairs.

Somewhat apprehensive, Dan had no choice but to speak. He stood, straightened his tie and walked briskly to the pulpit.

"Thank you," the nervous Dan said, quickly shaking hands with the Reverend. The pastor backed away and sat down.

Dan stepped in front of the wooden podium and adjusted the microphone upward. As a ranking official in the national banking system, Dan had spoken at such high-level affairs as the World Banking Conference in Zurich and the annual Federal Home Loan Bank Board meeting held in Chicago each year. His position with the bank had also required him to speak at numerous conventions and seminars over the span of his career. No stranger to being in front of people, he had become very polished and comfortable, but talking to the hometown crowd with all of the emotions and personal issues involved was a much different challenge. This would be one of the most difficult speeches of his life. He took a deep fortifying breath, squared his shoulders, and then slowly exhaled. He laid his hands on the podium and made eye contact with the crowd, as he always did, and began to speak.

Chapter 8

"On behalf of my family and friends, I would like to thank each of you for attending this celebration of the life of my father. The extraordinary turnout today only reinforces what I have always known to be true, that my father was indeed a blessed man to live in such a wonderful community." Dan looked out at the crowd; many were smiling in agreement.

"Brother Mark did a fine job of reminding us of the remarkable athletic accomplishments of our father, especially that memorable state championship game." Never tiring of references to that game, there were murmurs and soft conversation throughout the crowd. Dan paused briefly, and then continued. "But, my friends, my father was special for more reasons than his awesome athletic achievements. He was special because he truly understood the unique status that had been granted him here in Maple City."

Dan's handsome face broke into a smile. "And he wasn't afraid to show it. I can still remember to this day the many times my father would go out of his way to stop to talk with one of you. He adored this town and he loved all of you for making his life here so special." Some of those gathered dabbed away the tears at the mere mention of the Great One's affinity for their fine community.

Feeling like he was connecting, Dan gestured toward his family. "As we Kinsey's gather here today in this familiar place of worship whereas Mark reminded us earlier, we attended as small children, we feel the same deep sense of gratitude and love for all of you that our father did. My father's physical presence is gone from us now, soon to be laid to rest some miles from here at the peaceful Coming Home Cemetery, but I can assure you that while his physical body has been taken from us, his heart will always reside right here in Maple City with all of you." Smiles and affirming nods appeared across the room. Dan lifted his voice to a very commanding tone and prepared to conclude his brief talk. "God bless you for your love and kindness to my father and to all of us over the years. We will always be in your debt. No matter where I may live during my lifetime, I want all of you gathered here today to know that Maple City will always be home to me. The sting of my father's untimely death has sent us all reeling," Dan turned and nodded toward the casket, "but we know he won't be forgotten. May his legacy of profound love for this community lift you up and give you peace. On behalf of a grateful family, I want to thank all of you for coming here today and sharing our grief. God bless you all." His eyes glistening, Dan stepped back from the podium, nodded to acknowledge the loud applause, then quickly navigated off the stage. Smiling and nodding at the appreciative crowd, he walked directly back to his seat and received a congratulatory "thumbs up" from Mark. Ann patted his leg and with tears in her eyes, smiled at him. Throughout the audience, the hankies and tissues were coming out once again.

The pastor rose and stepped to his familiar position behind the podium. "Thank you so much, Danny. What wonderful remembrances from you and Mark. I'm certain that my good friend Beau would be so proud of his children today." The aging clergyman smiled warmly and then began to survey the room, "Are there others who would like to say a few words about Beau?" Several hands shot up in the room.

"To save time, why don't you just stand at your seat? One of our fine volunteers will bring you a microphone, so please just stay at your seat." Eyebrows raised, he looked across the room once again and mumbled into the microphone, "Hmmm, it's difficult to, uh, oh yes, Mayor Thompson, why don't you say a few words." An elderly man with a microphone scurried down the center aisle excusing himself as he entered the row. He stepped over several people and made his way to the popular mayor with the snake-like cord slithering along behind him.

The mayor quickly rose to his feet, took control of the microphone, cleared his throat and began to speak. "My friends, as the mayor of our fine community, words cannot express the sorrow I feel inside today. The very thought of my close friend passing away before his time has just been devastating to me and my family. When I was first told by my secretary, Betty, that Beau had been found dead in his home, I was shaken to the core, as I'm sure you were. After the initial shock had worn off, I started to think about all the memories that Beau and I had created together: the charity events, service club meetings, church dinners, social gatherings, and of course the occasional golf game." There were several chuckles from the crowd at the diminished status given to his and Beau's almost daily round of golf.

The mayor rambled on for several more minutes, turning the warm tribute into somewhat of a campaign speech. "Oh, and yes, yes, there was the time that my friend bent over to mark his favorite Titleist ball on that tricky fourth hole and much to his never ending chagrin, we all heard a pronounced ripping sound, and soon his light blue boxers were on full display!" Loud laughter filled the room.

The pastor finally had to gently remind the verbose mayor that others would like the opportunity to speak. Catching the talkative mayor's eye, the kindly preacher very discreetly pointed his index finger toward his watch. Acknowledging the subtle gesture from Pastor Jenkins, the mayor began to wrap things up. "If I may be serious for a moment my friends," the smile faded from the charismatic mayor's face and his lips began to quiver. "I sincerely hope that someday this hurting I feel inside will begin to subside a little. Right now, it's overwhelming. Beau Kinsey was more than an athlete to me, he was a dear friend, and I loved him like a brother. I know that every time I step on that first tee, I will think of Beau and the great times we shared. I will miss him more than words can say. My life will never be the same. Thank you for bearing with my ramblings. I will sit down now." The sighs were audible from those gathered. The mayor nodded, settled into his seat, and mouthed the word "sorry" toward the Kinsey family.

"Thank you so much Mayor, for your heartfelt sentiments," the pastor said, while searching the room and trying to decide which of the many waving hands he would select next. Finally, his bony hand shot forward. "John Owens, why don't you grace us all with a few words?"

The rather diminutive spectacled man in a crumpled blue suit stood slowly in front of his pew. It was obvious that he wasn't nearly as comfortable speaking before a crowd as were his predecessors. Receiving the microphone, the owner of Owens' Hardware cleared his throat, and began to speak very softly.

"When Alice and I moved here so many . . ." Pastor Jenkins quickly rose to the podium, "I'm sorry, John, could you speak up just a little? Our sound system's not the best here at First Church."

"Oh yes Everett, I'll speak up a little." Many in the crowd winced when the nervous man cleared his throat and spoke directly into the microphone. "As I started to say, when Alice and I moved here so many years ago to take over her ailing father's hardware store, I was a little apprehensive to say the least. Having grown up in the Boston area, I was used to the big city and its benefits. The thought of living in a small town out here in the middle of the cornfields of north central Indiana was indeed disconcerting. And I have to admit, at first I thought you were all just a little bit crazy. After all, what kinds of people go out of their way to just say 'hi' to a total stranger?" Quiet laughter rippled throughout the crowd. The popular store owner continued, "They don't do that out East. If you don't know someone, you don't speak to them. In fact, sometimes you don't even speak to the ones you know!" Mr. Owen chuckled. "But ya know what? This place grows on you. Over the years I have found the friendliness of the folks here in Indiana to be quite endearing, and I must confess I have changed. I never pass a person now that I don't smile and say 'hello'.

My next big adjustment to this nutty State of Indiana was high school basketball. Alice took me down to Memorial Coliseum for a game one night. When we got out of the car and I looked up at the huge building, I was astonished! I had never seen a high school gymnasium that big in my life. The largest high school gym in Boston would pale in comparison. When I told Alice how surprised I was, she said, 'Heck, John, all the gyms in Indiana are this big.' I remember thinking that these folks must really love their high school basketball." He paused as laughter stirred through the crowd.

"A couple of years later, now fully addicted to 'Giant mania' as I like to call it, I started to hear about this Kinsey boy. Several of my customers at the hardware store told me that they thought the young teenager might be the best basketball player to ever come out of Maple City. Even as a young boy, Beau Kinsey had this town in a buzz. After hearing about how he scored thirty-eight points in an eighth grade game one evening, I decided to take a look at this kid. Alice and I went to the next home game against an undefeated middle school team from Kokomo." The crowd groaned at the very mention of their dreaded rival.

The smallish balding man grinned. The longer he

spoke, the more comfortable he was becoming. "Well, it didn't take me long to find out what all the commotion was about. With a dazzling display of shot making and passing, that young Kinsey boy almost single-handedly dismantled the much taller team from Kokomo, winning the game by over twenty points. I knew then we had someone very special on our hands here in our little town."

Reverend Jenkins fidgeted nervously in his seat; the grinning storeowner glanced toward the pulpit. "Okay, Everett, I'll wrap it up." The minister smiled in relief.

His sagging eyes glistening, the old man continued, "Time has passed by so quickly for all of us. I, uh, I just can't believe I'm here today at Beau's funeral. It just doesn't seem possible. That polite young boy who used to shout, 'Hello, Mr. Owens' from clear across the street, is no longer with us. It's so hard to understand. He was such a gracious man, always going out of his way to make everybody feel special. I've never regretted moving to Maple City all those years ago and this community will never quite be the same without our friend, Beau. But, I also know that he will live on in my heart forever. I will never forget him. He has given my wife and me a lifetime of memories." The aging storeowner paused, extending his shaking arms skyward, "God bless you, my dear friend. God bless you! May your soul rest in peace." Several people nearby reached over and patted the aging man's narrow shoulders. He quietly thanked them and then nestled back into his seat. The crowd sat in reverent silence. The shy old man from the east coast had summed up their feelings about as well as anyone could.

The pastor waited a few seconds and then approached the podium, nodding at Mr. Owens and giving the town time to absorb his heartwarming talk. He finally spoke, "I don't know about the rest of you, but I wouldn't want to follow that one. If there are no objections, I would like to bring this service to a close." He looked out at the somber room. There were several nods of approval.

The pastor continued, "Thank you to everyone for coming and paying tribute to our friend, Beau Kinsey. Who, as so aptly described by our good friend John Owens, meant so much to all of us." The charismatic old preacher looked away briefly and then turned his attention to the crowd. He hesitated, and after what seemed like an eternity, he finally gathered his thoughts and led the family and friends of Beau Kinsey in prayer. "Our dear Lord and Savior, as the lights dim to darkness in that blessed locker room in the sky, we rejoice in your promise of everlasting life for our dear friend Beau Kinsey. I commend his soul to you, my Father, may you sanctify this fine man with your never ending grace now and forever more. Amen, and Amen!"

The pastor stepped back, looked across the crowded room and shared a warm smile with Dan and his family. Then, with arms raised he bellowed, "May the Lord bless all of you!" He immediately pointed toward the back of the room, "Departure will start with the back row! Our friends outside in the overflow areas can do the same."

Many of those in attendance stood in front of their chairs without leaving, wanting to relish the moment, reluctant to accept the final demise of their cherished hero. Finally, after being nudged by those near them, they began to turn and joined the lengthy procession out of the church.

Chapter 9

Dan's extended family joined them at his father's house after the funeral for the customary dinner and sharing time. After the familiar mob had settled in, it was no surprise to Dan that the ensuing discussion soon turned to the past athletic accomplishments of his much loved patriarch. It started with Dan's slightly bulbous Uncle Bud, who turned away from the punch bowl, smiled and approached him with a glass of the reddish liquid in one hand and handful of nuts in the other.

Although aging in years, Uncle Bud still had the same twinkle in his eye that he had as a young man. "I'll tell ya, Danny, I'll never forget that game against Tech. I've never seen anything like it. Your father was unstoppable. He had basketball sense, smarts you might say, and he was a helluva passer on top of it." The old man stared intently at Dan waiting for his reaction. Dan gave him a confirming nod of his head. On this day, and in Beau's house, anything less than full agreement with his uncle's analysis would have been treasonous.

"Dad was quite a player, no doubt about it," Dan replied.

"And, don't forget, he was an All State quarterback in football and a track star, too. He was really something," Uncle Bud quickly added.

A compliant Dan once again nodded in agreement. "He sure was."

Dan was always amazed at the goodwill his father continued to enjoy in Maple City. The drinking, gambling and serial womanizing all seemed to be overlooked by the eternally grateful community. Over the years, the local folks had managed to turn a blind eye to all sorts of bad behavior from his father. Dan could have found such loyalty endearing if his father's actions hadn't been so devastating to him and his family. Even his intuitive Uncle Bud seemed impervious to his father's questionable behavior. It was very difficult for Dan to understand.

"You and Annie are gonna have to come down to Florida for a visit this winter. We'd love ta have ya. We're down there six months now, ya know. You're welcome anytime. It'll give you a chance to get out of all that snow in Denver." His uncle's cherub face broke into a broad smile.

"Well, thank you, Uncle Bud, but it really doesn't snow that much in . . ."

Dan was interrupted by the familiar voice of his sister Maggie. "The food will be ready shortly, gang. Why don't we all move into the family room? There's more space in there."

With his Uncle Bud scurrying off to the buffet table, Dan took the opportunity to survey the Davis family, many of whom he hadn't seen for years. He loved the Davis side of his family. Although they were prone to unceremonious behavior at times, they were survivors and loyal to the end. Their kindness and genuine concern when Ann had a breast cancer scare several years ago had endeared them to Ann and the girls.

The Kinsey clan, on the other hand, was a much different story. Dan barely knew them. His Grandmother Kinsey had died of polio when he was very young. His grandfather Tom, visited the kids a couple of times when they were small, but had fallen off the radar completely as the kids got older. For some unknown reason, Beau and his father never talked to one another. He died ten years ago after a long and very difficult battle with lung cancer. Beau had surprised everyone by attending his father's funeral, but even though he attended, he later groused to Dan, "I got my ass outa there as soon as I could. It was a bummer."

Dan never fully understood the lack of closeness his troubled father had with his family. Grandma Carrie had once told him that Tom was a cold man and had been very hard on Beau when he was growing up. A few times he asked his father about his dad, but he would only say, "If he comes and sees me, I'll go and see him." *It was such a shame,* Dan thought.

Still surveying his family, Dan's eyes fastened on his youngest daughter, Meghan. She was standing next to the long bar near the kitchen talking to her cousin, Katie. Noticing the sudden attention from her dad, she smiled. He set his beer down and walked over next to her. Dan was struck by how pretty she looked in her blue cotton dress and dangly gold earrings.

"Hey Dad." She always said the two words so quickly it always sounded like one.

"Hi, honey," The two shared a quick hug, Meghan was much like her Aunt Maggie and hesitant to show public displays of affection.

"Grandpa was so popular, people loved him. I couldn't believe the tents outside the church today. They were all full," she mused.

"Well, ya know he set that scoring record at the State and all. That's really big here in Maple City."

"Did you see those four guys toward the back of the church? They didn't look the kind of people that would be friends with Grandpa," Meghan added, tossing an inquisitive look toward her father.

"No, uh, I didn't see them. Why?"

"Well, they were all covered with tattoos and stuff and they had on black T-shirts with Tug's Tavern printed across the front."

"You're kidding," Dan laughed. "I guess we're taking informality to new levels nowadays. He glanced over at his pretty daughter hoping she wouldn't question him further. But, like so many of those of the gentler gender, she wanted more information.

"Where's Tug's Tavern, Dad, and why were those guys at Grandpa's funeral?"

"Oh, it's just a little bar on the west side of town over near the old foundry." Dan hoped that would quench her curiosity.

Meghan hesitated. She knew her dad was holding out, but she loved her grandpa and didn't want to think negatively about him, so she did what any loving granddaughter would do—she answered her own question. "I'll bet they're old high school friends," she said confidently, certain that she had solved the puzzle.

"Yes, uh yes, that could be," Dan said quietly. Dan knew that his reply to his daughter had been somewhat disingenuous. In reality, the macho-looking guys in the Tug's T- shirts were certainly not his dad's old high school buds. They were a few of the local toughs that his dad hung out with at Tugs, his last place of refuge each day. Beau's daily routine consisted of eighteen holes of golf, drinks and a few hours of poker at the local country club, then a stop at Tug's on the way home for a few more drinks and more importantly, a chance of getting laid by one of the leggy young factory girls who frequented the bawdy bar.

Leaving Tug's, he would arrive home, revving the engine as he drove down the drive. He would back off the pipes several times before barging into the house drunk as a skunk.

Fortunately, on most nights, he would just stagger over and fall into his favorite recliner, click on the tail end of the Johnny Carson show, and smoke cigarettes one after another until he fell asleep. But on some nights, he found it within himself to get mean, and the slightest thing could set him off—a bicycle not put away or a pair of shoes taken off hastily near the back door. It didn't take much. On these occasions, he would bypass his favorite chair and stagger back to the boys' bedroom.

He would enter their room quietly, and then shake them awake and scream profanities at them in the middle of the night in a darkened bedroom. His pungent breath would burn into their terrified faces.

Although the explosion would be over in a matter of minutes, it was seared in their young minds forever. Shell-shocked, they would huddle together and sleep the rest of the night together in Mark's bed with Mark's strong arms surrounding Danny, who usually received the brunt of the attack. Thank goodness, he spared Maggie the terror of these late night outbreaks, reserving them for his undeserving sons.

Grandma was of no help on such demonic occasions. She yanked her hearing aids out every night and laid them on her nightstand next to the bed. You could have ignited an A-bomb in the house and she wouldn't have heard it.

Unbelievably, the following morning their amazingly resilient father was raring to go. One would never guess in a million years what had happened the night before. At six-thirty sharp, he would hop out of bed or the recliner, whichever was his sleeping place of choice, shower, dress to the nines, and then join all of them at the kitchen table for a quick bite of breakfast. He would joke with the kids for a while and then head off to work.

All the years he had played sports had given their father an incredibly strong body. He could saturate himself with massive doses of alcohol, smoke three packs of cigarettes a day and eat all the junk food in sight, but if you didn't know better, you would think he spent his evenings working out at the local gym while drinking healthy cocktails full of vitamins and minerals. Lean and incredibly handsome, he was a striking physical specimen.

But Danny and Mark were not impressed by their

father's recouping ability. His behavior confused and disgusted them. Dan could still feel the sting of those late night encounters. They still haunted him to this day.

"It seems like everybody liked Grandpa. He was pretty amazing," Meghan asserted, interrupting Dan's thoughts.

Dan smiled and nodded. *Thirty-two points in the state finals,* he thought. He felt a gentle touch on his arm and turned to see the lovely face of wife Ann next to him with older daughter Ali at her side.

"It's almost time for the fire drill," she whispered with a giggle. Ali and Meghan grinned, pursing their lips as if they had heard something naughty. The magical hour had arrived. It was time for the family to leave.

And leave they did! As if directed by some mystical force, everyone would get ready to leave at almost exactly the same time. One by one the family members would conclude their conversations, collect their belongings and prepare to leave. After a rapid-fire procession of hugs and sincere condolences to Dan, Mark, and the others, they filed out the door and piled into their awaiting vehicles. It was crazy and awe-inspiring to watch. The busy and noisy family room of just a few moments earlier was now dead quiet. The only sounds to be heard were car doors slamming, engines revving and tires squealing outside.

Ann's hazel eyes twinkled as she glanced around the room. "Look!" she exclaimed, "They picked everything up. The room's immaculate, as usual."

"They started this years ago, after mom died, and the ritual has been the same ever since. I just wish I knew why they were always in such a hurry to leave." Dan smiled, rubbing his forehead. "Don't ya just love 'em?"

"We sure do," Ann replied while zeroing in on her somewhat listless husband. "You feeling okay, honey?"

"Somewhere along the line, I've developed quite a headache," Dan grumbled.

"You've been on a fast track, honey. Why don't you lie down in the den for awhile? You'll feel better." Ann's request didn't surprise Dan. A woman of strong faith, she was always looking out for him and the girls. Raised in Maple City by two loving parents, she was a very giving person. Ann was the kind of wife every man dreamed of having. She was fun, pretty, and totally dedicated to her family. He couldn't imagine his life without her.

Dan gave Ann a peck on the cheek and exited the family room, making his way down the narrow hall to the den. Once inside the den, he leaned over and clicked on a small lamp near the old loveseat. He exhaled slowly and then collapsed on the small sofa. Trying to unwind and get comfortable, he folded his arms on his chest and surveyed the walls in the tiny den. The walls were covered with all sorts of memorabilia, all of which were a testament to his father's sports career.

Pictures, newspaper articles, certificates of achievement and ribbons were displayed on one wall, multiple glass shelves on the other wall held dozens of trophies for basketball, football and track. But the best spot was right above his dad's old black walnut desk. It was reserved for the very large and truly incredible photo of his famous father on the front page of the Indianapolis Star. The bold letters of the headline read, **Kinsey leads Giants over Tech for State Title**. The black and white photo showed his strapping young father standing in front of the scoreboard at the legendary Butler Field House with a basketball pushed against his hip.

In one sense, it was exciting for Dan to observe the many tributes to his father's fabled athletic career. In another sense it confused him. All these reminders of his father's success, also brought back many painful memories. Something still hurt deep inside of him, and he knew that he had to deal with it. He had to get past it and he had to get past it now.

Lifting the afghan off the back of the loveseat and tossing it over his legs, he fell back against the soft cushions, breathed deeply and then exhaled, letting his thoughts take him on what he was sure would be a deeply emotional journey back to those difficult and hurting days of his childhood.

Chapter 10

"Damn it, Danny!" An angry Beau Kinsey slammed the accelerator to the floor on his new red 409 Chevy and sped away from school. "When I tell you four o'clock, I mean four o'clock. I want you out in front of the school waiting for me. Do you hear me?"

"Yes, I hear you." Danny replied meekly. His teary eyes looked longingly at his father searching for any sign of kindness, but found none. The smell of whiskey permeated the interior of his dad's cluttered car. "I'm sorry, Dad, but the other boys were playing pick-up in the gym and they asked me to join them. I didn't want to, but they needed another player real bad. They said I had to play. I thought I would be able to see you coming through the window. I kept looking out the window all the time, but I guess I didn't see you."

"I guess you didn't and I had to run my ass all over the school looking for you! I was in the middle of a meeting at the club and I need to get back. People are waiting on me."

"A meeting or poker?" Danny murmured. Shocked

by what he had just said, he shot a frightened look at his father.

"What'd you say?" his father's face was red with fury.

"Nothing," Danny replied quickly.

Suddenly, without warning, his dad's huge state championship ring crashed into his bony rib cage. A horrible pain shot through the side of his slender body. He groaned, he grabbed his side and began rocking back and forth. His ribs were throbbing from the force of the stinging blow.

"Don't you ever smart talk your dad again! Do you understand?

Writhing in pain, Danny mumbled, "Yes," as he continued to rock back and forth in agony. He had learned from previous punches by a drunken father that the pain would eventually subside, but then it would be replaced by a sore aching feeling that would often last several days. Every movement would hurt and with tryouts for the seventh grade basketball team the next day, it was the last thing he needed. Not a star player, Danny had to be at his very best to make the team, which seemed impossible to him right now.

Things were quiet in the car for several minutes after the violent blow. The only sound was the huge engine roaring down the narrow streets on the west side of town. His dad, as always, was driving too fast, but he never worried about getting speeding tickets. The local cops wouldn't dream of stopping the well-known red Chevy.

Danny just stared at the floor, occasionally glancing up at that large state championship ring on his father's hand. The ring that had brought so much adulation and glory to his father was nothing more than a tool of torture for him.

His father down shifted and the brakes squealed as the big car banged over the curb in front of their house. The loose change lying in the center console rattled. A few seconds later, the car came to an abrupt stop at the back of the house. Danny elbowed the handle down and struggled to get out of the passenger side with the big engine still chugging. "Tell your grandma that you were hurt playing ball. Got it?"

"Okay." Danny slid quietly out of the car. Holding his aching side, he ran up to the back door. His drunken father revved the engine and spun the tires down the driveway spewing gravel in his wake. He was obviously in a hurry to get back to the club. Danny usually rode home from school with one of the neighbor kids, but this was one of the few occasions when his dad had to bring him home. He hoped it would be a long time before he needed his dad again.

The back door swung open, and apron-clad Grandma Carrie smiled at Danny. Seeing his grandma's kind face made the pain a little easier to tolerate. After the death of their mother a little less than a year ago, Grandma had moved in to care for the children. She did all the cleaning and cooking and anything else that needed to be done around the house. Their dad was hardly ever at home, so Grandma had become an elderly parent figure in the children's lives. Danny thanked God every night for Grandma Carrie. She was kind, soft-spoken and always there for them; and best of all, Danny was her favorite.

"Hi, Danny, it's nice your father could bring you

home today." She draped her arm over his shoulder and pulled him through the back door into the family room.

"Uh-huh," Danny was holding his side and trying not to cry. Once inside, he gave his grandma a painful hug and started for his room attempting to hide his discomfort, but it didn't work.

"What's the matter, honey? Are you alright? I saw you rubbing your side."

"Some big kid elbowed me when I was playing basketball after school today. It doesn't hurt much," Danny replied, hoping his Grandma would let the subject drop.

His concerned grandmother hurried over. "Well, just hold on there, young fella, and let me take a look." She yanked the tail of his shirt out of his jeans, and quickly surveyed his side and his back. "Oh my! He must have been a large boy alright. You have a huge welt on your side. Stay here!" she ordered. She then hurried off to the bathroom. Danny could hear her rummaging around in the medicine cabinet. She returned quickly with a large white tube with Ben Gay printed on the side in bright blue and red letters. She quickly unscrewed the cap, squeezed a little on her hand and began gently rubbing Danny's sore ribs. He stared at his grandma's kind face as she gently administered her treatment of choice for almost every bump or bruise that the children experienced. With the rubbing completed, she opened a soft, adhesive pad and stuck it carefully on the tender wound. Danny poked the spot gently at the wound to see if it still hurt. It did feel a little better.

"Thank you, Grandma."

"You're very welcome, dear." His grandma smiled.

"Did you tell your father about this?"

"Yeah."

"What'd he say?"

"Nothin' much. He just told me to be careful next time." Danny peered up at his grandma's face to see if she believed him. She gave him "the look"—the look of bewilderment that he had seen so many times before. As much as he loved his grandma, she was just like everyone else. Even if she suspected that his dad inflicted the injury, she just couldn't make herself believe it. It was the same old story—the great Beau Kinsey could do no wrong. In his heart he knew that his grandma doubted Danny's explanation about the origin of his sore rib, but he also knew she would never allow herself to admit it.

Suddenly, Mark came running out of the back room. He stopped and observed Danny gingerly tucking in his shirt. "Ya okay?" he asked.

"Yeah, I just got elbowed at school," Danny replied. "No practice today at the middle school?" he asked, wanting to change the subject.

"Naw, the sixth graders had the gym today."

"Where's Maggie?" Danny queried.

"She had Brownie Scouts," Grandma offered.

Mark looked at his younger brother. "Want to go over to the Old Golf?"

"What for?"

"Cardboard Hill, dummy!"

"We got any cardboard?" Danny asked excitedly.

"Timmy is on the way over, he will know."

Then, as if on cue, there was a skidding sound out in the drive followed by the rattle of a bike hitting the ground. Timmy, had just arrived. He burst through the porch and shouted, "Let's go," through the open back door.

Danny and Mark's questioning eyes looked toward their grandma for permission. They knew she'd say yes, but out of their undying respect for the selfless caregiver, they waited for her okay.

"Go ahead, but you boys be careful. Watch that side of yours, Danny, and you two need to be home before dark. I just started supper and it will be ready in about an hour or so."

"Okay!" the boys shouted in unison. The excited trio darted through the back door. Mark and Danny ran through an already open garage door and grabbed their bikes. Soon all three boys were peddling down the driveway toward Wesley Avenue. A few pedals later, they dipped their shoulders, took a hard right down Jeffries Street and raced toward the Old Golf—a hilly wooded area that was a former golf course.

....

The Old Golf consisted of a long valley surrounded by steep hills. A narrow creek wound through the grassy basin. The Lutheran Church, a beautiful red brick building with a tall white steeple, majestically overlooked the lovely valley from atop the highest hill.

The Old Golf was a great place for the kids to play. Over the years, the children had worn several long paths through the picturesque woods. One of the paths led to the popular Cardboard Hill, a regular destination for Danny and his friends. The tall hill was directly across from the church and featured the steepest and most dangerous slope in the woods.

Chapter 11

The cool breeze felt good on Danny's face as he raced along Jeffries Street. His side was aching, but that wasn't going to stop him from an opportunity to go to Cardboard Hill. He hoped there was enough cardboard for everyone.

"Is there cardboard over there?" Mark shouted to whoever would listen.

"Yeah, I got some at Kroger's last week," Timmy shouted in reply. Timmy had designated himself to be the one in charge of finding cardboard, but Timmy didn't always come through and good cardboard was in short supply at times.

"There better be!" Mark threatened.

Toward the end of Jeffries Street, Mark abruptly took a sharp turn and headed down a steep dirt path toward the creek, narrowly missing a large cement abutment by inches. The other boys followed Mark's lead with Danny gently brushing the structure.

The three expert bikers continued along the treacherous path dodging the many trees and large rocks that lined the snaky corridor. When the boys arrived at the final incline that would have to be conquered to get to the top of cardboard hill, Danny's side began to ache terribly. Unwilling to fail now, he pushed hard on the pedals of his beloved Western Flyer. Grunting and groaning, he pushed down on the pedal one last time and finally ascended to the summit. He glided for a moment to collect his breath and then pushed forward again, racing to keep up with the others.

When they rounded the final turn, Danny could see the huge oak tree that stood next to their favorite sliding place. With its monstrous trunk and long powerful limbs, it was like a giant colossus that stood guarding their special haunt, it appeared to scream out to anyone who could hear, 'Stay away! This hill is for kids!'

Arriving at the hill, Danny slammed hard on his brakes and skidded to a stop just behind Mark and Timmy. Jumping free of their two-wheeled chariots, the boys ran headfirst into the tall weeds that surrounded the big oak tree. Pushing the weeds apart, the boys searched desperately for a good piece of cardboard. The longer pieces were the best for sliding because you were able to fold them back at the top for greater speed.

The hunt was on and at times, it could get ugly. Pushing and shoving often ensued, followed by some quickly doubled fists. Fortunately, today each boy was able to find an acceptable piece and they were soon scampering up to the top of the hill for their first trip down. Mark was the first to reach the top.

"Eee-yak-eee!" Mark shouted just before launching. Danny watched in awe as Mark maneuvered his way down the steep descent leaning left and right to gain more speed. Mark skidded to a stop in the long weeds at the bottom of the hill and rolled to his feet, holding the flapping cardboard high above his head in a triumphant gesture.

Danny was next. Not as aggressive as Mark, he started more slowly, but soon he was skimming down the hill at top speed, his dark hair blowing in the breeze. As he neared the bottom, a bolt of panic shot through him. He was heading straight for the Devil's Backbone, the huge trunk of a sycamore tree that sat at the bottom of the hill. Due to the grotesque shape of the trunk, the boys had tagged it "Devil's Backbone." Danny's heart was in his throat. On more than one occasion, a slider had to be taken to the doctor's office after an encounter with the giant tree. Leaning hard to the left and pulling with all his strength on the end of the cardboard, he struggled mightily to avoid crashing into the granite-like edifice, but the sled wasn't responding. He pulled harder and harder, but to no avail. At the last minute, the sled moved just a smidgeon left and missed the trunk, but he bounced over a large root at the base of the trunk. After colliding with the root, Danny lost control and rocketed off the cardboard into the thick weeds at the bottom of the hill. A few seconds later, the cardboard sled landed gently on his head.

"Wow!" he exclaimed. "That was cool!"

"Smooth move, Ex-Lax!" Mark chided, as he ran past him and headed to the top of the hill for his next ride. Almost completely covered by dead grass, Danny struggled to his feet.

"Look out below!" came a shrill warning. Neighbor Timmy flew by Mark at what seemed to be supersonic speed crashing headfirst into a defenseless Danny. Danny let out a holler and went flying back into the thick weeds. Chests heaving, both boys laid in the grass laughing uncontrollably. When the laughing had subsided, Danny playfully punched Timmy in the arm, grabbed his cardboard slice and ran up the hill with Timmy in close pursuit.

As the boys neared the top of the hill, the red autumn sun was starting to drop behind the tall pines that bordered the popular woods. Mark paused, looked at the sun and then he looked at Danny and Timmy.

"Sorry fellas, but it's time to go," Mark shouted. "We have to be home before dark."

Disappointed, the boys shrugged their shoulders and did as ordered. They tossed their cardboard sleds into the weeds on the side of the hill and followed Mark over to the bikes. Mark quickly lifted his beautiful English Racer, a gift from his father for being named Athlete of The Year the previous year. He threw his leg over the narrow-wheeled bike, and while straddling the bike, he turned toward his little brother.

"How's your side, Danny?"

"Kind of sore."

Timmy interrupted, "Gotta go!" he shouted and then quickly rode away.

The two brothers were alone now and Mark's mood suddenly changed. His eyes locked on his little brother. "Did Dad hit you?" he asked.

Danny bent over to pick up his Flyer, paused for a second, and then replied softly, "Yeah."

Angry tears welled up in Mark's dark blue eyes. "If he ever does that to you again, I'll kill him!" The tough fourteen-year-old's face was contorted in rage. He slammed his beautiful Racer into first gear, stood up on the pedal and rapidly rode away.

Danny hopped aboard his Flyer and took off, straining mightily to keep up with his older brother. He wasn't sure if Mark would really kill his father, but it made him feel good that Mark loved him enough to say it. All of a sudden his side felt a little better.

Chapter 12

"Drive the lane, Danny! Drive the lane!" The younger brother glanced towards the sidelines at Mark, who was shouting instructions at him. Instinctively, he quickly dribbled back to center court, but was unable to drive the lane as ordered. Mark had apparently stayed after his practice to encourage Danny in his tryout for the seventh grade team.

With his side killing him, but reinvigorated by Mark's presence, Danny passed the ball to the center at the edge of the key. Faking his man, he raced toward the basket. The center spotted him and dropped a great bounce pass just in front of the trailing defender. Danny gathered up the ball, took one more dribble and leapt toward the basket for a sure lay-up. He could hear Mark yelling, "Atta boy, Danny!" But when he lifted the ball for the shot, a horrifying pain shot up his side forcing his shooting arm to withdraw slightly and causing the ball to hit the bottom of the rim and fall harmlessly to the ground. A sure basket had become an embarrassing miss for the youngster. In excruciating pain, he looked over at Coach Collins who was shaking his head and talking to his assistant coach. It was the fourth shot that Danny had missed during the tryout and the easiest one. Grimacing in pain, Danny hustled back on defense. Hoping to redeem himself, he turned and ran smack into the biggest kid on the court, his long-time nemesis, Tubby Shelton. The collision caused Danny to stumble and fall.

Tubby laughed, adding insult to injury.

Danny scowled at him and quickly jumped to his feet. He turned and charged headfirst down the court to catch up with his man. He glanced over at Coach Collins, desperately afraid that the coach would take him out of the game for poor play.

"Ball!" someone shouted. Danny turned quickly just in time to see the orange sphere sailing over his head. He reached up with his right hand to try and block the pass, but it traveled over his outstretched fingertips and into the hands of a hard charging Stretch Hamilton, the star of the team. Danny watched helplessly as Stretch laid it in the basket.

Humiliated by his poor play, Danny just stood under the basket with his hands on his hips. He was so distraught that he barely felt the ball bounce off his shoulder and hit the floor. Chasing after it, he corralled the ball, grabbed it firmly in both hands and prepared to take it out. Abruptly, the gym reverberated from the piercing sound of the buzzer. Danny's shoulders sank. He watched his replacement race toward him calling for the ball. Danny shot him a short bounce pass and headed for the sideline holding his aching side.

Looking up at the electronic scoreboard, he saw

there were two minutes left to play in the second quarter. He felt sick and discouraged knowing the coach hadn't seen him at his best. He arrived at the bench and fell into an open spot. He looked over and saw Mark talking to Coach Carter and pointing at his side, attempting to explain Danny's injury. The coach was listening intently to Mark with a level of respect that he would give few athletes in this school. Unfortunately, the coach didn't appear to be convinced by Mark's explanation. He patted Mark on the shoulder and turned away from the persistent youngster, concentrating once again on the play on the court.

Even the aggressive lobbying of the coach by his older brother couldn't save Danny this time. He was certain he would be off the team. Mark glanced over at him and gave him an obligatory thumbs up. Danny gave back a half-hearted thumbs up, snatched a towel from the student manager and angrily swiped the perspiration from his face.

"I'm screwed," he whispered. The first and second quarters ended with Danny not returning to action.

The ten-minute half time intermission seemed to fly by. The coach blew the whistle and ordered the boys to the bench area for final instructions before the start of the second half. The players huddled around the passionate coach. Danny waited anxiously to see if the coach might put him in at the start of the second half.

"Moorhead!" he shouted. "Get in there for Stretch and give him a little break." The gangly youngster quickly jumped off the bench and hustled over to the scorer's table and leaned over to announce his entry. The coach hunched down in the huddle. There would be no more substitutions. Danny shook his head, now certain that he didn't make the team.

It seemed like an eternity before he heard the buzzer announcing the end of the third quarter. The boys huddled up around the coach once again listening to instructions for the fourth quarter. When the coach was finished barking out his instructions, Danny waited to see if by some miracle he would make a change in the lineup.

"Same five!" the coach yelled.

The huddle broke up. A dejected Danny walked slowly over to the middle of the bench and took his seat. He was very angry at his father right now. He knew that if not for the punch to his ribs, he would have had a good chance to make the team. Although he didn't possess Mark's athletic ability, Danny was still a pretty good basketball player in his own right. This was his first appearance before the new seventh grade coach and the coach was judging him solely on his performance today. Horribly disappointed, Danny sat and stared down at the hardwood.

Players shuffled in and out of the game as the fourth quarter progressed. With each substitution, Danny found himself being pushed further down the bench. He had reached the end of the bench when the buzzer sounded ending the game.

"Gather round, fellas!" the coach shouted.

The young athletes quickly circled around their burly leader. "I want to thank all of you for coming out today. You gave it your very best. I wish I could put all of you on the team, but regrettably, only ten of you will make the squad. I will also select two alternates to be ready in case one of the first ten is unable to play for some reason. The alternates will practice daily with the team and dress for home games, but they will not dress for away games. I will post the names on the main bulletin board by the front entrance. The list will be there when you come to school in the morning." The coach smiled warmly and looked around at the boys, "Any questions?"

The boys were silent, too nervous and insecure at the age of twelve to ask the imposing coach a question.

"Well then, if there are no questions, hit the showers," he ordered. The boys turned and filed quietly down the narrow passageway between the bleachers. Danny, head hanging, took up the rear.

"Kinsey!" the coach shouted.

Surprised, Danny turned. The coach strolled over and stopped right next to him. He put his big hand on Danny's shoulder.

"You know Danny, you've got quite a big brother. Not too many boys his age would confront an adult coach the way he did today. He must really love you a lot."

Tears formed in Danny's eyes.

The coach tightened his grip on Danny's shoulder. "Keep this to yourself, okay?" Danny could smell the damp sweat on the big man's cotton shirt. "Yeah, uh, sure."

"You're on the team, Kinsey, as an alternate. I want to see how you do once that side heals. I saw potential out there today. In fact, I saw shades of your father. I want to give you a shot. If you play half as well as Mark says you can, I'll dress eleven for the away games. I've done it before. Now get in there, get dressed and don't tell a soul until after I post the list tomorrow. Got it?" He smiled gently, shoving the awestruck lad toward the locker room.

"Got it," Danny replied. His heart was racing. He felt like his feet were floating off the ground as he ran toward the locker room to join the other boys. "I can't believe it!" he mumbled. He shoved open the heavy metal door and hurried in to join the other boys. He looked back at the smiling coach and then he melded into the chaotic locker room.

Chapter 13

Dan lay staring up at the ceiling in the tiny den. Those were indeed bittersweet memories of his tryouts for the seventh grade basketball team and the heroic efforts of his older brother. His heart sank as he recalled the disturbing incident that occurred at the Kinsey house the morning following his tryout.

....

Spoons clinking in cereal bowls and crunching bites into heavily buttering bread were the only sounds to be heard around the table on this typical morning at the Kinsey house. Breakfast was a much quieter affair than the festive and enjoyable atmosphere they enjoyed during the evening meals and there was one big reason for that. The quiet was soon broken.

"How'd the tryouts go last night?" Their agitated father hurried into the room and quickly pulled up to the table.

"Okay, I guess," Danny replied quietly.

"You guess? You mean you don't know?" his father snapped.

"Well, uh, good," Danny replied, careful not to anger his thin-skinned father.

"So, you're on the team, I take it."

"No, uh, not exactly, Dad," Danny murmured with some trepidation. He shot a frightened glance at Mark as if to say 'here it comes'.

"Not exactly? Just what do you mean, boy? Tell me now!"

Danny could sense his father's impatience growing and he smelled trouble. "Well, I made it, but as an alternate."

"An alternate!" their father shouted. "That was the best you could do? An alternate?"

He glared at the little boy, upset at his son's inability to make the traveling team. But Danny knew what was really bothering his father. He wasn't concerned about Danny, he was concerned about what the guys at the club would think. For the great Beau Kinsey's son to be just an alternate would be humiliating for him.

A deep scowl crossed Mark's face. He had been closely watching the emotional exchange between Danny and his dad. The strong one once again interceded on behalf of his little brother. "He did good, Dad!"

His dad shot a hard stare at the insolent boy. "This doesn't involve you, Mark!" he ordered. "This is between me and Danny." Danny couldn't help but notice how his father's voice softened when he spoke to Mark.

Unfazed by the preferential tone in his father's voice,

the protective youngster shot back at his father, "He would have done better, Dad, but his ribs were sore where you punched him!"

Bright red spread quickly up his father's face, obviously taken back by the damning statement from his oldest son spoken in front of Grandma Carrie. He was beside himself. His eyes darted around the table at the shocked faces. In a fit of uncontrollable rage, he jumped up knocking his chair backward. He leaned over and grabbed Mark by the neck. "Why, you little smart ass!" he screamed. "I'll teach . . ."

"Stop! Stop!" Grandma shouted. She jumped up from her chair and grabbed the powerful man's arm with both of her hands, trying frantically to stop him from hurting the frightened boy.

Clutching Sadie tightly, the usually feisty Maggie screamed and unable to watch the violent actions of her angry father, ran out of the room.

Enraged, the cruel man struggled to free his arm from the determined matriarch. Turning his focus on Grandma Carrie, he let loose of Mark, and with a mighty jerk, he freed his arm, sending the screaming caretaker flying backward like a ragdoll. The stunned boys watched as Grandma crashed violently into a large vase of artificial flowers that sat in the corner of the room. The vase shattered into a million pieces. She slid slowly down the wall landing on the floor. A sickening, terrified look filled her face.

Young Mark jumped up from his seat and dove headfirst across the table at his father. Silverware, bowls and cereal went flying. He ducked to avoid a punch thrown by his father and wrapped his arms around his father's muscular waist, holding on for dear life. "Leave Grandma alone!" he screamed.

At almost the same time, Danny darted under the table and threw his slender arms around his father's leg. The boys fought desperately to protect their fallen grandmother from the seething brute.

Then as quickly as the outburst had started, their angry father suddenly stopped his assault. He stood still with beads of sweat glistening on his upper lip, his dark hair dangling over tormented eyes. He surveyed the carnage in the room. Grandma Carrie sat sobbing in the corner. His sons were holding fiercely to him, trying to stop him from hurting her more. Maggie had long since run screaming from the room. The beautiful table setting that Carrie had so diligently prepared lay in shambles. Dishes and food were strewn everywhere across the room. Apparently shocked by his own violent behavior, a somber Beau pushed his hair off his forehead and spoke quietly.

"Well, uh, now, no sense everyone getting all upset," he said with a nervous chuckle. "Why, uh, everyone, uh, loses his temper once in awhile." An unnatural smile broke out on his face. "You boys can let go. I'm not mad anymore. Go over and help your poor grandma up. She stumbled and fell in the corner."

The boys' grips slowly loosened on their father. They looked around the room in shocked dismay and then withdrew from their dad and hurried across the floor to comfort their whimpering grandmother. They each grabbed one of her shaking arms, struggling mightily to lift her to her feet. Once standing, they hugged her waist and they all stood sobbing in the corner, surrounded by shattered pottery.

A blank look covered their father's ashen face as he observed the destruction in the room. It was as if he was unable to comprehend what he had just done to his family.

"I, uh, have a lot to do at the, uh, car lot. I best be going." His hands were shaking. He stuffed his shirttail into his trousers and headed to the door. After adjusting his tie, he twisted the knob to leave and turned toward his weeping family again as if to say something. However, after several seconds of staring, he couldn't find the words. He spun around and darted through the back door. A short time later, they heard the roar of his car's powerful engine and the crunching of graved as he backed down the driveway and headed for work.

Completely overwhelmed by the sudden turn of events, Grandma gently hugged the boys and tried to compose herself. She pulled a hanky from her apron and wiped the tears from her eyes.

"You children get ready for school. I'll clean this mess up." She managed a warm smile for the boys. Lifting her head proudly, Grandma Carrie walked across the room toward the refrigerator.

Mark put his arm firmly around Danny's shoulder and the two boys watched their brave grandma pick up a washcloth, open the freezer door on the refrigerator and grab a hand full of ice. She wrapped the ice in the small rag and placed it firmly against her forehead.

"Grandma must have a bump on her head," Mark said solemnly.

"She probably hit the vase when she fell." Danny replied.

The boys felt something on their legs. They looked down and saw Maggie's small head pushing out from between them. Her terrified face was covered with tears. "What's wrong with Grandma?" she whimpered.

Danny dropped down on one knee, gently squeezing his little sister's shoulders. "Grandma's okay, she just fell down for a minute." Mark also knelt down next to Maggie.

Sensing the distress in the children, Grandma dropped the washcloth and hurried over.

"You poor things," she said sympathetically. She knelt down and surrounded the frightened brood with her arms. She hugged them, whispering reassurances.

"You're not going to leave us are you, Grandma?" Mark's eyes pleaded desperately.

Grandma looked over at the oldest boy and hesitated as if searching for the right words. "Come sit with me, children. I think we need to have a talk.

"We'll miss the bus!" Mark exclaimed.

"Don't worry about the bus, I will take you to school." She stood and held Maggie's hand and led the group over to the large sofa in the family room. They all sat down. Grandma pulled Maggie, and her ever present Sadie, upon her lap. Mark and Danny squeezed in on either side of her.

Chapter 14

With her hands still shaking from the horrifying event of a few moments earlier, Grandma spoke calmly to the children. "After your mother died, I promised myself that I would help raise you children, no matter what. I felt that it was very important that you have someone in your life that could fix your meals, do your laundry and clean the house. I also thought your father would need me." She paused and looked intently at each of the children. "And I have never once regretted my decision. I love you children dearly. What your father did today was inexcusable, but I also know that he loves you. I will have a talk with him when he has calmed down and tell him this must never happen again."

"Why is he so crazy?" Mark groaned.

Grandma smiled, "Mark, I've known your father since he was a small boy. Our families were friends, and he had a crush on your mom from the time he was just ten years old. He was a sweet boy growing up, very polite and always trying to do the right thing. From the time he was a little boy, your father excelled at sports.

When he started playing organized sports, people watched your father in amazement. It was obvious that he was something special. But no matter how much he excelled at sports or how many awards he won, it was never enough for his father."

"You mean Grandpa Tom?" Danny blurted. "He was nice."

"Yes, Tom was very nice to you children when he would come to visit, I know that. You never saw the hardness in your grandpa because he mellowed as he grew older, but as a young father he was very harsh with your dad. Verbal abuse and occasional beatings were not unusual. You see, I don't think your Grandpa Tom liked himself very much, so he took it out on your father. From the time your dad was a small boy, Tom would go to your dad's ball games and scream and berate him. No matter how well your dad played, he was never happy. I think that's one of the reasons why this town loves your father so much. They all marvel at how he was able to overcome his father's verbal abuse."

"Is that why Dad drinks so much beer and stuff . . . because of how his dad treated him?" Mark asked.

"I think so, Mark. I also think that's one of the reasons he becomes so angry at times and does some of the awful things he does."

"Like what he did today," Maggie whimpered.

"Yes, dear, I'm afraid so." She gently ran her fingers through Maggie's blond curls.

The strong woman's voice began to crack. "Oh, there have been several times when I've thought about packing it in. Every time he's mean to you kids I feel like walking out, but I understand your dad and I know what he's been through. He's basically a good person and he always treated your mother well and I know how very much he misses her. She always brought out the best in him."

Red-eyed, the children sat quietly, trying to comprehend everything they had just learned about their thin-skinned and volatile father.

"Will he get nicer someday like Grandpa Tom did?" Danny asked.

"I hope so, I certainly hope so." Grandma sighed.

"Uncle Bud told me that our dad's a hero. Why is he a hero?" Danny asked."

Danny and Mark knew that their dad's team had won the State, but they knew little else about their father's basketball career. It was something that Beau never really talked about much to the children. They had heard bits and pieces around town about their dad's exploits, but they had little comprehension of the significance of their dad's career and how the memories of his accomplishments were so indelibly etched in the minds of the folks in this basketball crazy city.

Grandma hesitated for a moment and then spoke, "Let me try to explain something to you children." She made eye contact and smiled at each of them. "Maple City is passionate about high school basketball." Mark and Danny sat up in their seats. "And about the biggest thing that can happen to a town like Maple City is for the high school basketball team to win a State Championship."

"Dad's team won the State," young Danny blurted.

"Sure did, Danny. When your father was a senior, Maple City had a pretty darn good team. We won sixteen games during the regular season and then the State tournament started. As usual, we had a tough time in the Sectional, winning a hard fought final over Oak Ridge. After that scare in the Sectional, our boys settled down and won the Regional easily. At the Semi-State, we won handily in the afternoon and then came on strong in the final game to beat Huntington by six points. Our town was so excited! There were posters all over town and a huge community pep rally! We were in the Final Four for the first time in forty years. It was off to Indianapolis and that giant Butler Field House."

"Did you go, Grandma?" Mark asked.

"Oh my, yes. I was a huge fan in those days. I knew a lot about basketball. I used to keep stats at every game. I knew every player's scoring average, rebounds, and shooting percentage. You could say, I was a basketball nut! Your grandpa said I knew more about basketball than anybody in town."

"Tell us about the games," an impatient Mark implored.

"Yeah, I hear people talking about it all the time," Danny added.

"Well, the Maple City Giants were not expected to win the tournament. We made the Final Four, but Indianapolis Tech was the huge favorite to win and if they didn't win, everyone thought Kokomo would. In fact, everyone was surprised that our school even made it to the finals. We weren't a highly rated team in the polls and we didn't have any tall players."

"Did Tech have tall players?" Mark asked.

"Oh my, yes. They had two boys over six feet five inches. Kokomo had one." The children could sense the excitement in their grandma's voice as she relived the story of the town's great success so many years ago. "Our tallest man was only six feet tall."

"Wow!" Danny exclaimed. "How'd we beat 'em?"

Grandma leaned up to the edge of the sofa. Her face beamed with excitement as she reminisced about that thrilling day so many years ago.

"We played Kokomo in the afternoon and they were ranked number three in the State. And boy, did they look big!" She lifted her hand high in the air to demonstrate. "At the beginning of the game, Kokomo got off to a big lead and things looked pretty grim for the Giants. Those Kokomo players were passing the ball behind their backs, dunking the ball and hitting everything they threw in the air. They were so quick! Our fans were getting pretty down."

"On the ground?" Maggie asked.

"Oh no, darling, I mean they weren't happy." Grandma smiled affectionately.

"Shut up, Maggie!" Mark ordered. "Let Grandma tell the story."

Maggie frowned and stuck her tongue out at him.

Grandma continued, "Then your father took over against those big Wildcats and he put on quite a show.

"What'd he do?" an excited Danny asked.

"What didn't he do?" Their enthusiastic Grandma continued, "He was stealing the ball and dribbling around and scoring at will. Soon we were only down a few points and our fans were cheering so loud you couldn't hear yourself think! Thanks to your dad, we were only two down at half time and our fans were going crazy, jumping around and screaming. But as the second half started, the Wildcats were growling. They came out of that locker room on a mission! They were hitting long ones, lay-ups, slam-dunking the ball and pretty much just having their own way." She smiled at the children. "But your father wasn't going to have any part of that. He turned it on, stealing the ball and tearing their zone defense apart. Your father wasn't quite six feet tall, but he was muscular and a great jumper. Kokomo's big guys were having a hard time stopping him. Their star player, Marcus Williams, got into foul trouble trying to guard your dad. Williams was furious when they called his fourth foul."

"Man! Dad must have been really good!" Mark exclaimed.

"Oh my, I should say so! Why, I've never seen anything like him. Your dad just kept coming at them. He was so quick and could jump so high that he made them look silly at times. At the end of the third quarter, we were only two points behind again and our fans were beside themselves. And then, just as the fourth quarter started, your father stole the ball and laid it in to tie the game. There was pandemonium in that gym."

"That's where Little Joe and Hoss live, at the Ponderonium." Maggie proudly announced.

"Butt out, Maggie! It's the Ponderosa anyhow!" Mark stared daggers at little Maggie. Danny smiled and patted her head.

"Marcus Williams soon fouled out and stormed over to the bench. Now it was 'Katie bar the door' for your father."

"Who is . . . ?"

"Knock it off, Maggie!" Mark yelled, interrupting his

confused sis.

Grandma continued, "I wish you could have seen your dad, scoring and feeding it off to his teammates for baskets. He was a one man show! He scored 29 points and we won 58 to 52. That game is etched in my memory forever."

"What happened in the next game?" an anxious Danny asked.

"Well, as you know, the first game was played in the afternoon and the final game in the evening, so between the games, all the Maple City fans went to get something to eat in downtown Indianapolis. We were soaking it all in, just walking along and gawking at the tall buildings and celebrating. Your dad was the talk of the town! People from the other schools were coming up to us and asking about your father. They couldn't believe what a good player he was. 'That Kinsey kid' sure had everyone's attention! We were so proud as we walked along the wide streets of the big city, waving our Giant banners and doing impromptu cheers, just acting like kids! Your dad put Maple City on the map that day."

"What about the next game?" Mark asked impatiently.

"Oh my, it was a doozy." Grandma chuckled. "Butler Field House was packed. The fans from the teams that lost in the afternoon would usually leave before the evening game, but not that night. Everybody wanted to stay and see if that 'Kinsey kid' and his Maple City teammates could pull off the upset of the year. Tech had been rated number one in the State all year. The Indianapolis Star also rated them number one in the entire country, and they were a very proud team. We sure had our work cut out for us."

"Number one in the whole country, wow!" Danny exclaimed.

"The night game got off to a slow start. The Tech coach was feeling us out a little bit. Naturally, he had a double team on your father. At the end of the first quarter, we were behind a few points, and your father was scoreless. Confident that they had found a way to stop your dad, the Titans came on strong in the second quarter. Their All Star guard, Darius Jones, really turned it on. A Sports Illustrated First Team High School All American, he was averaging over 30 points a game and was going to attend Purdue University that fall on a full ride. Their big six-foot seven-inch center, Ray Washington, was taking care of things underneath. They were impressive to watch! That Jones kid would float down the court and gently loft the ball to his big center for a hard dunk. At the end of the first half, I believe we were behind about twelve or fourteen points and it didn't look good for the Giants. Your dad had scored only six points and Tech seemed to be having its own way. You could hear a pin drop in our cheer block. We were stunned."

"Darn!" Mark shook his head.

"There's more." Grandma smiled and ruffled Mark's thick hair. "During half time, your father walked around the court talking to the other players, gesturing with his hands and encouraging them to play harder in the second half. He was smacking their fannies and shouting encouragement to them. My, how that boy hated to lose!"

"When the buzzer rang announcing the start of the

second half, our boys came out like gangbusters, hustling up and down the court and diving for loose balls. You could see those boys were determined to win that game and your daddy was leading the charge. He was beating the double team and feeding off to his teammates for easy lay-ups. The Giants were on the move and our guards were all over Jones on defense, causing their great star to become frustrated."

The children sat wide-eyed, listening intently as Grandma continued the story. "With Jones struggling, the Giants drew within four at the end of the third quarter. Our fans were ecstatic, jumping up and down and screaming for all they were worth, trying to inspire the team. The fans from the teams that had lost in the afternoon began cheering for us. It was so exciting!"

Grandma was beaming. "At the beginning of the fourth quarter, your father made a great steal and laid the ball in. The Giants were now only two behind and there was mayhem at Butler Field House. I thought the roof was going to blow off!"

The children were bug-eyed, hanging on every word.

"Frustrated, the Titans head coach called a time out. After the time out, he pulled the double team off your dad and went to a zone. Zone defenses had given your father a little trouble during the year, so it made sense. After the time out, Jones came down and quickly popped a fifteen-footer that quieted the crowd. Then he proceeded to steal the inbounds pass from one of our players and laid it in for another two points. The Titans were up six again, and now their fans were going wild. Maple City's Coach Ware quickly called a time out. I will never forget watching your father. He was moving around in that huddle and talking to his teammates, pushing them and shouting at them. He was obsessed with winning that game and even after the time out he didn't let up. As they came out on the court, your dad was waving his fist and rooting his teammates and the fans on. He had fire in his eyes and everyone had the sense that he wasn't going to be stopped.

As the second half continued, your father was hitting the jumper and keeping the game close with some great passing. The zone wasn't bothering him much, but Jones and company were not backing off. They were performing their magic also. The Tech boys were putting on quite a show, but so were our feisty Giants. It was obvious to everyone that something had to give." The smiling mother-figure hesitated and breathed deeply.

"What happened next, Grandma? Go on!" Danny urged.

She smiled and continued, "I will remember the end of that game for as long as I live. With two minutes to go, it was the Indianapolis Tech Titans 62 and the Maple City Giants 56. Jones stole the ball, shot a fifteen-footer and was fouled. He buried the foul shot. Now it was Tech 65 and Maple City 56 with less than two minutes left in the game. We were all sick inside. Exhausted from shouting all day, everyone was feeling pretty discouraged."

Grandma leaned up a little further on the sofa. "But it wasn't over yet. After a quick time out by the Giants, one of our boys, Wendell Small, took the ball out and tossed it to your father. Fighting off the double team, he carefully worked his way over the ten-second line and tossed the ball behind his back to Small, who hit the open jumper from the top of the key. We had a glimmer of hope again, but time was running out, and we were trailing by seven. Jones gathered up the loose ball in those big hands of his and stepped back to throw the inbounds pass. He must have been feeling overly confident and thought they had the game won, because the usually careful star threw a sloppy pass. One of our boys snatched it out of the air and fired a hard pass to your father who pulled up for a fifteen-footer and was fouled in the process. Your dad swished the foul shot and it was now 65 to 61 with less than a minute remaining."

Grandma took a deep breath and continued the story. "An angry Darius Jones gobbled up the inbounds pass and darted down the court, weaving quickly between our frustrated defenders. He was as smooth as velvet. He moved to the edge of the key and lofted one of those high soft passes to the tall Washington who went in for the dunk. But unbelievably, the ball bounced off the back of the rim and flew way out to center court. Your dad grabbed the long ricochet and tossed it ahead to one of our players who had stayed back on defense. He laid it in and it was now 65 to 63 with thirty seconds to go. The Tech coach was beside himself! He was storming up and down the sidelines, screaming at the ref for a time-out. The time-out was granted and all the boys from both teams gathered around their coaches. The bedlam in that gym almost brought down the rafters! Sure wish you kids could have seen it!"

"I'm gettin' goose bumps!" Mark said excitedly.

"Me, too!" Danny yelled.

"What are goose . . . ?"

Mark waved his fist at his little sister. She threw a nasty stare back at her big brother.

Grandma scooted up to the edge of the sofa, her arms extended as she began to recall the closing seconds of the exciting game. "After the time out, our coach put on a full court press. Our boys were jumping up and down in front of the Tech players and were trying to steal the inbounds pass." Grandma began waving her arms in the air to demonstrate the aggressive action. Maggie slid off her lap as Grandma leapt to her feet—much to the surprise of the children. Now standing, Grandma went on.

"Tech finally got the ball in to Jones, who broke our press and quickly dribbled across the center line. He waved his players into position and then proceeded to kill the clock. Washington hung around our end of the court so he would be in position to stop any fast breaks. He looked huge standing near the foul line with arms outstretched! Back at the other end, Jones was magnificent. He wove his way between our players, fainting to the left and right. He would charge under the basket and then dribbled back out behind the key. Our defense finally trapped him, but he quickly dished the ball to another player, who fired it right back to him.

Their coach was a nervous wreck, moving up and down the sidelines and shouting orders to his players. Soon there were only fifteen seconds to go and Tech's coach began yelling something at Jones, but with all of the noise, Jones couldn't hear his coach, so he continued to dribble. Only six seconds were on the clock when Jones finally heard his coach, he glanced toward the sidelines. With Jones distracted, your father moved in and swatted the ball away from him."

The children could feel the breeze from Grandma's hand as she demonstrated the famous steal.

"Your father gathered up the loose ball and raced across the ten-second line. We were jumping up and down on the bleachers and screaming at the top of our lungs. Our hearts were in our throats. Washington moved into position to stop your determined dad, but your father was at his amazing best. He charged headfirst toward the taller player."

Grandma dribbled an imaginary ball around the room, her excitement was growing.

"Your father fainted to the left, just enough to get the big center leaning, and then he ducked to the right." Grandma gyrated to the left and right mimicking the move.

"Washington righted himself and jumped toward your father who was driving in for the lay-up. We were all speechless. Washington's long arm swiped at the ball, but your father lowered the ball causing the big man's arm to glide just above the ball. While he was still in the air, your father brought the ball back up and let it fly toward the backboard. Washington crashed into him, just as the buzzer rang, ending the game. Both of them went sprawling to the gym floor. The ball hung in the air forever as the shocked crowd watched and waited. It finally bounced off the backboard and rolled clear around the rim. After teetering there for a second, it dropped through the hoop. There was nothing short of chaos in that big gymnasium. We were hugging each other and falling all over the bleachers. It was a moment

I will never forget!"

Grandma jumped into the air, fist doubled and screamed, "Yes!" Her feet landed gently on the shag carpet. Red faced, she glanced over at the wide-eyed children, quickly composed herself, stepped over and nestled between the boys again. Maggie quickly hopped up on her lap.

"What about the foul shot?" Mark asked.

Grandma cleared her throat and continued, "There was no time left on the clock and the score was tied at 65. The other players were milling around at center court while your father walked calmly to the line. He was as cool as a cucumber. He took two dribbles, as he always did, carefully placed the ball in the palm of his hand, bent his knees slightly and flipped his wrist. You could have heard a pin drop as the ball sailed through the air. Our mouths were hanging open as we waited for the ball to reach the basket. Finally, it reached the hoop and fell through the center of the rim, swishing the net. It had just happened! The Cinderella Maple City Giants had beaten the awesome Tech Titans and had won the Indiana State Basketball Championship, 66 to 65. Your father scored 16 points in the final period and ended up with 32 points for the game, a new State Tournament record. I couldn't talk for two days. I'd lost my voice."

"Did you ever find it?" a concerned Maggie asked.

"Yes, I did, darling," Grandma smiled and hugged her tightly.

"Wow!" Danny shouted. "I guess I can see why Dad's such a hero."

"Me, too!" Mark exclaimed.

"Oh yes, children, it was an incredible night. We all

stormed down to the gym floor, hugging and kissing our boys and more or less making fools of ourselves. The flashbulbs from the newsmen's cameras were flashing and the loudspeaker at Butler Field House was blaring when that ladder went up under the basket. A few minutes later, our boys, smiling from ear to ear, climbed up the ladder and cut off pieces of the net to keep as souvenirs. The team insisted that your father go first. There was another huge round of applause when he climbed up the ladder and cut off his piece of the net, a rather small piece, at that."

"Yeah, it's still in Dad's office in a frame on the wall behind his desk," Danny said.

"It sure is, Danny," Grandma said proudly. "A few minutes later, the crowd got real quiet. Our boys were lining up to receive the huge State Championship trophy."

"The trophy is down at the gym, I've seen it," Mark bragged. He shot a smug look at his brother, still smarting from Danny's answer about the piece of net above their dad's desk.

"It was wonderful, I was so proud of our team. After that day, your father became one of the best known basketball players in Indiana. Folks say he is a shoe-in for the Indiana Basketball Hall of Fame someday."

"Why didn't Dad play basketball in college?" Danny asked.

"Well, honey, he did for awhile. He went to Indiana University on a full scholarship," The children smiled at the mention of Indiana University. Everyone knew that their father was a huge IU fan.

Grandma continued, "But early in his first year at IU, your father injured his knee during practice and had to have an operation. After the surgery, his knee was never the same. He wasn't able to pivot or put any pressure on the bad knee, so he quit college after his first year, came back to Maple City and married your mom. Then you kids came along and he decided just to stay here and raise his family. I think the folks here are glad. They wanted their hero right here where they could see him. They idolized your father and still do to this day."

The kids got quiet as they tried to absorb everything they had just heard and seen. The dad they knew was so much different than the wonderful person their grandma had just described. A feeling of gloom settled over the room. The excitement of Grandma's story was soon replaced by the numbing reality of the violent scene that had so frightened and sickened them just a few moments earlier.

"Maybe he was nice once, but I still hate him," Mark grumbled.

Danny just stared at the floor.

Maggie held Sadie in her arms, gently rocking her back and forth, "Don't cry, it's okay. Our Daddy can't hurt us anymore. He's at work," she said gently.

Upset by the children's conflicted feelings, their grandmother tried to make sense of it all. "I think your father fought hard to be a good person, even though he was treated so poorly by his own father. It would be hard to come through all that abuse without being somewhat affected. I think your father's a good person, he just doesn't know how to show it."

The children sat quietly not making eye contact with

their grandma.

"Your mother had a wonderful calming effect on him. After her death, I could see a big . . ." Realizing what she had just said, the sensitive lady's eyes shot toward Mark.

Mark's head dropped at the mention of the day of his mom's tragic death. It brought back memories of the hateful words he said to her that day. His eyes glazed over and he jumped to his feet and raced from the room.

"Oh, no! Now what have I done?" Grandma immediately sat Maggie on the sofa next to Danny and hurried after Mark.

"That bump on Grandma's head is really getting big," Maggie whimpered.

"I know," Danny replied. "And she's worried about Mark."

"I love Grandma so much."

"So do I, Maggie."

Chapter 15

Dan rolled over on the loveseat, the smallish afghan slid to the floor. Half awake, he felt around on the floor until he located the evasive cover. Grabbing it securely, he pulled it back over him. The room had grown dark around him. He now realized the den had become his bedroom for the night. Nesting places were hard to find in the small house, and his Dad's old bedroom was definitely off limits. Dan felt certain that Ann had decided that the den was a good sleeping destination for him. He rolled to his side and looked down at the old shag carpet, the same shag that felt so good on his bare feet as a kid. Taking a long deep breath, he closed his eyes and once again let his thoughts take him back to his childhood days and growing up in Maple City, Indiana.

....

Busy doing his history homework, Danny's concentration was broken by the sound of a bicycle horn out in front of the house. He dropped his yellow

#2 lead pencil and watched it as it bounced on the kitchen table. Anxiously, he ran to the living room and brushed back the long green curtains for a look outside. Near the street, waving his arms frantically and motioning for Danny to come out was his best friend, Timmy Wortels.

Timmy was a slight boy, with freckles and dusty blond hair that always seemed to be about three weeks past a haircut. He lived with his brother and parents a few blocks from Danny in an undersized ramshackle house. The gutters sagged, and it was surrounded by large evergreen bushes that were in desperate need of a trimming. "That Wortel house is an eye sore," Danny's father would often complain.

Most evenings, after a hard day's work, Timmy's parents would end up at one of the many bars that were located near their factory, a massive plant that manufactured tires on the city's west side. Their lengthy absences from home left Timmy under the direct supervision of his fourteen-year-old brother, Frankie Wortels. Frankie, too young for such responsibility, proved to be a very weak parent figure. The result was that Timmy had a great deal of freedom with no curfew or geographical boundaries.

Being under the restriction of a nine-thirty curfew that was strictly enforced by his grandma, Danny sometimes envied his friend's freedom, but in reality, he felt kind of sorry for the slender boy with sad eyes and wrinkly clothes. *Maybe we kids need a few rules,* Danny often thought.

Danny's father never really approved of the unusual union between Danny and a factory worker's son; but preoccupied with his own drinking and gambling, he never said much about it. As a result, over the years, Danny and Timmy had become the best of friends. They spent most evenings together roaming the streets of the west side of Maple City on Timmy's 24- inch JC Higgins bike that was equipped with a light, a horn, and three red reflectors.

Danny's Western Flyer sat leaning on its kickstand at the back of the drive. It didn't have a light or horn and there was only one reflector. He wished his dad would buy him the necessary equipment for night riding so he and Timmy wouldn't have to ride double.

Mark's English Racer had four reflectors, a large light and a battery operated horn. "It came that way!" his father would grouse when Danny complained to him about the disparity between the two bicycles.

Danny quickly closed the living room curtain and raced back to the kitchen, "Grandma! Grandma! Timmy's here! Can I go play basketball?"

The kindly grandmother smiled at her adventuresome grandson. "Yes you may, but remember your curfew."

"Okay, Grandma," Danny shouted. He yanked his jacket off the wooden hook by the back door and raced through the living room, stumbling briefly on the door mat as he darted out the front door. With great excitement, he was looking forward to another evening of roaming the tough west side with his good friend Timmy. One advantage of having an absentee father was that their grandma gave them more freedom than their dad would have permitted. While Danny didn't enjoy as much freedom as Timmy, he could pretty well go where he wanted as long as he got home in time to meet curfew.

With a wide grin on his handsome face, the Kinsey boy ran toward his impatiently waiting friend. When he saw Danny coming, Timmy leaned up and began peddling slowly down the street. A running start was their way to get every minute out of the evening. Eyeing the empty seat below his friend's behind, and now at full stride, Danny took a mighty leap at just the right moment and landed on the empty seat just as Timmy was beginning to gain speed. It was an intricate maneuver, one that they had perfected over several months of trial and error and many scratches and bruises.

Now with Danny safely aboard and holding on for dear life, the two youthful nomads raced down Wesley toward Stanton Avenue, heading for another night of fun and mischief on the mean streets of the city's west side.

....

A short time later, Timmy lifted up and hit the brakes. They had arrived at the intersection of Wesley and Stanton, the end of the first leg of their journey. Danny glanced east, down Stanton at the expensive three-story homes and the beautifully manicured lawns. The wealthy east side was a far cry from their ultimate destination, which was the economically challenged and crime-ridden west side.

Maple City was a town where just a few blocks could mean the difference between being in a secure upscale neighborhood to being in a much poorer, less protected neighborhood. The west side was very much the latter—a blue-collar part of town made up of small unremarkable homes. The roads received less maintenance, reflecting the total lack of political pull in the area. French poodles and Great Danes roamed the well-manicured lawns on the east side, while pit bulls, Rottweilers and other breeds of aggressive dogs nervously paced back and forth behind rusty chain-link fences on the west side.

The town's manufacturing section had also been shoved over to the west side. On most nights, the air was filled with gray smoke that belched from the many factories that dotted the area. It was a tough blue-collar neighborhood, and after a long day's work in a hot dirty factory, many of the workers couldn't wait to stop by one of the many bars and taverns that were close by to have a few cold ones and blow off a little steam.

Both Danny and Mark found the rough west side fascinating. There weren't many kids from the east side hanging out in this part of town. It wasn't socially acceptable for them to be there, but the Kinsey boys loved it and went there anyway, especially Danny.

....

Timmy's thin, but strong legs powered the small bike along Stanton Avenue to the edge of the local bypass. The bypass is the major thoroughfare in town and widely accepted as the line of demarcation between the good and bad sides of town. Constructed some fifty years earlier when it was on the very edge of town, the bypass had become something quite different. Shortly after the construction of the bypass, the city fathers decided the prairie land on the west side of the highway would be a great place to expand their industrial base and provide jobs for the local folks. The weed covered fields soon became home for several factories of various shapes and sizes. This industrial expansion was soon followed by a major boom in housing construction. Cheap houses popped up overnight, providing living quarters for the thousands of workers flooding into town to work at the plants. It wasn't long before the bypass was surrounded on both sides by large neighborhoods and lined with all sorts of businesses including gas stations, restaurants, drug stores and car dealerships. Only a decade after it was constructed, it had become anything but a bypass.

The boys dismounted the bike and prepared to run across the highway. Timmy looked anxiously both ways. It was a perilous move to get across the busy four-lane highway with traffic speeding past at nearly fifty miles an hour. Finally, he saw an opening and ran frantically across the dangerous roadway with Danny running alongside him. Panting and out of breath, they reached the other side and quickly jumped back aboard their sturdy voyager and continued their journey into the dark and foreboding west side. As they sped along, the road was becoming narrower and bumpier.

A short time later, they were near their destination. Timmy leaned right and headed north down Railroad Street, which was the exact opposite direction of the basketball courts where Danny had told his grandmother he was going. Bouncing along behind

Timmy on the bike's narrow seat, pangs of guilt flooded through the conscientious Danny. He felt bad about fibbing to his grandmother about his destination, but the guilt would soon be outweighed by the thrill of hanging out with the home boys at the Bluebird Diner.

With his feet dangling to the side of the racing bike, Danny leaned forward and placed his chin over Timmy's shoulder, "Are we going to the Bluebird first?"

"Yeah," Timmy barked out the side of his mouth.

Within a few minutes, a large blue neon sign, in the shape of a giant bluebird, flashed above the small cinder block building. The busy diner was tucked between a large apartment building on the left and the infamous Tug's Tavern on the right.

Timmy peddled hard for another hundred feet and then jammed on the brakes. The bike skidded to a stop. He banged the kickstand down and the boys hopped off and headed for the front door of the dingy diner. Danny looked down at the many scratches and bare spots on the faded front door of the Bluebird. It looked like someone had started to paint it years ago and then gave up. The two boys pushed through the mottled door with Timmy leading the way.

It was dark inside the little café with only a few dim wall lamps providing light. The Bluebird always gave Danny an eerie feeling, but it was a feeling he liked. He found it exhilarating to be hanging out in such a dark mysterious place.

The many tables in the main room were occupied by men in soiled gray T-shirts, many sporting tattoos on their well-muscled arms. They spoke quietly to their lady friends who wore long cotton work dresses and had their hair pulled back in web-like hairnets. Several of the men displayed a pack of cigarettes rolled up in the sleeve of their cotton T-shirts. Unfiltered Camels and Lucky Strikes were the brands most preferred—only wimps and women smoked filtered cigarettes. These were hard tough men who worked in the nearby factories and foundries that dotted the west side. A few of the patrons glanced up at the boys and nodded hello to the familiar faces, and then returned to their conversations.

The boys paid little attention to the informal greetings. They were anxious to get to the backroom and the exciting pinball machines. Upon entering the backroom, they observed that several of their friends were already there as bells rang and bright lights flashed in the cramped little room.

Danny paused and watched the metal ball darting erratically inside one of the long, rectangular machines. "Awe, shit!" the boy operating the machine shouted.

"What's the matter, Spike?" Danny asked.

"I had a chance for the record and the damn ball took a crazy bounce and went down the slot on the side!"

Spike Lewis was one of the local tough guys on the west side. Spike lived on the second floor of a broken-down boarding house just across the street from the Bluebird. He was a year older than Danny and Timmy but in the same grade at school.

Danny thought it was cool that Spike swore like a sailor. It was something that neither he nor any of his "respectable friends" would ever dream of doing. But here in the dark eerie Bluebird Diner, in the bowels of the tough west side, that kind of language was accepted. Danny found it exhilarating.

"Timmy with ya?" Spike barked out of the side of his mouth without looking up from the machine.

"Right here," Timmy said quietly. He sheepishly stepped out from behind Danny. Timmy's parents both worked at the nearby General Tire Plant, so he was very much a part of the scene at the Bluebird. Spike and the other boys knew that Danny was from the better part of town, but they liked him and accepted him because he was friends with Timmy.

"How's Mark?" Spike asked. Mark was a good athlete and all the boys in school looked up to him, even these guys, and Mark sometimes accompanied the boys on their adventures. A late football practice prevented him from being with them this evening.

"Mark's good," Danny replied.

"Hey, Danny," a soft voice drifted out from the corner of the room. Danny looked over. He could see the silhouette of a thick stocky boy and the bright orange flame of a cigarette.

The boy laughed. "It's me . . .Eddie."

"Hey, Eddie, how ya doin'?"

"I'm okay. What about you, Danny?"

"I'm good," Danny answered cheerfully.

Eddie Gibbs was fourteen, soon to be fifteen, and he smoked nonfiltered Camels. Eddie's father died when he was very young forcing his mother to take a job at the local stamping plant. Working the night shift, she couldn't be there in the evenings for Eddie, and as a result, she soon lost control of her rebellious son. Just like Spike and Timmy, Eddie was free to roam the west side as late as he wanted. Soft-spoken and polite, Eddie was also the toughest kid in town and maybe the world, if you asked Danny. Danny found this contradiction fascinating. How could this sensitive nice kid become such a violent person at times? Even Mark wasn't as tough as Eddie. Mark told him once, "If I ever got into a fight with Eddie, I'd have to kill him to stop him." That would never happen though because Eddie liked Mark. Danny was certain that his kindhearted friend would never get mad enough to hurt any of his buddies. Danny had seen Eddie beat up some of the toughest kids on the rough west side, but he had never seen him lay a hand on a friend, no matter what the provocation. You had to love a kid like that.

Eddie slowly stepped out from the shadows. His broad shoulders and well-developed chest filled his loose gray T-shirt. He ambled over to the backdoor, opened it and flipped his cigarette into the cold night air. "Feels like winter," he said. A smile broke out on his square handsome face accentuated by a long scar—a memento of a slashing he received from a broken bottle in a bloody gang fight last spring. The nasty looking welt started just below his right eye and extended down to the corner of his mouth.

Danny watched every move Eddie made. He was certain, even at a young age, that he would never again meet another character as interesting as Eddie Gibbs.

"Hey, Eddie."

"Aye, Spike."

"Let's go to the clubhouse."

"Why?"

"This pinball machine's pissing me off."

The benevolent leader grinned at his foul-mouthed friend. "Okay, I'm tired of this place anyhow," Eddie replied.

This was high anxiety time for Danny. He stood motionless, as his eyes bounced back and forth from Spike to Eddie, waiting for some verification that it was okay for him to go along with them to the clubhouse. It was a given that Timmy would be invited, but Danny's status was not as certain. If Timmy went and he wasn't invited, he would lose his ride home and have to walk through some bad neighborhoods alone. Danny's heart was starting to pound rapidly. His palms were beginning to sweat as he anxiously awaited the verdict.

The observant Eddie, noticing Danny's uncertainty, walked slowly over and placed both of his thick hands on Danny's shoulders. "You're part of this gang, buddy, you and Mark both. You can go to the clubhouse anytime you want," he smiled warmly.

Spike frowned, probably annoyed by the open-ended nature of the invitation, but he would never question Eddie. Eddie was the leader—plain and simple.

Spike slammed hard on the push rod. A shiny ball bounced up to the slot. He pulled back hard on the spring driven lever and let go. The ball flew up the narrow passageway and began bouncing erratically at the top of the colorful machine.

Eddie slipped on his black leather jacket and hurried toward the backdoor. "Let's go," he ordered.

Spike and the other boys fell into line behind him. Lights flashed and a myriad of sounds echoed through the small room as Spike's unattended ball bounced its way harmlessly to the bottom of the machine. A wide-eyed Danny, amazed that Spike could put a quarter in the machine and then not care if he finished the game, watched the ball disappear into the black hole.

"Let's go," Timmy shouted. He and Danny ran out the door and raced for their bike. Danny was ecstatic at his new found status in the West Side Gang. They hopped aboard Timmy's bike. Timmy began pedaling with all his might, with Danny pushing the ground with his feet. They were both straining mightily to catch up with their rapidly departing friends, but it was to no avail. Timmy's bike was no match for the older boys' twenty-six inchers; and despite all their efforts, the other boys began pulling away from them.

Several blocks later and growing tired, an exhausted Timmy slowed to a normal pace. Danny looked over Timmy's shoulder and watched the other boys disappear around a distant corner.

Several blocks later, with the boys out of sight, Timmy turned sharply and ducked down an abandoned truck route that ran beside the rambling old box plant. The plant had been closed for years and was left unattended. Tall weeds grew in the cracks of the broken asphalt on the isolated roadway.

After riding a short distance, Timmy abruptly took a sharp left turn down a narrow pathway that wove its way through the thick brush and tall oak trees that were behind the huge plant. It was a dark and scary place. The only illumination provided to the nervous boys was a couple of rather dim security lights perched high above the dark abandoned plant. Fortunately, Timmy knew this path like the back of his hand. Before long, they found the opening and the two youngsters raced across the lot, dodging scattered chunks of broken asphalt.

The quiet scene was broken by the sound of large metal dippers banging into the huge castings at the nearby foundry. Danny glanced across an adjacent field just in time to see the glowing steel being poured into the waiting mold. *This is no place for kids at night,* Danny thought. The two boys finally reached the far side of the vacant lot and dove into a dark woods. After a few hundred feet, they turned right and rode up to the top of a small hill.

At the top of the hill, they could finally see it—the old security guard's hut that had become the secret hangout for the members of the West Side Gang. The fall moon shone brightly on the small wooden building giving it a foreboding appearance. To add to the surreal setting, Danny looked above the front door at the silhouette of a large hoot owl perched on top of the gray metal roof.

No longer able to ride the bike, the boys dropped it next to the others and climbed up the final incline to the hut. Up ahead, narrow slits of light bled through the sides of the loose-fitting front door. Voices could be heard coming from inside. Suddenly, Danny winced and ducked his head. The startled hoot owl screeched and flew past, just a few feet above him. The startled boys collected themselves and a reluctant Timmy approached the front door and gave the secret knock—three quick knocks, a pause and then one knock.

Danny had always been curious about what was inside the eerie looking building. He had been to the hideout with Timmy on other occasions when looking for Frankie, but he had never been inside. He didn't know what to expect.

"Who is it?" a gruff voice shouted from the back of the building.

"It's us, Timmy and Danny!" Timmy shouted.

Danny could hear feet shuffling across the wooden floor. A shadowy face peered at them through a large crack. After a brief pause, he heard the latch pop up and the door swing open.

"Come on in," Whitey Jones ordered. Whitey, so named because of his albino-looking eyes, stuck his head out the door and looked into the darkening night, as if looking for potential adversaries outside the hut. An anxious Danny skirted past the preoccupied sentry and stepped inside. He scanned the interior of the hideout. A dirty gas lantern hung from the center of the low ceiling, providing dim lighting for the small room. The shadowy light created a dark and spooky atmosphere. Over in the corner, just below a smaller lantern, the gang was sitting on a collection of old orange crates. They appeared to be just settling in for a poker game. Frankie Cantrell, Timmy's older brother, scooted his empty orange crate closer to the giant wood spool that they used for a table and barked, "Draw, okay?"

"Yeah, deal the damn cards," Spike ordered. Strands of black hair hung down over Spike's thin pocked face. Spike was the toughest looking one of the group, no doubt about that. Whitey hurried over and returned to the game, taking his customary spot next to Eddie.

Eddie took a hard drag on his Camel and exhaled. The smoke drifted slowly toward the ceiling. "Hand me the bag," he ordered. Spike immediately leaned back and reached behind his chair. He pulled up a heavy gray cloth bag and handed it to Eddie. Reaching inside the bag, Eddie pulled out a handful of loose change, mostly quarters, and set it on the table in front of him. Eddie passed the bag to his right to circulate around the table. Each player grabbed his own handful of coins and placed them on the table in plain view. The bag eventually ended up back with Spike, who dipped in the bag for his share and then dropped it behind his chair.

Danny was indeed awestruck by the ritual with the bag of coins. Playing poker for money was something only older people did, people like his father and the men at the club. He was astounded to see a group of boys his age playing poker for money. He knew he could never muster the courage to sit down and play the immoral game with the boys, but he loved being part of such scandalous behavior.

"Did ya hit the Sunoco Station?" the inquisitive leader asked.

"Naw, we hit Biggie's Jap Store and Wilson's Market," Frankie replied.

Eddie nodded.

This was the part of hanging with these boys that scared Danny the most. He knew where the money in that bag came from because Timmy had told him. About once a month or so, the boys would ride around late at night and break into the many vending machines that were in front of the stores and businesses in the area. They would empty the stolen money into a gray bag like the one on the floor. Danny had never been asked to join the boys' forays into the world of crime and he was glad. For the son of Beau Kinsey to be caught breaking into vending machines would be the talk of the town for months, and Danny knew it.

After robbing the machines, the boys would take their booty back to the clubhouse for safe keeping. When necessary, it would be distributed to the others as Eddie saw fit. During their frequent poker games, any one of them could grab a handful of money as needed. If someone appeared to grab too much, they had Eddie to deal with, so that never happened.

Danny shuddered to think what would happen if he was at the clubhouse and the police showed up and arrested all of them for breaking into vending machines. It would be the end of his life as he knew it. Chills shot up his spine just thinking about it.

"Aw, shit!" Spike exclaimed. "I can't get anything tonight." He angrily tossed his cards on the table.

The pale looking Whitey reached for the pot, his bony arm was covered with bruises and the gang knew why. Whitey's dad beat him regularly for little or no reason, often leaving bruises on his arms, face, and legs. Danny felt really sorry for the scrawny Whitey and was happy that the odd boy had won the pot.

Danny noticed that Frankie was staring at Eddie. The observant Eddie noticed the glare also, his brow raised begging more information. Frankie spoke, "After school today, Mose Jackson put Whitey in a headlock at Ogden Park and threw him on the ground, then he swiped all his money. He accused Whitey of stealing the money from his locker earlier in the day. Mose said it was his money."

Eddie looked over at Whitey, his brow furrowed. His

face slowly turned bright red. "That black bastard! Whitey doesn't even go to his school. Mose is in high school."

That was one of the few times he ever heard Eddie curse. He was obviously very angry. His antagonist, Moses 'Mose' Jackson, was fifteen and lived in the Carver neighborhood, a racially mixed area on the southwest side of Maple City. He was almost six feet tall with broad shoulders and a muscular frame. He was a bully and was feared by everyone. Stories of the beatings he had given to those who crossed him were legendary in Maple City.

With Eddie so angry and being protective of Whitey, Danny felt certain Eddie wouldn't let the big black boy get away with bullying and robbing his friend. He didn't want to see Eddie get hurt, but a fight between the stocky Eddie and the fearsome Mose would be awesome to see. It would be a fight to the end between two of the toughest kids in town.

"Mose plays ball 'bout every night at the lighted courts by the grade school," Spike offered.

Eddie angrily tossed his cards on the table. "Game's over." He scooted his crate back and spat on the wood floor. He stood and headed for the door, with Danny and the other boys in close pursuit.

Chapter 16

With Eddie leading the way, the boys rode hurriedly along the darkening streets of the far west side. Soon the bright lights of the Carver Elementary School basketball court came into view. After a bumpy ride through the school's side yard, Eddie jumped off his bike at court's edge and walked determinedly toward the middle of the court with Spike, Frankie, and Whitey close behind. Slowed by their smallish bike, Timmy and Danny arrived a few seconds later.

With the light growing in the large courtside lamps, Danny hopped off of Timmy's bike and caught a glimpse of Mose's gang playing ball at the far end of the court. The Carver boys gave little attention to the approaching gang at first, but as the boys got closer they stopped shooting around and took a closer look. The stage was being set, and an explosive confrontation was about to take place and somebody was going to get hurt.

Danny took a look round as the light dimmed over the surrounding neighborhood. The rest of the west side looked like Hollywood Hills when compared to the Carver neighborhood. Carver consisted of a sprawling collection of small one and two-bedroom shanties with dirt lawns and sagging gutters. The residents were a mixture of poor white folks, Mexican migrant workers who came here to pick tomatoes on the nearby farms, indigenous blacks, and a few gypsies. The area was bordered by U.S. 37 on the east, the Toledo, Peoria, and Western railroad on the north, State Road 18 on the south and a large General Motors axle plant on the west. And even though it was in close proximity to the high paying General Motors plant, few if any of its residents, benefited from employment there. The folks in Carver worked as laborers at nearby farms or took menial jobs in the local retail stores. Everyone in Maple City held status over the undereducated and underpaid folks in the Carver area.

But at this moment, one's status in the community meant very little. The toughest kid in Carver was about to do battle with the only kid in town who had the courage to confront him, Danny's soft-spoken friend Eddie Gibbs. The battle lines had been drawn, there would be no turning back.

"Look!" Timmy shouted as they neared the court. "It's him!"

Out of the courtside shadows on this darkening evening, a tall figure walked slowly into the light. Eyes-wide, Danny was filled with a sense of dread. It was him. It was Mose. He and the other boys watched with rapt attention as the dark figure moved across the court toward Eddie and the gang.

Undeterred by the appearance of the menacing boy,

the stocky Eddie, with his fists doubled, strolled forward and stopped under the bright lights in the middle of the large asphalt court. Spike and Frankie spread out on either side of Eddie with Whitey taking up the rear. Eddie looked plenty threatening with his black leather jacket and his dark brown hair combed back in an duck-tail hairstyle. The other Carver boys, taken aback by the sudden appearance of the notorious bad boy Eddie Gibbs, watched silently. Three of them quietly fell in behind Mose, while the others stayed beneath the basket at the far end of the court away from the action.

Danny and Timmy hurried over and took up their position at the middle of the court behind Eddie and the others. The huge and menacing Mose sauntered closer to Eddie. His black eyes seemed to glow like some primeval animal in the court's bright lights. Danny couldn't believe that these two tough guys were going to do battle. He kept hoping he would wake up and find that it was all just a very scary dream.

Mose stopped and surveyed the scene in front of him. With his eyes locked on Eddie, he slowly removed his full-length tan trench coat and tossed it to one of his boys behind him. Under the coat, his sleeveless T-shirt, gave emphasis to his long, muscular arms. His black shiny hair was slicked back against the sides of his head and combed up to a point on either side, forming an almost devil-like formation. His narrow evil-looking face was accentuated by black piercing eyes and a broad flat nose. A gold chain dangled from his thick leather belt and ended inside his right front jeans pocket. Danny wondered if a switchblade knife might be attached to the end of that chain.

The tension grew as Mose stepped closer to Eddie, opening and closing his fists in preparation for the ugly battle that was about to take place. Suddenly Mose stopped, spread his legs, and spoke calmly. "You boys lost or something?" He had an abnormally deep and powerful voice for a boy his age.

Unfazed by the intimidating Mose, Eddie replied angrily, "I'm here to get Whitey's money back. Six dollars and fifteen cents," he said coolly as he peeled off his leather jacket and handed it to Frankie. A terrified Whitey stepped forward and hooked his index finger on Frankie's belt loop, apparently to keep himself from falling down from sheer fright.

The announcement of the exact amount owed Whitey seemed to unnerve Mose. Such attention to detail at a time like this was impressive, but the large boy collected himself and replied, "That was my money. The little thief stole it from me."

Eddie grimaced and ground his fist into the palm of his hand several times. He became more agitated listening to Mose's remarks. He began to move around the center of the court like a cat stalking its prey, ready to pounce at any time. Danny had seen his hero do this before and it was very imposing. His strategy would be to prowl around for a while, have his say, and then at exactly the right moment, he would charge his opponent.

Eddie's broad shoulders seemed to get broader and his thick forearms seemed to get bigger as he paced back and forth on the asphalt court taunting Jackson. "Whitey goes to Ogden. He couldn't have been at your school today. You're lyin'!" His voice was quivering with rage.

Sensing the fury inside his tough opponent, Mose calmly doubled his fists. An ugly smile spread across his fearsome face, "I spent that money shooting pinball. It's all gone. Too bad, Eddie Boy."

The arrogant response intensified Eddie's anger. Abruptly, he charged forward, his thick neck and shoulders seemed to meld into a large battering ram. He leaped head first toward the threatening brute, all the while growling like some enraged grizzly bear. Mose bent down and braced for the coming assault. Now in full flight, Eddie swung wide and hard with his right fist. The tall boy ducked frantically to avoid the punch, but to no avail. Eddie's thick fist blasted into the side of his head. The powerful blow staggered the legendary bully. He grabbed hold of his right ear, hopping around and screaming in pain. Blood squirted out between his fingers.

Meanwhile, Eddie plunged to the ground and quickly rolled to his feet. Once again he turned and charged the taller boy. Like a wild animal going in for the kill, he knocked Mose to the ground and pounced on top of him. Mose's worst nightmare had just come true—he was on the ground with an enraged Eddie Gibbs on top of him. If Mose could have stayed on his feet, he could have won the fight. Champion of the local YMCA's light-heavy weight boxing division, he could have pummeled his shorter adversary from a distance; but now with Eddie on top of him, it was definitely advantage Gibbs.

With a powerful push with his muscular leg, Mose momentarily rolled on top of the grunting Eddie, but

Eddie grabbed the chin of the tall boy and pushed him off causing the two boys to roll over and over, punching and gouging one another as they rolled. Fortunately for Eddie after one final roll, he ended up on top. He hooked his arm around Mose's neck and squeezed it tightly. The Carver boy's eyes bulged as Eddie squeezed tighter on his neck. Eddie, with his feet braced against the tall chain link fence that bordered the side of the court, began viciously punching the larger boy around the head. The sound of his fist bashing into the helpless boy's skull filled the air. Propelled by a powerful force buried deep inside, Eddie continued to slam his fist into Mose's swollen head, one stomach-turning punch after another. Danny feared that Eddie was going to kill him.

"Stop! Stop!" Frankie shouted. "You're killing him!" He and Spike jumped on top of their leader in an attempt to pull him off. Danny and Timmy soon joined in. Tears were streaming down the terrified boys' faces as they tried to stop the brutal attack. The other Carver boys stayed at a safe distance, too frightened to intervene.

Making weird groaning sounds like some savage beast, Eddie fought loose from the pawing grips of his friends and continued to pummel his fallen foe. Blood splattered everywhere.

All of a sudden, the boys heard a siren. It was the police heading towards the school. Eddie's angry gaze seemed to lessen a little. Mercifully the sound of the nearby siren had temporarily distracted him. He looked down at his battered opponent and then toward the bright flashing light atop the distant squad car approaching at high speed. Eddie lessened his grip on

Mose's neck. The Carver boy's head rolled to the side and fell still.

Standing on his knees, Eddie dug around inside the boy's pant pockets. The other boys watched in astonishment as he carefully pulled out a wad of cash and peeled off a five and two singles. "You owe interest," he chided and then jumped to his feet. Frankie tossed him his leather jacket. He and the other boys ran as fast as they could to their bikes with Eddie struggling to put on his jacket.

Frightened, Danny looked back as he ran. The squad car was nearing the court. It was less than a block away. He watched the Carver boys rush over to help their bloodied leader. Dazed and injured, but still conscious, Mose struggled to his feet. He and the others staggered off the court and disappeared into the shadows at the edge of the court. Danny was relieved when he saw Mose get up and stumble away with his friends. He had been certain that Eddie had killed him.

Soon the boys reached their bikes, and clambered aboard. With Eddie leading, they peddled furiously across the far side of the playground toward a dark alley. Danny glanced over his shoulder and saw the squad car racing onto the playground. It skidded to a stop with its siren blaring. A bright spotlight protruding from the side of the car began combing the adjacent areas just as the boys ducked down a narrow gravel driveway and disappeared into the darkness. A big white spot passed on the ground just behind them.

"That was close," Spike yelled. "Let's get the hell outa here!"

The panicky boys headed back toward their

clubhouse, ducking down alleys and between houses to avoid the police. With Timmy straining to keep up with the larger bikes, Danny turned and tried to look back at the distant court one last time, but a row of small houses blocked his view. Danny was eager to know if the Carver boys had gotten away. If they hadn't, the cops would surely question them and the West Side Gang could get into big trouble. The very thought of being in trouble with the police caused a bolt of fear to shoot up Danny's spine. He grabbed tighter to Timmy and whispered a silent prayer, "Forgive me Jesus, I don't want to go to jail."

It wasn't long before the boys were approaching the familiar weed-covered gravel road that led back to the clubhouse. A frightened Danny glanced down at his Timex, it was 9:40. "I gotta get home!" he shouted to Timmy. Without saying a word, Timmy nodded and slammed on the brakes, causing the tires to squeal and the bike to skid to a stop.

Ahead, Eddie heard the noise and stopped his bike just before entering the road. He looked back at Timmy and Danny, and shouted, "Don't worry about anything, Danny!" He waved good-bye and headed to the clubhouse.

Danny waved at the back of the departing boy and shook his head in admiration. He knew what Eddie meant. The benevolent leader was reassuring Danny that if the gang got in trouble, they would leave Danny's name off the list of those present at the evening's events. For the boys on the west side, an arrest was almost a badge of honor but to a boy from Danny's world, it would be devastating.

"He's amazing," Danny exclaimed.

"Yeah, he is," Timmy said quickly, anxious to get Danny home so he could come back and join the others at the clubhouse.

Chapter 17

"Bye, Timmy!" Danny leapt off the bike and raced toward his house. Slowly opening the front door, Danny was hoping he wouldn't disturb his grandma, who usually fell asleep in the rocking chair just inside the door.

With the door partially open, he leaned forward and peaked into the dark room. A nearby street light illuminated the room well enough so Danny could see his grandma sitting motionless in the old rocking chair. *She looks asleep,* he thought. He warily reached around the door and turned the inside handle as far to the right as he could so it would close quietly. Then he slipped into the house, gently pushed the door shut and carefully released the handle. Once inside, he again turned toward his motionless grandma. Her eyes were shut and she was breathing deeply. Feeling relieved, Danny was certain she was asleep and headed for his bedroom. Smiling like a Cheshire cat, he tiptoed past her and down the darkened hall.

"Do you know what time it is, young man?" Danny

lurched at the sound of the commanding voice coming from the darkened corner of the room.

"Not sure," Danny said softly, still hoping that somehow his grandma was babbling in her sleep and not really awake. He paused in the hallway and waited apprehensively to see if there would be a follow-up question from the shadowy figure. If there was no follow up, he was safe; she was just talking in her sleep. If there was a follow up, that meant she was awake and he was dead meat. It didn't take long for Danny to get his answer.

"Do you know that it is after ten o'clock?" Without warning, the ancient chair creaked forward and panic rushed through Danny's body. Grandma stood up and walked deliberately toward the frightened boy.

"I was . . . uh over at the basketball court and I didn't realize what time it was," he replied. He felt her hand slide over his shoulder.

"I was worried sick about you, Danny. Don't you ever come home this late again! Next time I might have to tell your father." She pulled him out of his statue-like stance and drew him close for a hug. "I couldn't stand it if anything ever happened to one of you children. Why Danny, you're everything to me."

"Sorry Grandma," he gurgled, trying desperately to speak with his face pressed against her ample bosom. "Is Mark home?"

Grandma's eyebrows lifted. "He's back in your room. He got home when he was supposed to," she scolded and then gently pushed him toward the back bedroom. "You better get to bed now. You can take your bath in the morning."

"Okay, I won't be late again, I promise."

Relieved that his grandma was no longer upset with him, Danny left his grandma's arms and escaped to the bedroom he shared with Mark. The light in the room was still on and Mark was lying flat on his back staring at the ceiling. A thin wire coming from the transistor radio that sat on the headboard next to Mark's trophies snaked down to the bed and disappeared into his left ear. Mark was probably listening to the top-forty hits that came on the radio every night at about this time.

"Top forty?"

There was no response as Mark continued to stare blankly at the ceiling.

Danny was concerned. It wasn't like Mark to be so quiet. Wanting to know what was wrong, he tried again, "What's the matter?"

"Nothin'!" came the curt reply. Mark yanked the checkered quilt a little higher on his face. Only his eyes were visible now.

Frustrated and anxious to tell him about Eddie and Mose, Danny changed the subject.

"There was a big fight tonight! Eddie Gibbs and Mose Jackson got into it over at Carver school!"

An event this monumental could not be ignored, even by the apparently distressed Mark. Eyes wide, he yanked the little plastic radio plug from his ear and shot up in bed. "Eddie and Mose got into it?"

"Yeah, it was great!" Danny said excitedly, not wanting his big brother to know how scared he had been.

"Who won?"

"Eddie killed him. It was so cool!" Danny exclaimed,

rubbing it in a little that his brother had missed the titanic battle.

"He did? Mose is huge and he's fifteen!"

"I know, but Eddie got him on the ground and just kept hitting him."

"Did Mose give?"

"No, the cops came, but we got away. They had their spotlights on us and everything."

"Where you scared?"

"Naw, it was cool."

Mark stared skeptically at his brother. "I'll bet you weren't scared." He shook his head and then laid back and stared blankly at the ceiling again.

Danny was concerned. For Mark to stop talking about the fight of the century so soon meant that something was really bothering him.

"You okay?" he asked while slipping off his jeans and plaid shirt.

"Yeah, leave me alone."

"Something happen at school?"

"Shut up and leave me alone!" came the sharp reply.

Danny slid his soft cotton pajamas off the bed post and slipped them on. "You sure?"

"Yes."

"Okay," Danny lifted the blanket from under his pillow and started to get in bed.

"It's Dad," Mark said quickly.

Danny dropped the blanket and sat erect on the side of his bed, "Dad?"

"Yeah." Mark glanced over to be sure he had his brother's full attention.

"What about Dad?" an anxious Danny queried.

"I saw him tonight."

"You saw him? Where?"

"At Tug's Tavern."

"You saw Dad at Tug's Tavern?" his incredulous little brother inquired.

"Yeah," Mark replied. Tears welled in his eyes.

"What happened, Markie?" Sensing his distress, Danny used his more affectionate name for his older brother.

Mark threw his blanket off, rolled over and sat up on the edge of his bed. His dusty, blond hair dangled over his eyes. Danny hurried over and settled in next to him.

"When I, uh, got home from football practice, Grandma told me that you went over to the west side to play ball, so I went looking for you and Timmy. I headed for the Bluebird to see if you were there shooting pinball or something. When I got there, I didn't see any bikes, so I started for the basketball courts. Then I heard Dad's 409 coming down the alley between Tug's and the Bluebird."

"How'd ya know it was Dad's car?"

"I'd know those mufflers anywhere."

"I can't believe Dad was at Tug's. He's always telling us not to go to the west side," a shocked Danny replied.

"I know."

"Go ahead," Danny encouraged.

"Well . . . I, uh, looked around the corner of the diner and I saw Dad's car pulling into the parking lot behind Tug's, so I got off my bike while he was parking and ran behind the Bluebird and hid behind the big trash cans. Dad got out of his car and walked in the back door of Tug's. I could hear all the men talking inside. They all said 'hi'. I could tell they all knew Dad. One of them said, 'Your booth is waiting on you by the front door.' Dad thanked him and walked on in."

Mark's voice shook with emotion as he continued the story. "I hurried around to the front of the building and hid in the bushes by the big window. A little later, Dad sat down in the booth. I stood on my tiptoes and looked in the bottom of the window. I could see Dad's white pants and white shoes under the table. That's all I could see from where I was, but I knew it was him. His loafers have that little gold chain on the top. The window was open a little at the bottom and I could hear him talking to someone back in the bar. Then I saw a woman's legs slide in next to him in the booth. She said 'hi' and then she leaned toward dad and started rubbing his leg way up here." He pointed to the top of his thigh.

"Maybe Dad had a sore leg or something," came Danny's innocent reply.

Mark's eyes narrowed. He shot an incredulous glare at his naive brother. "He didn't have a sore leg, dummy, she was trying to get close to his thing."

"Maybe his thing was sore."

The older boy sighed in total disbelief, "She wanted sex, dumb butt!"

"Oh yeah, sex." An embarrassed Danny tightened his lips, lifted his eyebrows and glanced over at his brother. "Go ahead, know it all!"

Mark dropped the stare and continued, "Pretty soon Dad reached over and started rubbing her bottom."

"He's after sex," Danny announced proudly in a last ditch effort to save face.

Mark shook his head, "No crap, Sherlock."

Danny scowled.

Mark's mood seemed to change, his head dropped down, he stared at the floor. "Well, uh, then he said, uh, . . .uh."

An impatient Danny could sense the torment in his brother's voice, "What did he say?"

"He said . . .uh," Mark was speaking so softy now his younger sibling could barely hear him. "He said, 'Millie Cantrell, you're one sexy lady'."

Danny's eyes went wide. "What? What?" he yelled as he jumped up from the bed. "Dad was having sex with Timmy's mom? She's married to Mr. Cantrell!"

Danny was crushed. He stormed to his side of the room and dove into bed, violently yanking the blankets over his head.

Dismayed by Danny's grief, Mark hurried over to his brother and patted him gently on his arm, "It's okay, Danny," he said softly, temporarily regaining his fatherly role in an attempt to comfort his distressed brother.

"Leave me alone!" Danny growled, pulling the blankets further over his head.

Mark frowned. He patted Danny and then walked over and crawled back into bed. He stuck the earplug from the transistor radio back into his ear, reached up, turned off his bed light and yanked the heavy quilt over his head. The room fell dark while the two devastated youngsters lay in bed feeling alone and vulnerable—both trying to make sense, once again, of the disturbing and painful behavior of their celebrated father.

Chapter 18

"Oh, no!" Ann murmured. Just finishing a late night potty stop, she quickly spun the faucet's handle. She didn't want the noisy faucet to disturb her sleeping family members. She dried her hands, swiped off the light in the bathroom and tiptoed toward the den. She quietly pushed the door open and stepped in to check on Dan.

The brilliant moon shone through the sheer curtains partially illuminating a slumbering Dan, who was uncovered and lying in the fetal position on the small loveseat. Sleeping soundly, his deep breathing was very close to snoring. Ann bent down and lifted the fallen afghan off the carpet, carefully laid it over her snoozing husband and tucked it snugly around his body. She leaned over and kissed him tenderly on the forehead.

Breathing a sigh of relief, Ann left the den and pulled the door shut behind her. She walked quietly back to the bedroom that she was sharing with Ali and Meghan. She crept into the room and nestled back into her small twin with nary a whimper from her two slumbering daughters. *I could set off a bomb and those two wouldn't wake up,* she thought.

....

Back in the den, Dan had fallen into a deep sleep and began to dream. It was an astonishingly realistic dream prompted by his recent recollection of his father being at Tug's tavern with his best friend's mom, Millie Cantrell. The dream started with Beau stopping at Tug's Tavern after playing eighteen holes of golf at the country club.

....

"What's happening, Beau?" a young tough in a black, leather jacket shouted as Beau staggered in through the rear door.

"Not much Jake," Beau replied, making his way through the pool room and into the main bar area. The owner, Tug Langley, smiled and nodded quickly at the local celerity as he made his entrance. Tug sporting his usual red vest and white cotton shirt was glad Beau spent so many evenings in his bar. It was good for business.

Beau shook a few hands and then made his way to the front of the narrow room. Beau looked a little out of place in his white polyester slacks and bright red golf shirt, but the folks at Tugs didn't mind. They were glad to have him aboard, even though they knew that Beau's main reason for stopping at Tug's was to get laid.

Beau eventually reached the front of the room and

slid into his favorite booth by the big front window,
"Beau's booth", as Tug liked to call it. The little nook
was in the front corner of the building and overlooked
Railroad Street. A partition separated it from the other
tables in the bar area creating a quiet sanctuary for its
occupants.

Most of Tug's customers knew that Beau preferred
the booth and they would bypass it and find seats
elsewhere. On the rare occasion when some unknowing
newcomers would sit in the secluded booth, Tug would
hurry over and tell them it was reserved and scoot them
off to a more suitable location somewhere else in the
popular bar.

Beau felt safe at Tug's. He knew none of the
members of his First Christian Church or any of his
business associates would ever be caught dead at the
bawdy bar. He could make himself available to the
stable of young divorcees with hard bodies that hung
out here with little chance of being discovered. Also, it
was an unspoken rule in this tough factory town that
was consumed by high school basketball, that the girls
he bedded down would never tell anyone about their
intimate interludes with the over-sexed former hoops
star. And the proof was in the pudding. After twenty
years of frequenting the popular hangout and conquests
too many to count, none of his respectable friends had
ever mentioned having any knowledge of his other life.
He was certain they didn't know.

"How ya doin' tonight, Beau?" Tug slid a mug of
cold beer in front of Beau. Foam splashed on the table.
The wiry owner scooted into the booth across from his
old friend.

"Oh, uh, pretty good, Tugger." Beau smiled at his pal, a little surprised that the busy bar owner had taken a seat in the booth. It was something Tug very seldom did and he wondered why.

"How'd ya hit 'em today?"

"Not bad, shot seventy-eight, but the mayor still got me for twenty." He shook his head. "He always plays his ass off late in the season." Beau lifted his mug, swished the beer for an instant, took a swig and then made eye contact with the tired owner. "Somethin' up, Tug?"

Tug's bloodshot eyes stared down at the table. He seemed a little anxious. "I had some trouble in here earlier tonight."

Beau's eyebrows lifted slightly.

"A couple of the boys got into it in the backroom. They were shootin' for money and one of them accused the other of cheatin'. First thing I know, one of the boys ran up and told me someone had been stabbed."

"What the hell!" Beau exclaimed. "Anybody get hurt?"

"Not too bad, but someone ran out the back door and called the cops from the pay phone over at the Bluebird. They were here in ten minutes." Tug began to tremble. He ran his shaking fingers through his black hair.

"The guy with the knife hightailed it out the back door. The cops picked him up a short time later. They found him cowering underneath the water tower a few blocks from here. They said they were going to book him for assault with a deadly weapon in the mornin'. The other one was lying on the floor. He was bleedin' like crazy. I called the hospital. An ambulance came right away and took him to Maple General."

"How's he doing? Have you heard anything?"

"I called the emergency room a little while ago. They said the knife blade didn't hit any internal organs, and other than a lot of bleeding, they said he should be okay."

"Hmmm, well that's good."

"Yeah, but you see this is the third time someone's been arrested for fightin' in here this year. After the second one, the liquor board told me if I had one more incident, they were going to yank my license." Tug seemed very upset and agitated. "Hell, Beau, I can't lose my license. I've put my heart and soul into this business for twenty-five years. What would Esther and the kids do? I'm not qualified to do anything else, and the local plants have been layin' off lately anyhow."

Beau could see where this was going and he wanted to nip it in the bud. "Better get yourself a good attorney," he said matter-of-factly.

"I can't afford no attorney Beau, you know that." The distraught owner's eyes glazed over. "You and I go back a long ways, Beau. We played ball together at the high school for cryin' out loud!" Tug stared intently at his old pal. "I'm a nobody in this town, Beau, and you're a big shot, well connected and all that. I need you to talk to Chief Zollars before they book that fella tomorrow and get him to pull the file. Once they book him, it's too late."

Beau shook his head and fidgeted nervously with his gold ring. "I'd like to help you Tug, I really would, but I've had my own share of problems along the way and I don't have a hell of a lot of equity left with the Chief. In fact, I'd say he's just about had enough of me."

Suddenly, Tug's expression turned angry. His mouth curled down, he grabbed Beau by the forearm and squeezed it hard. "Now you listen to me, you arrogant son of a bitch! I've seen a hell of a lot in here over the years and I sure wouldn't want any of that to get out in the community. Why, the folks wouldn't believe some of things their great Beau Kinsey has been up to."

Beau yanked his arm free from the angry man's grip, "I don't know what the hell you're talking about!"

Tug leaned forward on the table—their faces were only inches apart. "How about Lavonda Weathersby? Folks around here don't cotton much to black on white," he whispered. "And that was before Anita died."

Beau felt his face turning red. He began to perspire, ". . . uh, you wouldn't, . . .uh . . ."

The desperate owner interrupted. "The hell I wouldn't."

Beau tried to collect himself. He didn't like being threatened by a lowlife like Tug Langley, but he knew that the one thing that could ruin him in this town was an affair with a black woman, particularly on the eve of his beloved Anita's death. "Okay, okay, I'll talk to the Chief first thing in the morning." He lifted his mug and drank it down, slamming the thick glass on the table.

"Call me as soon as you hang up from the Chief," the determined saloon owner ordered.

"Alright, alright."

Tug looked away, slid out of the booth and hurried over to the busy bar, leaving a despondent Beau alone with his thoughts.

Beau slid his hand into his front shirt pocket and

pulled out a pack of Marlboros. He bumped the pack against his wrist until a few brownish tips popped up. He pulled the tallest one out, yanked the Zippo from his pocket, flipped the lid back and lit up. He took a hard drag and exhaled. He stared aimlessly through the rising smoke at the dark street outside. He knew that the Chief would be furious. Over the years the tough Chief had bailed him out time and time again, but it was one thing to ask for help for himself—it was another to ask for help for a small-time bar owner on the west side. He had to do it though. He knew that Tug was serious about his threat and Beau had become accustomed to his life as a local hero. He sure as hell didn't want it all to come to an end over a knife fight in a bar. He had to convince Chief Zollars to pull that warrant, no doubt about it. Suddenly, he felt a tap on his shoulder, the sweet smell of Coty perfume filled the air.

"Ya okay, big guy?"

"Oh, . . . yeah sure. How are you?"

"I'm fine."

The nervous Beau, managed a weak smile.

The shapely Millie Cantrell, wearing skin-tight capris and a halter top, pushed in next to him, all the while rubbing his thigh. Beau felt himself becoming aroused as her hand moved higher on his leg.

"Where's Frank?"

"He passed out a little while ago. I kept feedin' him Scotches until he dropped. I wanted to get back here to my beautiful Beau before some bitch beat me to the punch."

"Sure he's out?"

"Yeah, I'm sure," she said softly. She laid her head on

his shoulder. He felt her delicate hand move ever so close to his groin area. The warmth and nearness of her hand made Beau forget his problem with Tug.

He took a final drag on his Marlboro and stuffed it out quickly in the ashtray. The sudden appearance of the very attractive Millie had really thrown him. His face was flushed. His heart was beating rapidly.

"Got the Nash tonight?" he asked.

"Yeah, she murmured. Her roving hand finally reached pay dirt. "And I parked in the back of the lot where it's very dark."

Beau loved the old Nash Ambassadors. The front seats folded down creating a large bed-like area in the interior of the auto. *Great for family vacations or screwing a girl,* he thought. Now fully aroused by Millie's roving fingers, Beau put his right arm carefully over her shoulder, His left hand slid cautiously inside the aggressive lady's halter top. He glanced down. The tight capris accentuated her long, shapely legs, a lovely sight for the intoxicated Beau. "We better go, before I lose it," he whispered.

"Okay." She reluctantly sat up and attempted to compose herself. She fluffed her long brown hair and slid out of the booth with Beau right behind her. The former basketball star watched in drunken delight as Millie's shapely backside wiggled down the aisle just in front of him. The bright lights on the large Wurlitzer jukebox flashed and the Rolling Stone's mega hit, "Satisfaction," blasted into the room.

When they passed Frank's booth, Beau glanced over at Millie's inebriated husband. A flood of guilt rushed through him. He was about to hit on the wife of a man who had risked life and limb to dig him out of a giant snow mound in the middle of a freezing blizzard last winter. "I'm such a son of a bitch," he whispered. The two lovers hurried past the pool players. Beau could hear the boys in the pool room snickering as he followed Millie toward the back door.

Suddenly, the pool room turned pitch black. "What the hell!" a bewildered Beau shouted. "I, uh, got something on my legs. There's something heavy on my lower legs. I can hardly walk!" His voice was filled with terror. He glanced down at his feet.

"What the . . ." Millie screamed.

"My God! My God!" It's my boys! They're hanging on my legs! It's Mark and Danny! My God! Where did they come from?"

The room grew quiet. Beau frantically pushed at the boys, trying to pry them loose. "Get off my legs, boys! Get off! You shouldn't be in here!"

"No, Dad! Stop, stop!" Dan shouted. He shot up on the loveseat, perspiration was pouring down his face and his chest was heaving. The dark room was spinning, his heart was racing. He fell back against the seat. Outside the room, he heard footsteps in the hall. He looked up as the door flew open. Ann rushed in and fell into the seat next to him, hugging him around the shoulders. "Dan, Dan! Are you alright, honey?"

Trying to collect himself, but still very much shaken by the vivid dream, Dan stammered. "Oh, uh, yeah, yeah, I'm okay. I just had an awful dream. It was so realistic." He pushed his drooping hair off his forehead and ran his fingers through it.

"You poor thing. Your shirt is soaked."

Ann retrieved a tissue from her pajamas pocket and dried his forehead. "What on earth were you dreaming about?" she asked with a chuckle. "Did you get fired from your new job or something?"

Dan exhaled, "No, I wish that's what it was about."

"Want to tell me about it?" she inquired as she rubbed his back.

Dan exhaled, "It was so real, Ann. Dad was in a bar and he was hitting on the mother of a friend of mine. Then, just as he was taking her out back to her car . . ."

He took another deep breath. "Mark and I were hanging on his legs and trying to stop him from leaving the bar and going to her car. That's when I woke up."

Ann's eyes softened as she said sympathetically, "That father of yours must have really been something."

Her husband just shook his head.

"Are you okay?"

Dan smiled, "Yeah, I'm fine, thanks, honey."

"It's the middle of the night, try to get some sleep," Ann ordered.

Dan nodded.

She rubbed his upper arm for a minute and gave him a peck on the cheek. "Good night, sweetheart."

"Good night, dear."

As Ann stood to leave the room, she asked, "Are you sure you're okay?"

"I'm fine. You go on back to bed."

Dan had been brave with Ann, but he was shattered by the dream. The dream was so detailed and it seemed so real. He knew in his heart of hearts that it was an accurate portrayal of his adulterous father and that he had just relived an event that very well could have happened in real time. Badly shaken, he desperately wanted to find a silver lining in this dark cloud that was slowly engulfing his past. Now wide awake and still feeling Ann's tender kiss, his thoughts took him once again to those heartrending days of his distressing childhood.

Chapter 19

The sun reflected through the beveled glass squares atop the large oak door as it slammed shut. "Hello, everyone!" came the call, "I'm home!"

Danny watched from above as the friendly doctor slipped off his long black topcoat revealing a pin-striped gray suit and blue silk tie.

Not hearing any response to his greeting, the big man looked around the house. With no one in sight, he hung the expensive coat on the rack next to the door and shouted, "Hello!" once again.

Breaking the silence, thirteen year old Bobby Burton shouted from the landing above, "Hi, Dad!"

Danny and Bobby were laying spread eagle on the carpeted landing above the main entrance playing their favorite board game, Monopoly. The Girls Athletic Association commandeered the gym every Wednesday after school, giving the boys a day off from basketball practice, and much to the delight of Danny's status-conscious father, he usually spent these free afternoons with the wealthy Burton boy at his big house on Stanton

Avenue.

Bobby's dad glanced up at the boys and smiled broadly, "Where's your mom?"

"She went to the store to get something for dinner," the boy answered as his father hustled up the spiral staircase toward them.

"Who's that little hooligan with you?" the doctor joked. He leaned down and ruffled Danny's wavy brown hair.

"Hi, Dr. Burton," Danny said shyly, his eyes never leaving the board.

Danny had been friends with Bobby Burton since kindergarten. Over the years, he had spent many hours playing games with him in his lavish home, but for some reason, he never felt totally comfortable there. Bobby and his parents went out of their way to be nice to him. It wasn't that. Maybe it was the big house or the expensive furniture, or Bobby's dad's fancy clothes that bothered him. He wasn't sure; he just felt a bit like a duck out of water.

"You played a nice game last evening, Danny."

"Thanks, Dr. Burton."

"We caught the fourth quarter of the ninth grade game also. Your brother Mark is just tremendous, he had us all buzzing."

Danny, used to such exclamations about his older brother, smiled and nodded in agreement. He sometimes wondered if anyone ever thought of how these comments about his older sibling's athletic prowess made him feel. Evidently they didn't, because they kept doing it.

"Now this little rascal's another story," the friendly

doctor jested. He grabbed the brass railing on the landing, leaned down and gave his shrinking son a peck on the forehead.

"Dad!" the embarrassed youngster cried, a deep crimson color flooded across his narrow face.

"You'll miss those little kisses someday when you're off to college and living on your own. Better enjoy them while you can, son!" He smiled at the mortified youngster and headed for the bedroom. Slipping off his suit coat, he hurried through the double doors into the master bedroom.

"Geesh, your turn," Bobby said as he rolled his eyes.

Danny gathered up the white cubes and scattered them on the colorful board. Double threes appeared.

"Oh, boy!" Danny quickly reached for his marker and tapped it along the squares that bordered the sides of the popular game. A smile broke out on his face when he landed on the prize of all prizes—the powerful Boardwalk. He had already acquired the cherished Park Place just a few minutes earlier.

"Darn!" Bobby groused, "You always get Boardwalk and Park Place."

Although from a well-to-do family and the owner of many expensive games and gadgets, Bobby, like most of the other kids at school, really looked up to the handsome and popular Kinsey boys. Danny had become accustomed to this fact and tried very hard not to abuse his special status, even though it was difficult at times.

"Just lucky," Danny replied.

"Lucky, my foot," Bobby lamented as he shook his head. Danny peeled off four hundred-dollar bills to pay for the coveted property.

"I suppose you're gonna get a couple hotels now," Bobby grumbled.

"Nope."

"You're not?" A happy Bobby grinned and quickly snatched the dice from the board.

"Nope, I'm gonna buy four!"

"No fair!" Bobby wailed. "I'm almost out of money. There's no way I could pay the fine if I landed there. I'm quitting."

"Let's keep playing," a disappointed Danny replied. "I can loan you some money. Come on!"

"Nope, you've got all of the utilities and all the best properties. I'm busted."

The frustrated boy threw the dice into the empty cardboard box and started collecting the cards, houses, hotels and loose cash from the board. Danny joined in.

"You'll win next time, Bobby," the tentative winner said.

Bobby was upset, but Danny was sure that he would want to play again. The shy twelve year old liked to hang out with Danny Kinsey. It was his connection to the "in" crowd at school.

"Same time next Wednesday?" a now contrite Bobby asked.

"Sounds good to me!"

Danny jumped up, grabbed his jacket off the stair post and hustled down the winding stairs to the front door. He hastily opened the door, ducked outside and ran down the stone pavers toward his trusty Flyer, which was lying on its side in the front yard right next to the fountain. He felt a cool mist on his face from the flowing water of the nearby fountain that featured a

Greek goddess pouring water from a clay vessel.

Pausing briefly to slip on his jacket, he quickly lifted his sturdy bike, hopped aboard and began pedaling toward the street. A short time later, he bumped over the curb and started down Stanton Avenue. He gawked at the many large homes and well-manicured lawns that bordered the tree-lined boulevard.

Approaching the intersection of Second and Stanton, he lifted up from the seat and pushed on the brakes, slowing dramatically to see if any cars were coming. Seeing none, he leaned back and bolted across the intersection. Once past the busy intersection, he slowed dramatically. He was getting close to HER house. Would she be out in her yard? Would he see her? Maybe she would be out watering the flowers or sitting on the porch. Deep down inside he was hoping she would be outside, the thought of it filled him with apprehension.

Trying desperately to look cool on his undersized Flyer, he approached her expensive home with his head held high. Nick Harrison, star of the eighth-grade basketball team and his main competition for the lovely Ann, rode a 26-inch Schwinn, the top of the line. Danny wished that he had a 26-inch Schwinn right now as he glided slowly past her house. He pushed his eyes to the edge of their sockets, trying desperately to get a glimpse of her house without being obvious and turning his head.

Much to his delight, he saw someone moving near the bushes on the side of the three-story limestone house. He turned his head slightly for a better view and panic rushed through him.

"It's her!" he said excitedly. She was in the side yard and walking toward the front of the house! Out of the blue, a strong breeze came up and blew her long brown hair back revealing her gorgeous face. Wearing a red skirt and a white cotton blouse, she looked stunning.

Then, much to his surprise, she smiled and lifted her hand slightly to acknowledge him. The subtle gesture caused his knees to get weak. The bike began to wobble beneath him and he started to lose control. The front tire began to skid on some loose gravel near the edge of the road. To his never ending horror and dismay, the cycle suddenly slid out from under him and crashed hard on the asphalt roadway. Danny was sent sprawling to the ground. The sharp gravel ripped into his shirt and dug into his back.

"Oh, no, Danny!" came the panicked cry of the lovely Ann. She raced toward the street.

With his back throbbing, Danny quickly jumped to his feet and scrambled over to his bike. Ann reached the wreckage a few seconds later. Standing on the grassy strip between the sidewalk and the street, her pretty brown eyes were full of concern. She spoke frantically to him, "Are you okay, Danny?"

The boy stood still. It was too late for him to make any kind of a getaway. She was there, in all her glory, standing right in front of him. He bent over and slowly grabbed the handle bars of his fallen chariot and lifted it up. Chin on his chest and his face bright red, Danny stood in the street next to his battered bike and mumbled, "Yeah, I'm okay."

"Want me to call the doctor or something? Your back's bleeding."

"Naw," the devastated boy replied softly. "I gotta get going."

He checked his bike for scratches and climbed aboard. Too embarrassed to look at the pretty Ann and feeling totally shattered inside, he gave her a quick sideways "Bye" and began to pedal away.

"Bye, Danny. See you at lunch tomorrow. I'll save the seat next to me."

Danny's jaw dropped and his eyes opened wide. "At lunch tomorrow she'll save the seat next to her for me!" he exclaimed under his breath. Ecstatic, he stood up and pushed hard on the pedals. The bike surged forward and fell side to side as he continued to gain speed. When he was finally out of earshot of Ann and her neighbors, he shouted, "Yes!" at the top of his lungs followed by, "She's beautiful and she's mine!"

Chapter 20

"Pass the beans, Lover Boy." Having overheard Danny telling Grandma Carrie about his episode with Ann Harper, Mark couldn't wait to give him a dig.

"Shut up, Mark," Danny snapped.

Maggie tossed a hard look Mark's way. She wasn't sure what the "lover boy" remark was about, but she knew Danny didn't like it. Mark crinkled his nose into an ugly contortion and glared at his little sister.

"Now, now, children, quit your fighting. It's time for the news."

Grandma didn't allow any talking during the 5:30 news on WISH-TV. It was her habit to watch it every evening on her nearly twenty-year old TV that sat in the corner on the kitchen counter.

The smiling matriarch hurried over and pulled out the protruding silver knob on the 16-inch Sylvania television. After patiently waiting, a white spot in the center of the dark gray screen gradually turned into a white horizontal line. The thin line eventually expanded into a dim shadowy picture that gradually began to clear.

After what seemed an eternity, the family could actually see the black and white images on the screen. The TV was officially on!

Grandma hurried back, scooted her chair under the table, and carefully replaced the white cloth napkin on her lap. A smile of contentment spread across her face. According to Mark, the reason Grandma liked the evening news so much was because she had a crush on the handsome anchor, Frank somebody.

Unexpectedly, Grandma's smile faded and her expression changed.

"Listen up, children. It sounds like there has been an accident or something in Maple City. Let's all pay attention!"

The three children stopped eating and turned toward the television and watched as the anchor's demeanor darkened.

"Ladies and gentlemen, we are sad to report to you this evening that there has been a tragic death in one of our sister cities in the greater WISH-TV listening area. Maple City Chief of Police, Jack Zollars, reported to us just moments ago that fifteen year old Edward D. Gibbs, better known to friends and family as Eddie, was tragically stabbed to death earlier this afternoon in a vacant lot on the west side of the city. The suspected assailant is a juvenile, so the police are withholding his name."

"What?" Danny shouted. The glass of milk slid out of his hand and shattered on the kitchen floor.

The boys listened in stunned silence at the announcement.

"The stabbing appears to be the result of a long-standing feud between two local gangs in Maple City, the Gibbs boy's West Side Gang and an opposing gang in the Carver school area. Recently, tensions had been escalating between the rival gangs due to a brutal beating administered by Gibbs to one of the Carver gang members on a school playground just a few days earlier. After several threats and counter threats, members of the Carver gang, apparently seeking revenge, went to the west side and hunted down their unsuspecting victim. According to several eye witnesses, one of the Carver boys attacked the young victim with a switch blade knife after surrounding him in a vacant lot. Known locally as a tough kid, the eye witnesses say the Gibbs boy fought ferociously, not succumbing until multiple stab wounds had been administered to his chest, neck and shoulders. Funeral services for the young man will be held this Saturday morning at the Nelson Funeral Home in Maple City. Gibbs is preceded in death by his father Earl A. Gibbs. He is survived by his mother Bernice Gibbs of Maple City and a stepsister, Martha Boxer of Little Rock, Arkansas. The suspect has been apprehended and is being held without bond in the Grant County Court House, pending a hearing. Chief Zollars indicated that he will request that the young assailant be tried as an adult. Now turning to other news, today in New Castle . . ."

"Now, you eat your carrot." Maggie pushed the steaming vegetable toward her doll, Sadie. Maggie was totally unaware of the devastating news her brothers were attempting to digest.

"It was Mose. It had to be Mose," a teary-eyed Mark mumbled.

Stunned, Danny stared at his plate, tears rolling down his cheeks. His tough friend and hero Eddie Gibbs, was dead! How could that happen? How could it be? Trying to come to grips with the shocking news, Danny felt like the room was moving in some surrealistic dance around him. Shaking his head violently back and forth, he attempted to wake up from this awful dream. He was starting to feel sick inside. Just yesterday, Danny had joined the gang at the clubhouse for an impromptu fifteenth birthday party for Eddie. He had been in great spirits, thanking all of them over and over again for the cake and the new Zippo lighter they gave him as a gift. It had been a fun night. Little did young Danny know that his brave friend would be dead a day later. It was almost more than the young boy could bear.

Distraught, he jumped up from the table and raced from the room, clutching his churning stomach. He banged off the wall in the narrow hallway and charged toward the bathroom. Once inside, he dropped to his knees in front of the porcelain stool. His stomach pushed violently up to his throat. Bits of food and hot bile blasted into the tank. His stomach heaved over and over again until he could throw up no more. Nearby, he could hear Mark wailing in the bedroom. He wondered if either of them would ever get over this shocking day.

Wiping her wet hands on her apron, Grandma hurried in the bathroom and knelt down next to the horror struck boy. "Oh, Danny, are you okay?"

Danny fell back on his heels, staring blankly ahead. Strangely, he could hear his father's intemperate voice yelling at him and telling him to pull himself together.

Eyes red with grief, he paused for a moment and did just what his powerful father would have ordered—he pulled himself together.

"Sorry, Grandma," he said softly. He grabbed the end of his shirtsleeve and swiped his nose and eyes clean.

"Oh, don't be sorry, my boy," Grandma said as she embraced the distressed boy. "A young boy has died. Someone you knew well. Your reaction is completely understandable, darling. I can't imagine how you must feel. You're just too young to have to face something like this!" She gently lifted him to his feet.

"I'll bet he . . . " Grandma was interrupted by a loud bike horn coming from the front of the house.

"It's Timmy!" Danny shouted. Mark and Danny both hastily headed for the front of the house at the sound of the horn. They hurried through the front door and joined Timmy and his brother Frankie on the front sidewalk.

Grandma followed them to the front door. "Boys! Boys!"

The boys talked animatedly with their friends, gesturing wildly, and then they turned and ran toward Grandma.

"Can we go with Timmy and Frankie, Grandma?" Mark shouted. "All the kids are meeting at the school to talk about Eddie."

"You boys have barely had any supper, I, uh, just don't . . ."

Danny interrupted, "Please, Grandma, please! Everyone is going to be there."

Grandma felt Maggie's hands slide around her leg.

"Okay, boys, but be home by curfew time."

The boys both gave her and Maggie a quick hug. Mark raced to the back of the house to get his English Racer. Danny ran down the narrow sidewalk and hopped aboard Timmy's trusty Higgins. Timmy's skinny body shot up. His right leg leaned hard on the pedal and the little bike lurched forward.

"I love you!" Grandma shouted. "Be careful and remember, nine-thirty!"

Chapter 21

The boys raced along Wesley Avenue to the clubhouse. Danny held tightly to Timmy, he could feel his chest heaving beneath his arms and the splash of warm tears on his bare forearms.

When they finally reached the clubhouse and began the ascent up the hill, they could see Whitey lying on the ground in front of the clubhouse wailing in grief. The boys mounted the hill, jumped off their bikes and hurried over to Whitey and knelt on the ground next to the distraught boy. The fast riding Mark was already on the ground trying to console him.

After what seemed an agonizingly long time, Whitey finally fell silent and rolled to his back. His tortured eyes stared aimlessly toward the sky. His slender torso shivered in grief. Mark leaned down and gently slid his arms under the exhausted boy's back and legs and lifted him up. Whitey's ashen face, covered with welts from a recent beating by his father, fell into the larger boy's chest.

"Let's go inside," Mark said softly. "We need to talk."

Danny ran ahead and quickly yanked the door open for Mark and Whitey. The other boys followed close behind. Frankie and Spike were already inside. Frankie kicked one of the gang's empty orange crates out from under the poker table and Mark walked over and carefully seated Whitey on the crate. The other boys gathered around, just standing and staring at each other not knowing what to say.

Mark glanced out of the corner of his eye at Danny. Danny was the one who volunteered grace at their evening meals at home and said the prayer every third week at Sunday School. Mark narrowed his eyes, urging his younger brother to say something.

Realizing that he was the chosen one, Danny sighed and took a deep breath. "Why don't we . . . uh all hold hands, fellas?" Much to his surprise, the tough gang bangers clasped their hands together and moved in close forming an impromptu huddle around the reluctant youngster.

"I'm, uh going to, uh, say a prayer for our friend, Eddie." Danny felt a squeeze on his hand and glanced left at Spike. His pocked face was covered with tears. His upper body was jerking in spasms of grief. The other boys stood with their heads bowed, tears streaming down their cheeks.

"God, we never thought Eddie was gonna die today." The words were simple, but they exploded inside the heads of the frightened youths. The sobbing got louder with each word from Danny. "We loved our friend Eddie. He fought some, but he was a good boy. Please take him to heaven, God. We all think Eddie should go to heaven. Uh . . . Amen."

Danny felt another squeeze to his hand, "Thanks, Danny," Frankie said softly, "That was beautiful."

Danny turned toward Frankie, the tough kid fell into Danny's waiting arms. The two terrified youngsters embraced and soon it was a gang hug. All the boys pushed in together, crying unashamedly while they tried to make sense of the tragic death of their young friend. The grieving continued for some time and then gradually broke apart, one boy at a time.

Shoulders slumped, Spike sauntered over and fell onto a nearby crate. "Eddie's dead," he murmured as if by saying it out loud it might help him understand the tragic event.

His eyes locked on Eddie's favorite spot at the poker table. "Damn that Mose. Damn him!" he screamed and violently swept a pile of poker chips off the table with the back of his hand. The other boys stood still and stared at the multi-colored chips scattered across the floor.

Danny looked at the grief-stricken eyes of the other boys. To all of them, the brave Eddie had been the father figure that was so sorely missing in all of their lives, including Danny and Mark. His strong, yet affectionate manner had touched them deeply. He was the last person on earth they expected to die. Eddie had seemed invincible to all of them, yet he was gone— killed over six dollars and fifteen cents. They would never see his kind blue eyes again. They would never again play cards with him. They would never again ride bikes with him. He was gone from their lives forever, and they were feeling a pain that was so horrific and so agonizing that it was almost too much for their young souls to bear. The sobbing continued as the room darkened around them. Their hearts were breaking, their young lives had been turned upside down and they were trying to understand why.

Danny glanced at his watch. "We gotta go, Mark," he grumbled, "It's ten after nine and Grandma told us to be home no later than nine-thirty."

"Okay, we'll ride double on the Racer so Timmy can stay."

Timmy's freckled face broke into a wisp of a smile. "Thanks, Mark," he said quietly.

"See you guys later," Mark said softly to the other boys.

"See ya, Mark. See ya, Danny," the boys replied. A quiet Spike just sat staring at the wooden floor, unable to muster a good-bye to his departing buddies.

The boys pushed through the wobbly front door, ran over and jumped on Mark's English Racer and headed home. Bouncing on the seat of the skinny bike, Danny glanced up at the full moon that was filtering through the tall oak trees that surrounded the isolated clubhouse. "Eddie will never see the moon again," he moaned.

"I know," Mark murmured, "I know."

....

For Danny, the legacy of Eddie Gibbs would reach far beyond this tragic evening. The leadership Eddie had exhibited, his compassionate manner and sharp decision making turned out to be a life lesson for Danny. Modeling Eddie's leadership style, Danny climbed to the top of the corporate ladder and was promoted to president at one of the largest banks in the world. Danny knew that he owed much of his success in life to Eddie Gibbs, a tough, under-educated kid from the west side of Maple City, Indiana.

Chapter 22

Mark leaned right, skidded briefly on some loose gravel, and darted down the drive toward the back of the house. It was after nine-thirty and the sun had long since fallen beneath the distant landscape. The only light on this dark evening emanated from the pole lamp in the family room that filtered through the kitchen window and fell across the narrow driveway, briefly illuminating the boy's pathway. Grandma was probably reading by the lamp and waiting for the boys to get home.

"Think Grandma's upset?" Mark asked, knowing that his little brother understood their grandmother's moods a little better than he did.

"Naw, she's worried, that's all." Danny replied. The sullen boys hopped off Mark's bike and hurried through the shadowy back porch. The back door suddenly swung open. "Right on time!" Grandma said briskly. "Are you boys okay?"

"Yeah," they mumbled in unison.

"Come in, I've got hot chocolate waiting for you."

The boys smiled. They loved Grandma's hot chocolate. She made it with real milk and always tossed a pile of tiny marshmallows on top.

Grandma held the door open and pointed toward the kitchen. The boys slipped past her and headed for the kitchen. Two thick brown cups were sitting on the Formica counter waiting to be filled. An open bag of miniature marshmallows sat next to the cups.

"Sit down there at the table, fellas. I'll get your hot chocolate."

The boys slumped down in their usual seats. They watched their grandma pour the hot milk into the cups, stir the mixture together and dump in the tiny puffs of marshmallows. Grasping the thick handles, she carried the steaming cups over to the table and set a cup of the delicious concoction in front of each of the boys.

Grandma sat down with them, her eyes were tired and sad. She looked sympathetically at the boys and then choosing her words carefully, she spoke to them. "Death is a difficult thing for adults to comprehend. It must be terribly difficult for you boys to understand. I can't imagine how you must feel right now."

The boys sat staring at the steaming hot chocolate sitting in front of them. Danny squirmed nervously in his seat and then blurted out, "Grandma, I fibbed to you earlier," Danny was feeling remorseful about what he had told his Grandma earlier in the evening.

The usually honest Mark kicked Danny under the table while staring daggers at him. He didn't want Grandma, and more importantly, his father to know about the boys' association with the West Side Gang.

Flinching from the pain, Danny nonetheless,

continued to come clean. "There wasn't a bunch of kids over there tonight. There were just a few of us. Mark and I are in a . . ."

A horrified Mark quickly interrupted his confessing sibling, "Yeah, it's just a little group of guys, that's all."

Grandma smiled. "Well, it doesn't matter to me who you boys met with tonight. You're good boys and you never give me the first bit of trouble. I trust you boys completely and I'm sure this Eddie was a nice boy."

Still nervous about Grandma discovering who he and Danny were hanging with, Mark continued, "Dad doesn't know we hang out with the guys on the west side and stuff. You won't tell him, will you?"

"Of course not! What your father doesn't know won't hurt him," she replied.

She stood and walked to the counter to fill her teacup and then she returned to the table. She took a sip of her tea and then spoke deliberately to the boys. "I want to tell you boys something and you have to promise that you will never tell your father. It's something he is very sensitive about and he would not want you boys to know."

"We won't tell, we promise," Mark declared.

The boys sat up in their chairs. Their tear-soaked eyes were locked on their grandmother. Getting the skinny on their dad was a big deal.

Grandma exhaled slowly, "You know those tall apartments next to the Bluebird Diner on Railroad Street?"

"Yeah, that's where the poor people live," Danny blurted.

"That's correct, my boy. Those are government

subsidized apartments where people of little means are forced to live."

"What's subsidized mean?" Mark asked.

"It means the government pays part of their rent for them."

"You mean they're on welfare," Danny said, repeating a word he had heard in his government class.

"Yes, many of them are on welfare," Grandma replied.

"People on welfare are really poor!" Danny blurted, attempting to express his great knowledge of the subject.

Mark scowled at him.

"Well, let's just say they're people who need a helping hand."

"Go on, Grandma," an impatient Mark urged, anxious to get the inside scoop on his father.

The hesitant lady looked away from the boys toward the family room, "Oh, I don't know if I should really tell you boys this right now with the death of your friend and all. I just . . . uh . . ."

"Come on Grandma, you gotta tell us now!" Danny pleaded.

Grandma sighed, "Well, I guess you're right. I brought it up, so I suppose I can't back out now."

The boys leaned forward.

Grandma's eyebrow twitched as she struggled to continue with her story. She took a deep breath and continued, "Your father has kind of an affinity for the west side. That's why he goes to Tug's Tavern occasionally."

"Yeah, I saw him go in there one night," Mark

bragged.

"Why does Dad like the west side?" Danny asked.

Grandma studied the boys' faces, tapping the table nervously with her fingers. She cleared her throat and continued, "Well you see, my dear boys, your father was born in those apartments next to the Bluebird Diner and he lived there until he was about ten years old. Your Grandpa Tom had a tough time finding work, so it was all they could afford."

"Huh?" a surprised Mark questioned. "Dad was born in those apartments next to the Bluebird?"

"Yes, dear, he certainly was."

Danny fell back in his chair, shocked by the news.

"Your father's a proud man, sometimes a little too proud, I believe. He never talks about his childhood. Oh, there are certainly many people around here who know where he was born, but nobody ever brings it up. I don't think the folks here in town want their hero to be from the poor part of town."

"Wow." Danny mumbled. "Dad was born on the west side in those crummy apartments."

"Yes, he certainly was, and like I say, he lived there until he was in the fourth grade."

She paused and looked at the stunned boys. "I was born in a poor part of town also, so there's no shame in not having money. There are plenty of good folks over on the west side. In fact, some are good friends of mine. I only tell you this so you'll know that it doesn't matter a twit to me that you have some friends on the west side." She pulled her hanky from her apron pocket and dabbed her eyes.

"Thanks, Grandma," the boys replied.

Grandma's revelations explained why Danny often felt a connection with the west side, kind of like he had lived there or something.

Grandma smiled warmly and glanced at the cups of hot chocolate. They hadn't been touched.

"Well enough of that. You boys have had a lot to deal with today and it's getting late. You better get your baths and get ready for bed. That school bus will be here before we know it!"

The shocking news about their dad soon faded and Danny's thoughts once again went back to Eddie. His heart was heavy with grief.

Grandma stood and the two boys slowly scooted back from the table.

"Goodnight Grandma," Mark mumbled.

"Goodnight, Grandma." Danny followed Mark down the narrow hall to their bedroom.

"Goodnight, boys. I love you."

"Love you too."

"Love you too, Grandma."

Chapter 23

"Where are those darn things?" Maggie grumbled as she shut the door on yet another small oak cabinet in her father's kitchen. "One more to go,' she sighed and reached up to open the tiny cupboard above the refrigerator.

To her delight, she found the unseen coffee filters. "What do you know," she whispered. A smile curled on the corner of her mouth.

Standing on her tiptoes and stretching to reach them, she lifted the package off the shelf, carefully peeled one loose from the stack, and stuffed it in the flimsy plastic basket on the coffee machine. She scooped a few heaping tablespoons of coffee from a can of Folgers and dumped them in the basket. She poked the "On" button, and the rickety machine groaned into action.

After wiping the counter clean, Maggie reached up and grabbed a few coffee mugs from the cabinet. She turned and smiled when she saw Dan coming through the small swinging doors that separated the kitchen from the living room.

"Mornin', Sis," he grumbled at the tail-end of a hearty yawn.

"Good morning, Dan. Did you sleep okay?"

Knuckling sleep from his eyes, Dan replied, "As well as one can on a loveseat!"

"I used to love that little sofa. I spent a lot of time in the den playing with Sadie—that was until . . ." Her voice trailed off.

Dan glanced her way, waiting for her to finish the provocative announcement, but as usual, she didn't. Curious, but not wanting to make her uncomfortable, he changed the subject. "Up kind of early, aren't you?"

"Oh, you know me, Dan, I never was much for sleeping late."

"I know. You and I were always the first ones up in the morning. Some things never change."

"I guess we just couldn't wait for the daily 'chewing-out session' from Dad at breakfast."

"Guess not," Dan said quietly.

"Coffee? I think enough has brewed to grab us a couple of cups."

"Thought you'd never ask."

"Black?"

"You know me, Sis. Remember, I'm the wimp."

"Okay, cream it is."

Maggie dumped a teaspoon of powdered cream in Dan's cup and then lifted the carafe from the midst of the brewing session and poured the steaming black liquid into their cups.

"Oh good, just enough coffee was brewed to fill both cups," Maggie sighed in relief. "Why don't we go out to the screened porch so we don't wake the kids?"

She nodded toward the brightly decorated room just outside the kitchen. She pushed the carafe back in the machine and lifted both cups, handing one to Dan.

"Okay." Dan glanced over at the family room at the motionless figures of Mark's Kris and Katie who had chosen to sleep in the family room and were snuggled up in two sleeping bags next to the TV. "Lead the way, Sis."

Maggie pushed the handle on the sliding door that opened to the porch and headed for her favorite spot on the old wooden swing that hung front and center in the comfortable room.

Close behind, Dan quietly closed the slider and bent down to click on the space heater on this chilly fall morning. Then he joined his younger sister, burrowing in next to her on the creaky old swing.

"I was always afraid one of these things might break when we were kids," Maggie laughed, sliding her hand up and down one of the rusty chains that held up the ageless glider. "Now here they are twenty years later still doing the job."

A grin broke out on Dan's face. His blue eyes sparkled. Maggie glanced toward him. She missed those reassuring smiles from her older brother. There were times when as a child, she felt alone and frightened, and Danny would flash her one of those smiles and she would suddenly feel like everything was going to be okay.

She often lamented to her family that the hardest part of growing up was parting ways with Danny. Struck down by the dreaded Crohn's disease in her early adolescence, life from that point on became a fight to survive. The awful malady that inflames and eventually destroys the bowel, sapped essential nutrients from her body making her vulnerable to pneumonia and other infectious diseases. Adding insult to injury were the many extremely embarrassing episodes of abdominal cramping, often resulting in a mad dash to the nearest restroom to relieve herself.

In many ways, her illness had caused her life to be a living hell. Three husbands had left her—none of them willing to spend the time and energy it took to care for someone with her condition. A Christian woman, she believed very much in the sanctity of marriage and had been totally devastated by each of her divorces, always blaming herself for the break ups.

Danny was the only person in her life who had always completely understood her illness and its embarrassing ramifications. She never felt the least bit uncomfortable around him, or Mark for that matter. She had never been able to find anyone in her adult life who was as accepting as her older brothers.

"Did you sell your house in Van Haven?" Dan asked.

"Yes, I sure did. Got eighty grand for it. I bought a small condo near the school. Now someone else mows the grass and shovels the snow."

Dan smiled. "Living so close, did you see much of Dad?'

"No, not really. Oh, he'd call once in a while and we'd talk for a few minutes. I guess he was busy doing his thing, golfing at the club, gambling, playing the big shot here in Maple City."

"Yeah, the turnout at the funeral was huge."

"It didn't surprise me. The folks around here still

love him, that's for sure."

Dan surveyed the outside room. "We spent a lot of time out here on this porch watching Johnny Carson and Maverick," he said quietly. "I miss it."

Tears began to well in Maggie's eyes. She took a deep breath to keep from crying and gently tapped the floor to get the swing going. "I know," she replied softly. "So do I."

Dan gently slid his hand over hers and squeezed it gently. "We've all suffered so much, Maggie. I've been reflecting a lot on our childhood the past couple of days."

Maggie's eyebrow raised. She looked quizzically at her brother.

"Since Dad died, it seems easier for me to look back at things. I'm starting to deal with his, uh, I guess you might say all of my pain and unresolved feelings. Our father could be so insensitive."

Dan's revelations seemed to affect Maggie. Her eyes began to cloud over. "Insensitive? How about cruel?" she snapped.

"You're right. He could be awful at times, and it was hard for all of us, especially you being so frail and small. I tried to help but . . . "

Maggie quickly interrupted. A stern but loving expression spread over her face. "Sorry Dan, but I just can't let you go on. I'm thinking of all those nights when my Crohn's disease was at its worst and I was so sick and frightened. I would lie in bed at night shaking. Then I would hear the door to my room open and there you were. You would walk in and take out that folding chair, unfold it, and sit down next to my bed. And you would sit there for as long as it took for me to forget my fears. You would tell me funny stories about things that happened at school that day. I thought you were the funniest person in the whole world. I would laugh like crazy until I could laugh no more and then I would fall fast asleep and sleep like a baby until morning. In the morning, I would wake up and yank the blanket back to see if you were there. Of course you weren't, the chair wasn't there either, and the door was closed. I swear I never heard you leave that room—ever. I don't know how you made everything so bearable for me, but you did. It meant so much to me."

Danny laughed, "I'm glad my bedtime was an hour later than yours."

Maggie smiled, "It wouldn't have mattered. You would have been there for me anyway."

"I'll never forget the day we had to admit you to the hospital. The doctor said if dad had waited a few more days, you wouldn't have made it."

"I know. Nothing like massive doses of steroids to make one better."

Maggie sighed. "We were buds back then, you and me." She leaned closer and laid her head on his shoulder.

"You've been so strong and brave throughout your life, Maggie. The way you've dealt with your illness and all, it's been an inspiration to everyone."

"I don't feel like I've been much of an inspiration, but thank you."

Dan sensed an opportunity to get his tight-lipped sister to open up.

"I always tried to imagine what it was like for a little

girl growing up with a man like Dad. I can't imagine how you must have felt at times."

Maggie's eyes clouded over. She sat up and stopped the swing. Pushing her blond curls off her forehead and tucking them behind her ear, she slid off the swing and walked over to the edge of the porch. It appeared as though he had struck a nerve. Maybe she would talk.

Maggie spoke quietly, "My childhood was very lonely. I was too shy to make many friends and you boys and Dad were never home, so I stayed home alone and played with Sadie and my imaginary friends."

Dan pushed on. "You must have felt so alone."

She shook her head, "I don't think it really helps to dredge up the past."

Dan quickly retorted, "Sometimes you need to talk about the past. We all do. Please, Maggie, for me."

A hardened non-communicator, Maggie got quiet for a moment and when she finally began to speak again, she chose her words carefully. "I guess there were times when . . ."

The youngest sibling quickly stopped in mid-sentence as if catching herself before she said something wrong. "I see no need to talk about this now."

Dan hurried off the swing and walked over and stood next to her. "Tell me about those times, Maggie, please!" He laid his hand gently on the back of her neck.

She took another deep breath and sighed, "Okay, I'll try." She slipped a tissue from her robe and dabbed her watery eyes.

"I'm sure you'll remember this night. It took place

several months after Mom's death when Dad was
starting to drink heavily. It was before supper one
evening and you boys were out playing with your
friends. I remember it like it was yesterday. I was only
seven at the time and I was in the den playing with
Sadie. I was standing and barking out my usual list of
orders to little Sadie, who was tucked in the corner of
your lovely sofa."

"You mean the loveseat?"

"No, sorry! It's a sofa to me. I can't see any love in
that piece of furniture, and when I'm finished, I think
you'll know why."

Dan nodded, "Go on, Sis."

"Like I said, I was playing with Sadie when I heard
Grandma calling me for dinner. I turned and barked
some final marching orders to Sadie and then hurried
off to the kitchen. You boys were late and Grandma
was getting worried. I was worried too, but then she set
a steaming bowl of her famous noodles in front of me
and I instantly felt better."

Maggie playfully poked Dan's bicep and grinned. "I
guess you can see where you stood with me, Big Bro."

Dan smiled.

"Grandma was grumbling about how you boys were
going to put her in her grave. Thankfully, her concerns
were soon alleviated. The back door burst open and you
boys came running into the house, punching and
shoving each other as usual. Grandma scolded you a
good one and then quickly started the evening prayer,
even before you boys had a chance to wash your hands
and sit down."

"Ah, the evening prayer. I remember it well. How

'bout you?"

"Sure do."

Slowly, in unison, and without any prompting, the two kindred souls began to say the prayer they had recited for so many years as kids. "Dear God, please bless this family and bless this food to the nourishment of our bodies. Amen."

Maggie's eyes began to fill with tears. "I still love that little prayer."

Dan nodded.

Maggie took a breath and continued, "While we were sitting there having dinner, we suddenly heard Dad's loud mufflers coming down the drive. We all got real quiet and stared at each other. All of us, I'm sure, were wondering what Dad was doing home at that time of day. We heard his car door slam shut and then we heard him yell, 'Damn bikes!' I could hear your bikes bouncing on the gravel as he tossed them aside. Then he came staggering in the backdoor smelling like a brewery."

"You're right, Maggie, I remember that evening."

Maggie went on. "He seemed to be taken aback by the scene inside the house. Not being at home much in the evenings, I don't believe he realized what our dinner times were like. I think he was surprised by the intimacy of it all. I remember his black hair was hanging down over his face and he obviously had had too much to drink. Grandma suggested he sit down and eat with us, attempting to divert his attention. Grandma would never challenge Dad directly. I think she was a little afraid of him also."

"I agree," Dan replied.

"Well, he refused to eat with us. Said he just came

home to get something from the den and was in a hurry to get back. Stumbling toward the back of the house, he almost knocked over that tall lamp by the sofa. Remember that ugly lamp?"

"Who could forget it?" Dan chuckled.

"A short time later, we could hear him throwing things around in the den and rustling through drawers. No one was eating a bite; our stomachs were in our throats. Then it happened. He must have seen Sadie on the sofa and knew I had been in his den. He screamed, 'Maggie! Get in here!' His powerful voice reverberated throughout the entire house. I looked at you and Mark and I could tell you were both scared for me. I knew that you both wished that it was one of you going into that den instead of me."

Dan nodded.

"I got up and walked slowly back to the den. Filled with dread, I was shaking like a leaf. When I finally arrived, he grabbed me by my arm and yanked me in the den and closed the door. I knew it was going to get ugly when he closed that door. I started to whimper. He kept his voice low so you boys and Grandma couldn't hear. He told me to knock off the crying, and then he asked me if I had been playing with his ribbons. I shook my head yes. All of a sudden, his eyes narrowed and he exploded in rage. He grabbed my chin with his huge hand and began squeezing it and shaking my head violently back and forth. His eyes were black with anger, 'I told you to never mess with my stuff!' he said furiously. Pointing to the cluttered desk, he demanded to know where they were. I told him I didn't know for sure. Maybe they were in my bedroom. I was so scared I couldn't think. My whole world was falling apart. Even though he was hurting me physically, the pain inside was so much worse. No matter what Dad had done before, I always thought that he loved me; but that night, I wondered if he had ever loved me at all."

"Oh my God, you were just a little girl." Dan grimaced.

"Dad stormed out of the den and charged into my bedroom. I could hear my Cinderella lamp rattling on my dressing table. A few seconds later, he came storming back in a frenzy, waving those stupid ribbons in my face. 'Here they are!' he yelled, 'They were in your room!' I was sobbing uncontrollably at this point. Then it happened. The worst thing of all. As he was leaving the den, he spun toward me, and without saying a word, he popped me on the head with his knuckle. Just like this."

She poked her hand violently toward Dan's forehead with her second knuckle protruding.

"I'm sure he had hit you boys just as hard, but he had never hit me like that before. It wasn't the force of the blow that mattered to me. It was the symbolism of that act that was so demoralizing. Even as a little girl I understood that a punch like that from a man, whether it's your father or any other man, is a totally violent and disrespectful act to inflict upon a woman. I will never forget that day as long as I live. I was devastated and still carry those memories to this day."

Dan laid his arm on Maggie's shoulder and pulled her close.

"You boys must have heard me groan because you both came running down the hall with your little fists doubled up. He swore at you, pushed you aside and hurried out to his car and left. You and Mark huddled around me, hugging me and asking me what happened."

"Yes, but we never knew he hit you. We never knew that. Oh Maggie, I'm so sorry we didn't do more," Dan said regretfully.

Maggie paused and wiped a tear from her eye.

"You couldn't have known. My hair covered the bump. And I just couldn't tell you boys. I was too humiliated. I swear to this day Dan, I can't remember taking those stupid ribbons to my room." She laughed nervously. "Why were they so damned important anyway?"

"More than likely, he was bragging to the guys at the club about his track prowess and someone doubted him. That would have embarrassed him. A lot of people didn't know he ran track. I can only imagine he felt insulted and ran home to get the evidence." Dan gently rubbed Maggie's back. "When he couldn't find the proof, he became enraged and took it out on you."

"After that night, Dad tried to be nice to me, but it just seemed so insincere. I was never able to trust him after that happened. Our relationship became very distant." She pushed in closer to Dan. "That's another reason you were so important to me. After that night, you and Mark were all the family I had. I felt like there was a wall between Dad and me. Grandma tried to fill the void, but no one can really replace a parent."

"I'm so sorry," Dan said softly.

"I know you are," Maggie replied. "There were so many times as a child that I fantasized about a big white chariot dropping out of the sky and sweeping us all up into its beautiful cushy seats and carrying us away, far, far away."

Dan pursed his lips and smiled, "I swear, I don't know how we all turned out so normal."

"Relatively normal, may be a better description," Maggie joked.

"Maybe so," a smiling Dan replied. "Uh-oh, I hear the girls. They must be up."

Maggie stepped back and dabbed her eyes one last time before she greeted the girls. "I best try and pull myself together a little here. I don't need to burden the kids with my problems. They're sad enough about their grandpa dying."

Dan smiled, "Don't worry, Sis, they're sensitive girls. They expect a few tears at a time like this."

"Guess so."

"I'm so glad you opened up today, Maggie."

She squeezed his arm. "I feel like a load has been lifted off my shoulders. Thanks for insisting. Let's go inside and spend some time with your girls. Some of us have to go to work in the morning."

Maggie smiled and slipped her hand under Dan's protruding elbow as they went to greet the giggling girls. Just before stepping into the family room, Dan paused and looked back at the old swing still swaying gently in the morning breeze. "That old swing holds a bunch of memories for us," he whispered.

"Sure does," Maggie replied.

Chapter 24

Mark slammed his generous backside against Dan, sending him sprawling onto the ground and then dropped in a short jumper for two.

"16 to 12, Chicago Kinseys!" Mark blared.

"No foul there?" Dan shot back at his brother, shaking his head in disgust. He rolled up to his feet and gathered up the ball.

"I was establishing position!"

"Position, my foot," Dan tossed the ball quickly to daughter Meghan.

Not athletically inclined, Meghan caught the soft inbounds pass and threw it like a hot potato to her sister Ali, the star of her high school basketball team. Ali snapped the ball up in her hands, took a quick dribble past her cousin Kris, and shot a lofty fifteen-footer. The elusive sphere ricocheted off the rim and back into the hands of a startled Meghan, who once again quickly shoved it away, this time to her dad.

Dan could feel Mark's fingers poking him in the middle of his back as he began to dribble toward the basket.

"Show me what you got, Danny boy," Mark taunted, poking harder on his brother's spine.

Dan saw his opening and quickly spun toward the basket and laid it in. Even though he wasn't the athlete that Mark was, the taller Dan always seemed to get the best of his brother when they played one on one.

"Lucky shot!" Mark shouted.

"The Denver Kinseys rock!" Meghan cheered.

The back screen door swung open. "Phone for you!" Ann shouted at Meghan. "It's Jenny."

A smiling Meghan raced toward the house, happy to have an excuse to leave the game.

"I'll sit out since Meghan's on the phone," cousin Kris offered. Never too enthused about these time honored pickup games, the slender Kris looked relieved as she trotted off the court.

"Okay, two-on-two," an anxious Mark replied, not wanting the game to end before the game got to twenty, the winning total.

"16 to 14 and our out!" Mark yelled. He tossed the ball toward his oldest daughter Katie, who fumbled the errant pass.

"Keep your eye on the ball!" he bawled.

"I did!" Katie shouted defensively. "You didn't throw it right!"

"Didn't throw it right? Didn't throw it right?" Mark shouted sarcastically, mocking his daughter.

She angrily tossed the ball back to her dad.

"Come on, big mouth, show me what you got" Dan barked at Mark. He crouched down on defense with arms extended.

"Big mouth, is it?" Mark showed a nasty grin, and then threw a head fake at his younger brother, pulled back, took a jump shot and swished one through the net. "18 to 14," he shouted.

"I quit," a frustrated Katie said. "Dad does all the shooting and all I get is grief." She turned and stormed off the court.

"What the . . ." Mark's arms shot in the air. "I'm sorry, Katie. I was just kidding. Come on, sweetheart, don't quit."

Undeterred, the disgruntled daughter disappeared into the crowded screened porch, the screen door banging shut in her wake.

Dan looked toward his sixteen year old daughter Ali, standing with the ball pressed against her protruding hip. Always one to enjoy a challenge, she didn't want to quit.

"The two of us against Uncle Mark wouldn't be fair," she grumbled. She hurled a hard bounce pass to her dad and strolled dejectedly off the court.

"Sorry Ali," Dan said. He threw her a kiss and then turned his attention back to his brother. "Okay, you old fart, let's see what you got."

"We'll see who the old fart is!" Mark said, waving his hands in his brother's face.

Dan turned his back to Mark and spun the ball into the air and watched it bounce off the hard asphalt surface and back toward his waiting hands. He hunkered down. It was a fight to the death now, and he knew it. He was down four, and Mark was only one basket away from winning. He had to score now and hold his brother scoreless on the next possession—no easy task.

Mark planted his thick fingers on Dan's back. He grunted nervously, an annoying habit of his during these pickup games. "It's your move, big shot," he said in a mocking reference to Dan's recent promotion.

Dan dribbled out to the backcourt to get a little breathing room, putting himself outside his normal shooting range. Knowing Dan was out of range, the savvy Mark laid back, saving energy.

"Palming! Palming!" Mark bawled at his brother.

"This is how the pros dribble!" Dan bellowed. "Get over it!"

The painfully regressive behavior of the two middle-aged men seemed to grow progressively worse as the game continued. Their insults and bickering had descended into full teenage mode at this point.

Dan plotted out his next move with a sudden shift to the left. He grinned when Mark went for the nifty fake and gave him an opening to the right. Leaning forward with his head down, Dan charged aggressively toward the basket. Mark tried frantically to right himself and get back on defense, but it was to no avail. The smirking Dan dribbled twice, jumped in the air and took the shot. The ball fell through the rusty rim for two.

"18 to 16, win by four!" he shouted.

"Win by four?" Mark complained loudly. "Who said that?"

"We always play 'win by four', barf breath!" A sheepish grin spread across Dan's face at his own recognition of the childish epitaph.

Mark flashed a nasty glare. He flipped the ball into the air, caught it, and leaned forward. Dan crouched down on defense. Mark was grunting profanities under his breath and tossing the ball from hand to hand. Concerned, Dan knew that bodily harm was a distinct possibility at this point in the ugly fray.

Mark's right foot pawed the ground like some angry bull preparing for the attack. Imagining small curved horns popping out of the top of Mark's head, Dan knew the battle would be epic. Surprisingly, Mark leapt forward and barged headfirst toward his unprepared brother with no attempt to fake. He lowered his broad shoulder and crashed into Dan's midsection, knocking him backward. Dan fought valiantly to stay afoot while his brother drove toward the basket. Flailing helplessly backward toward a crash landing on the gravel driveway, Dan braced for the fall. An evil smile appeared on his brother's face and Danny was certain that he could see smoke shooting from his ears.

Nonetheless, Dan wasn't going to be daunted. While falling backwards, he lifted his foot just enough to make contact with Mark's ankle.

"You weasel!" Mark shouted. He stumbled on the protruding appendage and lost his balance, causing the ball to fly from his hands and settle harmlessly at middle court as both men went sprawling.

Dan was the first to fall on the gravelly courtside, the heavy grit ripped into his back. Pain shot up his spine. Ignoring it, he quickly rolled to his feet, righted himself, and dove headfirst toward the ball at middle court. He grabbed the ball and clutched it firmly in both hands. Spinning around, he charged toward the basket for the tying shot. The soaring sphere flew toward the weathered backboard like some brilliant comet streaking across the sky. Mark, lying in the yard next to the court, watched helplessly as the ball bounced ever so softly against the ancient backboard. It fell through the rim and swished the tattered net. All color drained from Mark's face.

"18 to 18," Dan shouted, jumping and punching his fist in the air.

Mark got to his feet and began making grunting sounds again sounding like a wild boar. Dan watched the growling man-beast chase down the ball. Grasping it firmly in his hands, he prepared for another assault.

Winded and exhausted Dan glanced toward the end of the screened porch. Not surprisingly, the ferocity of their endeavor had attracted an audience. Just below the blinds that dangled on the large screen at the end of the porch, the entire Kinsey family was huddled together watching the barbaric struggle. Grandma Carrie sitting center stage had a shocked look on her face. The rest of the family was used to such animalistic behavior from the Kinsey men and were talking, smiling and enjoying the action.

Dan decided to use the unexpected audience to his advantage. He began to fantasize that he was in front of a royal court in the Roman Coliseum with thousands of spectators watching him. Like some powerful gladiator, he turned and acknowledged the crowd with a nod of his head and took a deep bow. Then he pushed up his sleeves and turned to face the evil opponent on the other side of the court.

"You're mine," Mark taunted, once again tossing the ball back and forth between his hands. Beads of perspiration glistened on his forehead. With his chest heaving from near exhaustion, he leaned forward, bent down and prepared for his next charge to the basket.

Dan crouched down on defense. His tired, middle-aged knees were shaking. He was struggling to get his breath. Then, just for an instant, thoughts of the many childhood games between him and his brother flashed through his mind—games he usually won. *I can do this*, he thought.

Trying to get the jump on his weary brother, Mark pivoted on his right foot and pushed hard against the ground, but the abrupt move caused his tired leg to give out. Mark struggled to regain his balance, but to no avail. Needing both hands to protect himself during his fall, Mark reluctantly was forced to let go of the ball. He watched in stark terror as the ball began to roll away from him. Attempting to seize the moment, Dan immediately dove for the loose ball, but his tired legs were also failing him.

Like two bad actors in some slow-motion movie, the two dog-tired men were starting to tumble. Ever the opportunist, Mark tried to regain his balance by grabbing his brother's shoulder with his free hand. Dan in desperation, reached his sweaty hand forward and grabbed onto Mark's cotton sweatshirt.

The extra weight from Dan's grip caused Mark's tired legs to give out completely. Hanging on to one another for dear life, the middle-aged gladiators seemed to be doing some macabre dance as they charged helplessly toward the rough edge of the ancient court. Out of control and falling helplessly, Dan glanced over at the horrified faces on the wide-eyed bystanders.

The two men bounced hard off the stony rim on the edge of the court and then rolled like two giant sacks of potatoes toward the soft thick grasses that covered the backyard. Coming to a abrupt stop, his chest heaving from almost total exhaustion, Dan turned slowly toward his moaning brother lying on the ground beside him. Mark's grim expression began to soften. His blue eyes began to twinkle. It wasn't long before a slight wisp of a grin appeared on Mark's sweaty face. Dan smiled, surprised by the unexpected metamorphosis of his gritty opponent.

"That was great!" Mark moaned in delight. He rolled to his side, lifting his hand toward Dan for a high-five. "We still got it, Bro! We still got it!" he exclaimed. Their hands bumped together.

Dan smiled warmly "We sure do."

The screen door on the back porch suddenly banged open, and a horde of concerned family members raced across the yard toward their fallen heroes.

"Are you alright?" Ann asked, holding back her giggles. "Why, you two could have killed each other out there!"

The others pushed in next to Ann and stared down at the two aging protagonists.

Red crept up Dan's face, embarrassed by the remarkably juvenile exhibition put on by him and his unrepentant and smiling brother.

"We're fine, everybody. We just got a little carried away."

Mark punched him gently in the arm, "Let's call it a tie, Bro. What do you say?"

"Sounds good." Dan rolled to his feet and the two dog-tired warriors shared an awkward hug. The family roared their approval, relieved that the brutal affair had finally come to an end.

"Excuse me, fellas," Grandma Carrie said in a commanding voice. Both men looked wide-eyed at their beloved grandmother.

She smiled, deep wrinkles spread across her face. She cleared her throat and spoke ever so slowly to the winded combatants. "We buried your father yesterday and I thought we had seen the last of him, but I can see he still lives on in you boys. I saw a lot of your dad out there on that court just now. Both of you boys got your father's grit and determination."

The men nodded politely. Grandma suddenly jerked up on the aluminum walker and poked both of them firmly in the backside.

"And that's not all I wanted to say. From now on, act like you've got some sense! You were both acting like a couple of fools out there!" The tired men, grinning from ear to ear, stepped over and gave their grandma a sweaty hug.

A few moments later, the group began to disperse and go their separate ways. Dan took the opportunity to pause for a moment and look up at the tattered net dangling below the old rusty rim. Surprisingly, a vision of his father's face appeared inside that rim. It was an hallucination for sure, but it felt very real to Dan. Unexpectedly, his loving grandmother had turned the ritual of blood and guts with Mark into something very special. As much as Dan resented his father and the pain he had caused him, he truly had given Mark and him that competitive drive that had helped push them to the top of their chosen professions. That fire in their bellies and their never-give-up attitude were indeed positive gifts from an otherwise, very troubled father.

It was encouraging for Dan to contemplate the possibility that something positive had been passed on to him from his father. The thought comforted him, even if it was only for the moment.

Ann walked over and gently picked pieces of dead grass from Dan's hair. "You have a problem," she said softly.

"Ann, it was only a game!"

Ann poked his shoulder playfully, knocking him off stride. "Not that silly."

Dan's brow lifted.

"We're almost out of beer."

"Hmmm, that is serious. We better take care of that."

He looked around for Mark and found him demonstrating his jump shot to his daughters. He interrupted the hedonistic display. "Hey, Bro!"

"Yeah, Dan."

"Beer trip?"

"Think I'll pass. The Denver clan hogged the shower all morning, I gotta clean up a little."

"Good idea," Dan mocked.

Mark grinned. "Don't dally. I'm a little dry."

"There's still a couple in the fridge, Mark," Ann interjected.

"Oh good, then take your time, Bro. Give us all a break."

Dan smiled, slid a comb out of his back pocket, and ran it through his ruffled hair.

"Don't worry, you look great, honey," Ann said as she winked at her persnickety husband.

"Oh, uh thanks."

"Our girls are still pretty down about your dad. I thought it might be a good idea to get them out of this house for a while. We're going to run over to the mall and do a little shopping with Grandma. Ellen and her girls have a few errands to run and then they're going to try and catch up with us. We'll see you after a while, honey." Ann gave him a peck on the cheek and started to leave.

Dan gently grabbed her hand. "Are we really short of beer or are you just trying to get rid of me so you and the ladies can go shopping?"

Ann squeezed his hand tenderly and moved closer, her expression changing. "You know how much I love you, Dan. You are a great husband and father, always there for me and the girls, but I think you need a little more time to sort things out. I want you to deal with whatever these powerful emotions are that seem to be overwhelming you. It's obvious that your father's passing has had a major effect on you. So please, Figure it out while we're here, and then let it go. Don't take this back to Denver. Okay?"

"Okay."

She kissed him tenderly. "Gotta go."

She gave his hand a last firm squeeze and hurried off to join the girls.

"I love you," Dan said quietly.

Chapter 25

Encouraged by Ann's perceptiveness, and still trying to make sense of his difficult journey through adolescence, Dan felt compelled to visit Tug's Tavern for his mid-afternoon beer run. Tug's was his father's favorite drinking hole, and the scene of the troubling Millie Cantrell episode so many years ago.

The turn signal chimed as Dan turned onto the crumbling, pothole-laden Railroad Street. Dan quickly darted into an open parking spot right across from the aging tavern. He turned the engine off and sat in the car for a moment just surveying the old neighborhood. Gone was his favorite childhood haunt, the Bluebird Diner. The big blue neon sign he loved so much had been replaced by a makeshift wood sign that read, 'Hank's Gun Shop'. Strong feelings of nostalgia stirred inside of him. Memories flooded back from his childhood days. He remembered the many dark winter nights that he and the boys spent huddled together shooting pinball in the tiny room at the back of the ramshackle diner. And even though it was over twenty years ago, the feelings were still very real.

He looked past the gun shop to the space where the tall apartments with the long porches had stood. They were also gone. His father's childhood home had been torn down and converted into a parking lot and for what appeared to be a topless bar at the other end of the long lot. The curvy figure of a scantily clad woman protruded just above the front door of a large one story building that sat some two hundred feet away with a sign that read, "Girls! Girls! Girls!" a dead giveaway as to what was going on inside. Dan watched as two men in grimy T-shirts climbed out of an old dilapidated pickup truck and hurried inside.

Tug's Tavern appeared to be the exception to the urban decay that seemed to be taking over the rest of the neighborhood. Except for a burnt out "g" on the Tug's sign out front, the old place appeared to be in remarkably good condition.

Still gazing, Dan pushed the handle down and opened the door. Stepping out onto the rutted street, he adjusted his dark glasses against the bright afternoon sun. He suddenly leaned back against the car, startled by a loud rumbling sound. He turned left to see four Harley Davidson motorcycles turning onto Railroad Street. The riders roared past him, their apparent destination was the topless bar at the end of the block. The words "West Side Bikers" were embossed across the backs of their black leather jackets.

With the smell of exhaust from the big motorcycle engines still hanging in the air, Dan looked both ways and hurried across the street. He hopped up on the sidewalk and paused to read a small sign tacked on the front door of Tug's. It read "Carry Out" and featured a black arrow pointing to the rear of the elongated building.

He glanced in the front window and was shocked to see the old corner booth, his dad's booth, still looking very much the same as did so many years ago. For an instant, the pain of Mark's shocking revelation about his father's tryst with his best friend's mother in that booth shot through him. Dan took a deep breath, collected himself and walked around the corner of the building and down the well-grooved alley toward the back of the building.

Once in the alley, he was overwhelmed by a feeling of sadness. His heart yearned to see his old friends again, the ones he had roamed these very streets with so many years ago. He regretted the fact that after junior high school they had gone their separate ways.

Dan and Mark, blessed with almost princely status because of their legendary father, had found other interests as they grew older. They dated the prettiest girls in school and were privy to all the "coolest" parties and goings-on around town. A girlfriend had once told Dan that a party was not a success unless one of the handsome Kinsey boys was in attendance.

The fate of his tough friends who lived on the west side was much different. Not being favored with the economic and social advantages of the Kinsey boys, they had traveled a much different road through life. Very few even made it to high school. Following in their parent's footsteps, most of the gang quit school as soon as they reached the qualifying age of sixteen.

One of the exceptions to this was Frankie Cantrell, the brightest one of the bunch. Blessed with a love of science, he went on to finish high school, getting average grades and winning some small awards in the science department. Unfortunately, without parents to encourage him and with no money for college, he eventually ended up like the others—taking a job at one of the local plants earning slightly more than four bucks an hour.

It pained Dan to think of how callously he had treated his old friends back in those days. How he would stroll down the halls of junior high school, often with a pretty girl hanging on his arm, brushing past his old friends without speaking. *How arrogant of me,* he thought. *How cruel and arrogant of me!*

Dan now knew, after so many years had gone by, that these boys from the tough west side had truly been the best friends he had ever had. They shared with him in ways that his popular friends from the "good" families never did. And although he was less than gracious to them, they remained amazingly undeterred in their affection for him.

He remembered the crudely written notes of congratulations from Timmy and Frankie when he graduated from college, telling him how proud they were that one of the members of their old gang had gone on to the "big time." It was a truly magnanimous gesture from two kids of meager means, who lived in broken-down apartments in a poor part of town and spent their days working in a hot dirty factory.

Saddened and ashamed, Dan stopped and fell back against the old wood frame building in the dusty alley. "Damn!" he murmured. He kicked at the loose gravel, scattering several small rocks. "How could I be so callous?" he lamented. His Grandma was right, whether he liked to admit it or not, there was a lot of Beau Kinsey in him.

Dan was distracted by the groan of an old truck engine coming out from the rear of the building. He turned and watched as a rickety pickup pulled out from the parking lot behind the building and started down the alley toward him. Dan pushed up closer to the building and smiled at the bearded driver as he drove past. He watched the truck disappear onto Railroad Street, and then proceeded to walk to the back of the building.

Looking up, he saw a sign protruding from the side of the building that read, "Carry Out Inside." Dan walked around the end of the building and opened the rickety screen door and headed inside. Once inside, he suddenly realized that for all the hurting this place had caused him, he had never been inside the popular bar. He paused for a moment and looked around the small back room. The pool tables that he could see through the window as a boy had been replaced by a large assortment of gambling machines.

Dan navigated past the machines into the long main room. It was bright and rather cheery inside the bar, much different than the dark foreboding room of his recent dream. Old oak booths lined the right side of the main room. They bore a nice sheen and were very well preserved. Expensive looking stained glass chandeliers hung down from the ceiling and stopped just a few feet above the tabletops. Several paintings of hunting scenes dotted the walls above the booths and were interspersed with colorful beer signs. Behind the bar, a huge moose head seemed to extend halfway across the bar and was surrounded on either side by large beveled glass mirrors. The spectacular moose was most certainly the prize of the legendary proprietor, who was well-known for his hunting prowess.

The patrons at Tug's for the most part were older. Many appeared to be retired or near retirement age, reflecting the changing economy of the area. The prevalence of cheap labor overseas had forced many of the local companies to close their doors and move out of the country, causing the loss of hundreds of jobs. The plants that did manage to remain open fell victim to major streamlining efforts and eliminated many jobs with the exception of those with the highest seniority. Such migrations and cutbacks left the local community with a much smaller and older work force. The net effect of all this was that it forced the younger folks in town to look elsewhere for employment, usually in the nearby large cities of Indianapolis and Chicago.

Dan was distracted by a loud, hardy laugh from a young man wearing a plaid vest and working behind the bar. He turned and watched as the bartender directed a narrow stream of a clear fluid into a small shot glass.

Then to Dan's surprise, a mess of gray hair popped up from under the bar. Dan looked closely at the humped man as he slammed down two bottles of beer and quickly wiped them dry with a small white towel.

My God! It's Tug! He's still here. Dan quickly approached the end of the long oak bar still looking intently at the old gentlemen. He wanted to be certain it was Tug, as he didn't want to make a fool of himself. As he got closer to the man, he was convinced it was him. He could never forget the deep creases in that face that he had seen so often at little league games when he was a kid. Tug rarely missed a game back then, cheering and encouraging his son, Johnny.

"Tug, how are you?" Dan called out.

The puffy-eyed old bar owner glanced toward Dan without commenting. Busy with a customer, he grabbed a five-dollar bill from the bar top and yanked the metal arm on the ancient cash register. The old bell clanked weakly and the worn wooden drawer popped open. He pushed the bill into the drawer, removed some change from the ancient register and handed it to the waiting customer. His gaze soon returned to Dan. He seemed somewhat puzzled by the greeting from the young stranger.

"I'm okay, thank ya," he said, still looking confused. Always friendly to his patrons, he turned and walked toward Dan, his hand outstretched for a shake. "Tug McGibben, what I can I do for you, young fella?"

"I'm Dan Kinsey, Tug," Dan smiled, shaking his hand firmly while Tug continued to stare dubiously at Dan. Reeking with the odor of alcohol, his eyes narrowed and then went wide as he recognized Dan. A big smile spread across his scraggily mug. "My God! Danny! How the hell are you?" The handshake resumed with new vigor. The surprised owner was now smiling from ear to ear. "I haven't seen you in years, my boy. You sure look different! I didn't recognize you with your fancy haircut and nice clothes and all. You've put on a pound or two, but ya look good."

"Thanks Tug. I didn't expect to see you in here today either."

"I ain't got nothin' else to do since Ella died. I'd

probably die myself if I didn't have this place to come to everyday. It keeps me busy and outa trouble."

Dan nodded agreeably.

The busy tavern owner, never one for small talk, shifted gears to a more serious tone. "Sorry I missed your dad's funeral," he said sincerely. "I had it all arranged to have my right hand gal take over for me, and at the last minute she got a bad case of the flu. There's only two of us that can handle the money 'round here, so I had to stay and run this joint. I hated it, Danny. I loved your dad like a brother."

Dan smiled, "I understand, Tug. Those things happen."

"Several of the boys went. Wish I coulda joined them, I truly do." Tug winced. Tears welled in his sagging eyes. Obviously, he was still sincerely disappointed that he had not been able to attend his good friend's funeral.

"No problem, Tug. I know Dad thought a lot of you."

"What'll ya have, son?" Tug fired back, wanting to change the subject before things got too emotional.

"Bud Light would be fine, thanks."

Tug pushed the door open and reached down into the stainless steel cooler and pulled up a couple of Bud Lights, set them on the bar, and wiped them dry.

"Hey, Josh!"

"Yeah, Boss?" the young bartender replied.

"It ain't too busy right now. Take over for a while. I got an old friend to talk to."

"Okay, Boss."

Chapter 26

Tug's weathered face cracked a grin; he winked at Dan and pointed to an empty booth in the back corner of the room. "Got a minute?" he asked.

"Sure do, Tug. My wife and daughters had some things to pick up at the store and Mark's taking a nap."

Tug beamed, "And how the hell is Mark?" he asked as he placed a couple of small glasses on top of the cold beers and slid around the end of the bar.

"Ornery as ever."

"He was a good kid, like you, Danny, and one helluva athlete."

"That's for sure," Dan replied.

Tug slid into the booth, looking slightly embarrassed. "You were a good athlete too, Danny, it just . . ."

Dan interrupted, "No apology necessary, Tug. Mark was the better athlete, but I got all the girls."

Tug burst out in laughter followed by a few hoarse coughs. Setting the beers on the table, he slid his hand inside the pocket on his white cotton shirt and pulled out a pack of Camels. "Ya mind?"

"No, no, that's fine."

Dan slipped into the booth, lifted the glass off the beer, set it on the table and poured it full. He was delighted that Tug, a west side icon, was taking time out of his busy day to visit with him. It made him feel special.

"I hope to hell that 'no smokin' stuff doesn't come to Maple City," the rough owner groused.

He tapped the nearly full pack of cigarettes on his index finger, and several of the white sticks popped up. He snatched the tallest one from the pack and stuck it carefully in his mouth.

Not a smoker, Dan watched in awe as Tug went through the time-tested ritual. He nimbly slid the heavy, steel Zippo lighter out of his jeans pocket with his right hand. He then clicked the lid open with the palm of his left hand, sparking the flint with the thumb of his right hand in one fascinating motion. The yellow flame exploded. Tug squinted through the flame, dragging hard on the little bonfire. Red coals spread up the end of his cigarette. Without pausing, he snapped the lid shut against the thigh of his right leg and slid it ever so gently back into his pocket. There wasn't one hesitation or one wasted motion during the entire process. It was poetry in motion.

Dan was always captivated by the cool, macho way the west side boys used to light their cigarettes. It still fascinated him to this day.

"How's Johnny doing? Last I heard he was joining the Marines."

"Aw hell, he's alright. After he left the Marines, he got into dope pretty heavy. He got busted a couple of times and decided to kick the habit. He's still a little edgy from his dopin' days, but he's hangin' in there. Works at the Foster Forbes plant, been married a couple of times, has two kids. He lives alone right now. But he's okay, nothin' serious."

His sad eyes squinted through the cigarette smoke toward Dan, belying the somewhat positive exultation about his son.

"Next time you see him, would you please tell him I said hello?"

"Will do, sure will."

Tug quickly changed the subject. "How you and Mark doin'? Where ya livin' and all?"

"Mark's a bond manager in Chicago, married with two girls, and I'm a banker in Denver, married with two girls also."

Tug grinned, "Well, I'll be, a bond manager and a banker. I gotta say, my boy, it doesn't surprise me. You boys were always good students and all. I always wished Johnny had done better in school, but he chose to go huntin' and chase the girls."

"Nothing wrong with that," Dan smiled.

"Guess not," the old man murmured.

"Speaking of hunting, is that your moose head hanging above the bar?"

Tug's face lit up like the old neon sign out front. "Sure enough is. Got him in Montana years ago. Sixteen point bull, I'm damn proud of it."

"I'll bet," Dan replied. "What were you using?" Not well versed about hunting, Dan was attempting to show some knowledge regarding the ancient sport.

"I was usin' 250 grain, .338 caliber Winchesters in

my Ruger M77. He was hidin' behind a stand of birch trees. I stunned 'em with the first shot, dropped him with the second."

Dan nodded awkwardly.

"Do much huntin'?" the cagey old hunter asked with a sly grin.

"N, . . . not lately," Dan said quietly. "How's your business?" he shot back wanting to move on.

"Not bad, considerin' they opened that damned titty bar down the road a while back. It was darn slow in here for awhile. All my horny customers were racing down there like a bunch of teenagers in heat."

"What happened?"

With a twinkle in his eye, Tug took a drag on his rapidly shrinking cigarette and leaned back in the booth. The grayish smoke plumed upward.

"It was simple," he said with a mischievous grin. "The topless owner, Red Jenkins, was chargin' $2.50 for a bottle of beer. I was charging $2.00 at the time, so I lowered mine to $1.50. Those tight S.O.B.'s from the plants will do anything to save a buck." He grinned smugly. "So now the sorry bastards come here first, drink a few and get a buzz on with my buck-fifty beers. Then they go down there and play tuck-a-buck with the girls and nurse a couple o' those high priced beers for the rest of the night."

His tired sagging eyes scanned the room. "Hell, there's probably five or six of the ingrates in here right now drinkin' up a storm. There'll be more in a little while, when the 3:45 shift gets here."

"Sounds like you beat the system."

"Sure enough did. I'm selling more beer than I ever

did. I found a new distributor who gave me a better price. I'm still makin' seventy-five cents a bottle, 'bout what I was makin' before that joint opened, and my volume's up twenty-five per cent. And now I'm bringing in a few hookers. The ancient art, ya know."

Dan grinned, "Now I see why you've survived so long."

A tint of crimson spread across the Tug's deeply lined face.

"Do you ever hear what my old friends Timmy, Frankie, and Spike are doing?"

Tug coughed. "Did ya hear those Harley's go past awhile ago?" The watery-eyed Tug hacked a couple of more times.

"Sure enough did. They almost ran over me."

"Well, one of them was Spike Lewis. He's in that motorcycle gang now. He's rougher'n a cob. He used to come in here, but he was always startin' trouble with someone; hittin' on a guy's girlfriend, wife or something. I finally got so many complaints that I had to throw him out. Now he goes down the street every day to that topless bar with his motorcycle buddies. Good riddance." Tug scowled.

"Sorry to hear that."

Although he wasn't truly surprised, Dan was a little disappointed to hear this about his old friend. Spike was always the dark one of the group. Out of all the members of the old gang, he probably had the most distant relationship with Spike.

Satisfied with the information about Spike, he pressed on. "What about Timmy and Frankie?"

"Frankie used to come in here once in awhile. He'd

settle on one of those bar stools over there and just soak himself full o' booze. It made me sick to watch him. I called him a cab a couple of times because he was too drunk to drive home. That made him mad, so he quit comin' in. He died about five years ago. I think the young man drank himself to death. It was a real bad scene. It was sad."

Dan leaned up in his seat and rolled his eyes, shocked and saddened by the news about Frankie. He hesitated, not sure if he wanted to hear about Timmy.

Tug paused, took a sip of his beer, swiped the lingering foam from his thin lips and looked directly at Dan. "I know you and Timmy were real close as kids, ridin' all over town on that little bike of his and all." He smiled briefly and looked back at the foam swirling in the mug.

"Yeah, we sure were."

"Timmy was quiet and kind of shy."

A nervous Dan nodded, gulping down the foamy beer while he waited for the news on Timmy.

"Well, he never really changed that much when he got older. He hung out here quite a bit. He and Frankie would come in together sometimes, but for the most part he came in alone. I think Frankie was a little hard to get along with. A couple of years ago, some tough from the south side named Cord Hamilton started movin' in on Timmy's girlfriend. Timmy was divorced at the time and dating that Shelton girl."

"Daisy Shelton?" Dan asked.

"Yeah, . . . yeah, that was her."

"Pretty girl," an impatient Dan took another sip of beer.

"Cord got off work at three, same time as Daisy, but Timmy didn't get off until half past three. So Cord and Daisy would get here a half hour sooner than your old friend. Cord was a handsome sort—a big, tough fella and he had a way with the women. He kinda liked Daisy and was always hangin' around here buyin' her drinks and such. At first, he would beg off quickly when Timmy got here; but as time passed, he became more reluctant to leave her side. Timmy could see what was goin' on, but he's just a thin little guy, and like I say, Cord was a big raw-boned fella."

Tug punched out the amazingly short stub of his cigarette in the ashtray. Smoke drifted to the ceiling.

"Timmy was tough enough," Dan said in defense of his old mate.

"Yeah, he was, and he didn't like Cord Hamilton one little bit. Ya could see trouble comin' from a mile away."

Dan leaned forward on the table. "After the news about Frankie, I'm afraid to ask what happened next."

"Ya want me to go on?" the old man warned.

"Yeah, I guess so." Dan said warily.

"One day Cord got off a little early. The heating system at the plant broke down or somethin'. So he got here 'bout noon and started hittin' the b-booze pretty hard right from the get go. By the time Daisy got here, he was feelin' no pain. Daisy always kinda tolerated the scallywag. In fact, I think it's fair to say she led him on a little bit at times. He was a handsome dude and all that, but she was just playin' with him. It was obvious that she really cared about Timmy. The drunken Cord kept laying his hands on her and whisperin' sweet nothins' in her ear that day. She kept half-heartedly pushin' him away and tellin' him to leave her be."

Tug paused and flipped the lid open on his old Zippo to light another smoke. Sparks flew when his blackened, sandpaper-like thumb snapped down on the flint wheel. He leaned down and took a hard drag. Smoke drifted from the corner of his mouth, away from Dan.

Dan waited anxiously.

"I remember dreadin' Timmy's arrival. I kept watchin' the backdoor, hopin' that somehow he wouldn't show. But sure enough, at four o'clock sharp, he walked in, smiling and looking around for Daisy."

Tug gulped down the rest of his beer and glanced at Dan. Dan nodded to the negative when the boss signaled the young bartender for a refill and then continued.

"About the time Timmy arrived, Cord had just wrapped his arm around Daisy's shoulder. He didn't know Timmy was here. Timmy's face darkened. He just froze in the doorway, glaring at Cord. Just then, Cord reached over with his other hand and pinched Daisy right on the boob. She screamed and jumped back and yelled 'keep your dirty hands off me!' Timmy went crazy! All of the anger that had been buildin' up inside of him exploded. I'll never forget it as long as I live."

The bartender slid another beer in front of Tug. He paused and took a long drink. Impatient, Dan encouraged his friend to continue, "Go ahead Tug, what happened next."

The hardened saloon owner frowned. "Well, like I said, Timmy was madder 'en a hornet by this time. He charged across the room and dove straight at Cord. He caught him totally off guard. Cord raised his arms like this."

Tug's elbows went up, demonstrating the protective position.

"Timmy's left arm hooked around the brute's neck as he flew by. They both went sprawling to the floor with ashtrays, beer mugs, and bar stools flyin' ever which way. Timmy landed on top of 'em and started to pummel the larger man. Daisy started screamin', her eyes were big as saucers. Your old friend had caught the bigger man totally by surprise and was beatin' up on 'em pretty good. But Timmy was no fool. He knew that eventually the bigger and stronger Cord would be able to get the best of him. Cord was swearin' and holdin' his hands over his face. Then it happened. Timmy started looking around on the floor next to him for a weapon. Next thing I knew, he had ripped a leg off the broken barstool."

As Dan listened to the frightening story, a sense of dread came over him. Tug continued the story.

"I shouted "No, Timmy!" I started around the end of the bar, but before I could get there, Timmy was already beatin' the sorry bastard with the leg of that stool. I was yellin' 'Stop!' 'Stop!' Timmy was poundin' on him unmercifully. It was sickening to watch. Blood poured from Cord's face, and his arms dropped to his side. Several of the patrons and I got there about the same time. It took all of us to get Timmy to stop beaten' him."

"Oh, my God," Dan murmured.

"Cord wasn't movin'. His head was swellin' up like a muskmelon, and his eyes had this blank look to them, just starin' at the ceiling and not blinkin'. Timmy was standing there, his eyes still glazed over with rage. That bloody stub of a barstool was hangin' down from his hand. I had a sick feelin' inside me. Daisy ran over and started sobbin' and huggin' Timmy's back."

"Oh Lord, that's awful." Tears welled in Dan's eyes. "Was this Cord fella, was he, uh, uh, . . ."

The observant bar owner interrupted. "Not quite. He was still breathin' at that point. We rushed him to the hospital, but he never regained consciousness. He died a week later from a-all those head injuries. Timmy was hauled in that night by the local cops and never saw the light of day again. A few months later, he was convicted of s-second degree murder and got twenty to thirty in the state pen. He's up in Michigan City."

"Oh, that's awful!" Dan fell back against the booth. "Poor Timmy, he was never one to make trouble."

Tug shook his head, "Ya know, Danny, I've th-thought 'bout that night a hunnert times, and y-ya know what?

"What?"

"I really don't think Timmy had much choice. That Cord was a mean S.O.B. and as drunk as he was, if he'd gotten up, he woulda' killed Timmy or at least beaten him silly. I'm damn sorry Cord died, but I blame him for everything. He started it, and Timmy finished it."

Dan sat still, staring blankly into space, attempting to absorb the shocking news he had just heard. Eddie and Frankie were dead, his best friend was in prison for murder, and Spike had become a biker thug.

"How tragic," he mumbled. He thought of his wonderful life, his great job, his large home in an upscale neighborhood in Denver. It was all so tragically clear, just how vastly different his life was from than that of his old friends.

Tug swiped the foam from his mouth and slammed the empty mug on the table. He signaled for a refill. As his intoxication deepened, his weathered face became more sad and expressionless.

Dan was speechless for a while and then he spoke. "Thank you, Tug, for bringing things full circle for me, I really appreciate it, but I think I best be going."

He patted Tug's hand. "I'll need a twelve pack of Bud to go if you don't mind." He made a weak attempt at a smile, still shaken by the revelations about his old friend.

Tug reached forward and squeezed Dan's forearm. "I'm sorry, Danny, I truly am. Ya come in here right after your dad's funeral for a beer, and I dump all this stuff on ya."

"Oh, . . .no, no, I'm the one who asked you, Tug. You only told me because I asked. It's just that it's kind of difficult to digest."

Tug interrupted, "Please stay for just a few more minutes. I have something I want to show you."

"Well, I, uh."

"Please Danny, just for a minute. It's startin' to get busy in here anyway. I'll be back behind the bar before ya know it."

"Okay, sure, Tug, I got a minute."

Chapter 27

"Not today, honey. We just bought you two new tops before the funeral," Ann stated firmly to her oldest daughter.

"Mom! Come on!" Ali cried.

"You heard me!"

Ali's eyes narrowed, her tight fist landed on her protruding hip. She stood motionless, staring daggers at her mother.

Ann turned away from Ali and grinned, always a little tickled by the predictable exhibition.

"Hey, Mom!"

"Yes, Meghan."

"I love this department store. Sure wish we had one in Denver."

"Oh yes, it's very nice," Ann mumbled.

"Look here," the younger daughter continued, "These earrings are only $12.95."

She carefully lifted the earrings off the display on the jewelry counter, walked over to her beleaguered mom, and dangled the jewelry directly in front of her face.

Still a victim of the stare down from Ali, Ann's resolve to resist two persistent teenagers was weakening. She was hoping to enjoy the day just a little herself and did not want to spend the whole day arguing with her determined daughters.

"OK girls, you win," Ann said with reluctance. She was astonished at how quickly Ali's angry pose disappeared when she stepped around the counter and handed the oldest daughter her MasterCard. "Use this to pay for your top and Meghan's earrings."

"Thanks, Mom!" a smiling Ali replied.

With the new top firmly in hand, she looked around desperately for the nearest checkout counter.

Meghan removed one of the earrings from the holder and held it up to her ear. She tipped her head from side to side admiring herself in the small mirror on the wobbly display.

Ann glimpsed over at a smiling Grandma Carrie, who had been standing nearby observing the entire affair. Grandma, a God-fearing woman of traditional values, was very intuitive and wise, and she was always more than willing to inject her two cents whenever possible. Ann, a strong and savvy woman of similar values, looked forward to such advice from Grandma— particularly at maddening moments such as these.

"They're such kind girls, Ann, so warm and loving. You've never spoiled those girls. You did the right thing." Her face broke into a warm smile.

"Thank you, Grandma, I needed that." Ann kissed the eldest of the Kinsey family on the forehead and returned to the same sale rack she had been digging through earlier.

Grandma had more to say. "Ann?"

"Yes, Grandma?"

"Something's happening with Dan. He seems so intent on talking about the past. I think he's trying to make sense of it all."

Ann paused and looked toward the old lady. "I know."

"It doesn't surprise me. His childhood was anything but easy."

Grandma struggled forward and laid her hand on Ann's forearm.

Ann's brow narrowed. "I don't want to speak ill of the dead, so please forgive me. But was he that bad, that father of his?"

Grandma paused for a second, and then continued, "Well, Beau was a very complex man. He could be self-centered, and he had quite a temper at times," she replied, choosing her words carefully.

"What do you mean?" Ann asked, her gaze begging more information.

"Those poor kids had a go of it. They sure did."

Tears began to well up in her sad eyes. She retrieved a hanky from her purse to dab them away.

A sympathetic Ann listened intently to the aging matriarch, knowing that she must have suffered also at the hands of Beau Kinsey.

"Sometimes I feel like I let them down. I should have done more, much . . ."

Ann quickly spoke. "I'm sorry to interrupt but my goodness, Grandma, don't let me ever hear you say that again!" she became more animated. "You dedicated your life to those children. You sacrificed all of your own hopes and dreams so those kids. I hope I don't hear anything like that from you again!"

Ann put her arm around Grandma's sagging shoulder. She wanted to throw both her arms around her and give her a big hug, but the constraints of being in the middle of a busy department store called for a more reserved display of affection. "You were wonderful to those children." She smiled warmly.

Grandma was now dabbing frantically, trying to keep pace with the growing number of tears. "Thank you for the kind words, Ann, but there were times when I, uh," trying desperately to finish her thought, she just couldn't get the words to come out.

"It's okay, Grandma. It's okay." Ann rubbed her back gently.

Grandma finally composed herself and then a transformation suddenly came over her. The tears began to slow and a look of anger moved across her face; her eyes filled with rage.

"There were times I should have stood up to that arrogant son-of-a-bitch! I should've knocked the shit out of him!"

Grandma suddenly became quiet, hand over mouth. She scanned the room to see of anyone nearby had hear the uncharacteristic outburst.

Ann's eyes widened, she stood in stunned silence. Gradually, the corner of her mouth turned up in a smile.

"Grandma!" she said, "That just didn't sound like you." Her smile soon exploded into all-out laughter.

Grandma looking wide-eyed at her laughing granddaughter-in-law, started with a couple of nervous chuckles, and then her body began to convulse in waves of laughter.

"I c-can't believe I said that. Why, the poor man's not even cold in the grave yet!"

Unconcerned about their surroundings, both women were soon doubled over in laughter and hugging in the aisle of the crowded department store.

The girls, noticing the commotion, grabbed their shopping bags and rushed over to see what was going on. Falling victim to the power of suggestion, they were soon drawn into the merriment. Nearby shoppers detoured down nearby aisles to avoid the unsettling display.

"What happened?" a giggling Meghan asked.

Ann, finally able to speak, answered her youngest daughter. "We were, uh, just, uh, reminiscing about your grandpa and talking about some of the crazy things we've done over the years. That's all, honey." Ann said.

"Like when Uncle Mark knocked over the birdbath and it fell on Aunt Marie's poodle?" Meghan asked.

"Yes, yes, things like that," her mother replied quickly.

"How about the time Dad passed gas in church," a seriously blushing Ali added.

All of a sudden the roaring display of laughter was at full force again when they all thought back to the embarrassing expulsion during a very solemn sermon a few years back at the First Christian Church.

"That was a doozie!" Grandma shouted. Her walker rattled as she pounded it on the tile floor, all the while laughing with abandon.

With a growing number of curious stares and

incredulous looks coming their way, the merriment soon began to wane. The giggling females composed themselves, wiped away the final remnants of their tears of laughter and strolled toward the nearest exit. Just before reaching the revolving door, Grandma tugged gently on Ann's sweater. Ann leaned toward her. "I hope you know how I feel now," she whispered.

Ann whispered back, "I think I get the picture. Thanks Grandma."

Chapter 28

"Damn it! I know it's in here somewhere."

A frustrated Tug rummaged around in his cluttered office at the back of the bar. Dan listened closely to the commotion coming from the nearby cubicle. After what seemed like an eternity, he heard a metal file cabinet slam shut. The room went dark and a somewhat disheveled Tug emerged from the room clutching a folded piece of paper firmly in his left hand. He staggered over and fell into the booth across from Dan. The leathery wrinkles around his eyes seemed to deepen.

"I'm gonna organize that office someday," he mumbled.

Dan smiled.

Tug cleared his throat, "Your father was a helluva guy. He came in here for years, clear up till he died in here last week."

Dan shot up in his seat, eyes wide, "He died where? The local paper said he died at home!"

"Naw, he died right here last, uh Wednesday night.

I'll never forget it as long as I live. He was right here, no doubt about it. I'm the one who found 'em, but the town doesn't know that. They don't want their great Beau Kinsey dying in some bar on the bad side of town."

A shocked Danny replied, "I can't believe it!"

"Hell, you'd better believe it because it's the truth! Mayor Thompson, one of your dad's golfin' buddies, called me early the next morning and t-told me in no uncertain terms that your dad died at home. He said if he finds out I told anyone anything different, he'll close me down. So I'm keepin' my mouth shut, I don't want to lose my business."

Dan was speechless, his mind racing.

The drunken owner went on. "Yeah, your dad was sittin' right over there with that blond hook . . ." The old man caught himself, his eyes shot toward Dan. "With a friend of his."

Tug took another drink. He swiped away the foam with his shirt-sleeve and mumbled on. "I saw when I brought his drinks over that he was r-rubbin' his chest, like it was bothering him or somethin'. When he and his friend left, I saw him rubbin' his chest again on his way out. A short time later I heard a h-horn blarin' out back. His friend came runnin' in and told me your dad had passed out or somethin' in the car. I ran out to the back parking lot and yanked your dad's car door open. He was lyin' on the horn, and his gray hair was hangin' down over the steering wheel. I yanked his t-trousers up and me and another fella laid him on the ground."

The tipsy owner's eyes squeezed shut. He took a deep breath and continued to spew out the shocking news. "He didn't look worth a damn. I had one of the boys call the hospital. B-By the time the ambulance got here, he was already gone, Danny. One of my c-customers gave him, uh, CPS or whatever the hell you call it, but it didn't do no good. He never regained consciousness."

Crestfallen, Dan's frantic eyes searched the face of the drunken bar owner.

The old man paused. A wave of sympathy rushed over his face. "Hell, I'm sorry, Danny. I guess I just figured somehow ya knew."

"No, uh, I didn't know," Dan mumbled.

"Look here, Danny," Tug blubbered, "I have a whole bunch o' folks your d-dad helped out here at one time or another on this list."

He pointed at the crinkled piece of paper that he was smoothing out on the table top. "That's what I was huntin' for in my office. I w-wanted to show it to ya."

The babbling owner's voice sounded more and more distant as Dan fell into deep thought, trying to absorb yet another disturbing revelation about his conflicted father. He ran his fingers nervously through his hair. He felt warm and nauseated.

Starting to notice the impact his words were having on Dan, Tug went into full compliment mode about his dad. "He was a g-good guy, Danny. He really was. He loaned me money a couple a . . ."

Dan interrupted, "What do I owe you, Tug?"

"Oh hell, Danny, it's on me. It's the l-least I can do."

Dan collected himself momentarily. "Thanks."

"Hold on a minute; I'll b-be right back," Tug staggered over to the bar and returned with a cold twelve pack and handed it to Dan, "On the house," he said with a sheepish grin.

Dan nodded. "Thanks Tug, I almost forgot why I came here."

Tug leaned forward in the booth. Their faces were only inches apart. "Do me a favor, Danny."

Dan looked intently at the anxious owner, repelling slightly from the strong scent of alcohol on his breath.

"Don't tell nobody, p-please. They'll close me down. I just figured ya knew, Danny, that's all."

"Don't worry, Tug. I won't tell anyone. It's not something of which I'm very proud."

Tug's old face sagged to a frown. "Guess ya wouldn't be," he mumbled.

Dan and Tug slid out of the booth and shared a quick handshake.

"Good seein' ya Danny," Tug said meekly.

"Uh, yeah, same here," Dan replied. "And don't worry Tug, I won't tell anyone."

He smiled weakly at the drunken owner, turned and walked quickly through the gambling room and out the backdoor.

Dan was in a daze as he walked toward his rental car, twelve-pack in hand. Reaching the car, he leaned against the top of the sun-baked auto and stuck the key in the door. The metal felt warm on his bare forearm. *Another punch in the gut from the great Beau Kinsey!* he thought.

The car door clicked open. Slipping into the bucket seat, he slammed the door shut. He carefully placed the twelve pack on the passenger side and for some inexplicable reason, he turned for one last painful look at Tug's Tavern and then looked quickly away. Feeling disgusted, he started the engine, pulled out to Railroad Street, and gunned it spewing dust and gravel in his wake.

Passing the topless bar, Dan took a quick glance to the left at four shiny Harleys that were tucked in between several pickups in the crowded parking lot. Earlier in the afternoon, he had considered a surprise visit to his old friend Spike, but after the shocking revelations about his father's death, all he wanted to do was get home.

Dan was reeling emotionally from the disgusting and disgraceful news about his father's death, but deep down it didn't surprise him—a vile man dying in a vile way could almost be expected.

Driving aggressively through his old neighborhood, Danny was upset by the news from Tug, but he was also upset by the growing book of evidence about his own likeness to his father. It was a comparison that he had scoffed at so many times over the years, always certain that he was a much better person than his terribly flawed father. And while not the womanizer his father was, he was discovering to his growing dismay that the proverbial apple had not fallen far from the tree.

A picture was beginning to form in his mind of a middle-aged son who was driven, over competitive and very self-absorbed at times. This realization disturbed him as he reflected on himself. He wondered just how many more likenesses to his troubled father he would uncover as he continued on this unexpected journey into his troubled past.

Chapter 29

"This is not ground round," Ann complained. She shook her head disgustedly. The large batch of ground beef crackled in the hot skillet.

"Ann's famous tacos and beans tonight?" Dan mused as he walked into the small kitchen and stopped behind Ann. He placed his hands gently on her slender shoulders.

"What else?" Ann smiled and patted his hand. "You've been kind of quiet since you got back from the beer run, honey, anything wrong?"

Ann was right. Dan had been very much to himself since his return, still trying to come to grips with the stunning news he had heard from Tug.

"Sorry," he replied.

"Where did you go? You barely got back before we got home from shopping."

At this point, nobody knew where he had gone for the afternoon beer run. And except for Ann, he wanted to keep it that way. Dan saw no need to burden the rest of the family with the ugly news about his father's death. He felt it best to leave Tug's Tavern off the family radar for right now, yet he knew he had to tell someone. The shocking news was eating him up.

Although Ann had always been respectful toward his father, she was never very close to him. He was certain the one person he trusted most in this world would be able to bring him the solace and comfort he so desperately needed.

With the kids huddled in the family room listening to music on the radio and the rest of the family out on the screened porch engrossed in conversation, Dan seized the opportunity to open up to his lovely wife.

"Remember when I told you that I used to run on the west side quite a bit as a kid?"

Ann nodded, opened the refrigerator door and pulled out a tray of vegetables. She set the tray on the counter, lifted an onion from the tray and began chopping. "Yes, you've mentioned that a few times," she replied.

Dan fell back against the countertop across from Ann, placing his hands firmly against it.

"Well, I went to the west side today to get the beer, for old time's sake, you might say."

"Sounds like a good idea."

"Well, that's what I thought, but as it turned out, it wasn't such a good idea."

Ann's brow furrowed slightly. "Oh, and why is that?"

"Well, I decided to go to Tug's Tavern, my dad's favorite hangout."

"I remember those fellas at the funeral wearing the Tug's Tavern shirts."

"Yeah, just a few of the boys." Dan fainted a smile.

"Tug must have quite a few years on him," Ann surmised as she tossed the chopped onions into a small ceramic dish and reached for the lettuce.

Dan chuckled. "Yeah, he's getting up there alright. In fact, I was surprised to see him in there."

"And how is Tug?" Ann smiled warmly.

"Okay, I guess. He's getting old and he drinks too much. He was about half in the bag when I left—not a good thing for a bar owner."

Ann shook her head, "Probably one of those ten percenters I read about. They can do about anything to their body and still live be to a hundred years old—smoke, drink, you name it."

"That's Tug, alright." Dan grunted and then paused. Weary of the small talk, he wanted to get to the subject.

"Tug was really happy to see me. We go back a long way. His boy and I played little league baseball together as kids. He didn't recognize me at first. It's been about thirty years since he last saw me. But once he did, things started to move. First thing I knew, he had us in a booth and we were having a drink, and talking about old times."

"Of course," Ann smiled.

Dan ran his fingers steadily through his dark hair, pushing it back over his head.

"I was anxious to catch up on what had been going on with my old friends from the west side."

"How are they, Dan? You've mentioned those boys a few times."

"Not good. The news wasn't good at all. My best friend, Timmy Cantrell, is in prison. His brother, Frankie's dead, and my old friend Spike is a biker thug."

"Oh my!"

"Yeah, it was upsetting," Dan grimaced. "But that wasn't the worst news I got from Tug today by any stretch."

Sensing the tone in her husband's voice, concern flooded across Ann's face. She stopped stirring, turned the gas flame down and turned to face him.

"I can't imagine what could be worse news than that."

"It's Dad," he whispered so softly that Ann could barely hear him.

"Your dad?" she asked incredulously. "Why, we just buried the man. What on earth could he say that would be so terrible about your father at this point?"

Dan glanced quickly at the screened porch to be sure that no one was listening. He rubbed his hands together apprehensively. "Tug was getting pretty drunk and all."

Ann's eyes darted up and down her husband's sullen face, "What is it, Dan? What did he say?"

Dan hesitated and tears began to well up.

"Dad didn't die at home," he whispered.

"He didn't what?"

Anxious to burst the bubble and get the damning news out, Dan replied rapidly, "He didn't die at home. He died at Tug's Tavern last Wednesday night, and that's not the worst of it."

"Oh, my God! He died at Tug's, and that's not the worst of it? What in the world are you talking about?"

Ann's face showed bewilderment. She whipped around, turned off the hot flame on the stove and quickly slid the sizzling meat to a cool burner.

"He was, uh, uh."

Ann turned to face her husband again, hot pad in hand. "Go ahead, honey, let it go!"

The answer exploded from the tormented son, "He was in his car with a hooker when he died!"

Dan shook his head. "Tug was so drunk he told me the whole ugly story before he thought about it. It was horrifying to hear. Tug's the one who found him with pants down and his head lying on the horn of the car. It was just . . ."

Ann abruptly interrupted, "Oh my God, Dan! You poor thing!" She turned and slid her arms around his waist, hugging him tightly.

"I'm so sorry to burden you with this, honey, it just . . ."

"Oh, Dan, I would have been angry if you hadn't told me."

She rubbed his back gently and surveyed the scene.

"Everyone seems to be busy right now and the meat needs to cool. Let's go in the dining room where we can talk privately."

Dan nodded in agreement. Ann yanked several tissues from a box on the end of the kitchen counter and handed some to Dan. They pushed through the small bat-wing doors and stepped into the cozy dining room. Dan pulled two chairs out from under the oak dining table. After seating Ann, he settled in next to her. Filled with anger, disgust, sadness and disappointment, he was anxious to share his feelings with Ann.

"I'm sorry that I have been preoccupied for the last two days, but so much has happened, and now I really need to talk about it."

"It's obvious that something has been on your mind,

honey. Let's take a look at everything. It must have been such a shock when you got the news about your father in Europe."

"Yes, it really was."

Dan folded his hands on the table. "I was in the middle of the merger meetings when Carolyn interrupted me with the news. It was as if someone had punched me in the gut. Dad seemed so invincible. I always thought he would live forever, even with his drinking and all. I just wasn't prepared for him to die. I was shocked. I quickly explained the situation to my colleagues who were at the meeting and asked Chuck Wilson to finish for me. Carolyn whispered in my ear that she had already begun making arrangements for me to get home, so I excused myself and hurried from the meeting."

Dan sighed and glanced toward the front window.

"Go on, sweetheart." Ann pleaded.

"So many things were going through my mind when I boarded that jet in Paris. You and the girls, my difficult life as a child, Mark and Maggie and how all this would affect them. Somehow it was all the repressed memories that began to bubble up inside of me. When I finally landed in Cleveland after a long layover in New York, I was emotionally drained. Dad was such a powerful presence in my life, and having to come to grips with his death was starting to overwhelm me. I could almost hear my father telling me to quit moping around and pull myself together—one of his favorite phrases. There was no sentimentality with him, it was always just 'suck it up and deal with it.' But I didn't want to just 'suck it up' right then. I wanted to feel his death."

Ann gently rubbed his forearm.

"Later, after I left the Cleveland airport and drove into the Ohio countryside, something weird happened. I just started crying. I couldn't believe it, honey. I just cried and cried," Dan chuckled nervously. "Hell, I couldn't even see the road."

"Oh, Dan! Were you able to drive?"

"No, not really, I pulled off the road at some rest area and just sat there and bawled. I was just so overcome with the powerful emotions I had kept bottled up all of my life. After I calmed down a little, I got out of the car and walked past some picnic tables into a nearby wooded area. After a short walk, I went down a steep hill to a narrow stream. I looked at that creek and wooded area and it looked so much like the woods where we played as kids. You know, that creek and woods behind our house?"

Ann nodded her head in agreement.

"I thought back to all the times that Mark and I and the other boys played in that woods, and I started to cry again—just like a baby."

"Oh, Dan, I wish I could have been there for you."

He smiled appreciatively at his devoted wife. "Dad's passing was causing me to face things I had ignored my entire adult life—totally unexpected things. Am I making sense?"

"Of course, I think it's only natural to examine your life a bit when a loved one dies. And your childhood was, to say the least, a bit more challenging than most."

Dan looked away and sighed, "Yes it was, but there's more."

"What on earth do you mean?"

Dan blinked nervously, "I'm finding out that I'm not the person I thought I was."

Ann leaned forward, "I don't understand. Grandma Carrie confirmed to me today that your childhood was very difficult. Surely you're not blaming yourself for the actions of your father, are you?"

Dan stood and walked to a nearby window. He carefully lifted the faded curtain and gazed at an empty lot across the street. The tall grasses swayed in the late afternoon breeze.

"That's just it, Ann," he said quietly. "It's not about Dad anymore. He's dead, and I'm forty-one years old. I can't go on blaming him for everything that goes wrong in my life. It's about me now." He turned toward her. "I'm discovering I'm more like my father that I could ever admit to myself.

"What are you talking about? You're a wonderful father and husband!" She was unbelieving.

Dan sighed and walked over to her. "Strangely enough, as difficult as my trip home was, it was just the beginning. The real journey started once I got here. Seeing our house and this town, has caused me to examine and reflect on the past, and I'm discovering things about myself that I was never seemed possible to me."

The oven timer beeped. "I only have a minute, Dan. I need to get back to the kitchen before the food gets cold, but please, quickly tell me what is so disturbing? I must know, then we can talk more later."

"Okay. Well, growing up, I was always certain that I was nothing like my father. Everyone agreed that it was Mark who was like Dad. Mark was so aggressive, assertive, and such a good athlete. I was always the kinder, gentler son. I was sure of it. But I'm finding that not to be true. If there's another son-of-a-bitch in this family, it's me."

"Oh, come on, Dan!" Ann said emphatically, "You're not at all like your father!"

Dan's eyes softened, "I understand, honey, it's very difficult for you to see anything bad in someone you love, but it's there, Ann. It's true, it's real."

Ann lifted her head slightly, her eyes shooting toward the ceiling in frustration.

"Okay, dear, if you must, go ahead," she shook her head.

Dan continued, "My dad loved to avoid the issue, if things didn't go his way, he would spin events to fit his version of reality. Mark never does that. He says it like it is, whether you agree with him or not. I'm the one who is always spinning things to make a point. I do it all the time."

Ann's blank expression didn't change.

"Also, Dad was a manipulator. He used the force of his personality to sway the argument in his favor—just like me, Ann. I do it all the time. Mark's aggressive alright, but he's not a manipulator."

"Neither are you, Dan. My God, what are you going to say next?"

Dan pressed on. "Remember when everyone wanted our community center to be in the middle of our subdivision, and I wanted it by Brad Stuckey's house so it would be closer to us? It only took me fifteen minutes to sway the argument in our favor. Only fifteen minutes, Ann. We now have a beautiful clubhouse just a few hundred feet from our home."

"You're a good salesman, that's all." Ann turned to leave. "I don't want to hear any more of this nonsense. I have things to do."

"Please, honey, hear me out."

Ann paused facing the kitchen.

"It's not salesmanship. That's what I have always attributed it to, but it's not. I seek out the weakest personalities in the group and I give them the stare. If that doesn't work, I overpower their comments with opposing arguments until they give up and concede. Since most people are totally non-assertive, I soon have a nice majority on my side. It works like a charm every time, even at work."

"Is that all?" Ann grumbled.

"No, there's more."

His wife's shoulders slumped.

Dan pushed on. "You know that when Mark and I were in elementary and junior high we hung out with the kids from the west side?"

"Yes, you told me," Ann moaned impatiently.

"Well, when we got into high school, I suddenly realized that it was no longer cool to run around with those rough boys from the west side of town. So I turned my back on them. I didn't want anything to do with them."

"Dan, you were just a kid." Ann, still looking away, seemed irritated.

"So was Mark, but he didn't turn his back on them. At our high school dances, Mark would go over where the so called "hoods" congregated and he would sit and talk with Frankie and Timmy. He didn't care what people thought, they were his friends. I never did that. I was arrogant and full of myself, just like Dad. I didn't want anything to do with those boys from the west side."

Ann spun around, "So you didn't sit with some boys when you were a kid, and you convinced our neighbors to move the location of the clubhouse. So what? You're a wonderful husband and father and a good friend. I won't hear any more of this!"

She hurried over and gave him a peck on the cheek, just as Meghan shouted from the back bedroom.

"When we gonna eat, Mom? We're starving."

"In a few, dear, I have to warm the beans." Ann hurried into the kitchen.

"Okay, Mom."

Dan shook his head, "She loves me too much and is blind to my faults," he whispered.

He watched the girls, earphones on and hips swiveling to the music come parading down the hall toward the family room.

Ann popped out from the swinging doors, "I almost forgot, honey, Grandma's getting tired of all the commotion. She wants to go home after dinner. Would you take her? Mark's going out with some of his old high school buddies, and Maggie went home while you were gone. She told me to tell you 'bye.' Said she'll call you tomorrow."

"Okay, and I'll be happy to take Grandma home."

Ann popped out again from the still swinging doors, "And don't forget to mention 'you know what' to Grandma. What we talked about in Denver."

"Gotcha."

Chapter 30

"Oh, Danny, it's been so nice seeing all of you. I miss you all so much."

Carefully navigating the narrow country lane to his grandmother's farm, Dan smiled warmly and gently patted his smiling grandmother's frail arm.

"You, know, it's odd, Danny. Since your father's funeral, I can see a difference in you. I'm not exactly sure what it is, but there seems to be more openness in your eyes. And please don't misunderstand, you have always been a nice boy, but there's just a little more softness in you now."

"Hmm, that's interesting. I guess it shows."

"What shows, dear?"

"Well, I've been thinking about Dad a lot the past couple of days and what it was like to live with him. I think I'm starting to understand myself a little better."

"He was hard on you kids, that's for sure!" Grandma looked toward her handsome grandson, "And you, my boy, carried the heaviest burden of all. Back in those days, I saw a little boy who had the weight of the world on his shoulders. Your little eyebrows were always furrowed. There was always a tinge of sadness in those pretty blue eyes."

Spotting the lush green lawns of the softball fields where he played as a boy, Dan made a sudden right turn into the parking area and came to a stop. He gripped the steering wheel tightly and stared straight ahead at the perfectly manicured field.

Gathering his thoughts, he spoke softly, "This has been such an emotional time for me—searching for the truth about myself, about Dad, just trying to understand my childhood and the person I've become. At first it was just a matter of trying to make sense of all the pain and suffering, but then something very unexpected happened."

He let go of the steering wheel and sat back, his hands dropped to his lap. He sighed deeply and went on, "Much to my dismay, I'm discovering that I'm a lot like my Dad. It is something that I never dreamed possible until now."

Grandma leaned over. Her slender hand gently squeezed his forearm. Eyes glistening, she spoke. "Yes, Danny, you are like your father in many ways. When I looked into your face as a boy, I saw your father. Your inflections and facial expressions were so much like his, and you're competitive and driven, but that's where the comparison ends. You my boy, have taken a much different journey in life. I only wish your poor departed father could have been half the man you've become."

The kind words from his wonderful grandmother hit Dan hard. He looked away from her and back at the ball field.

She leaned toward Danny. "I'm so proud of the way you've turned out. I thank the Lord every day for allowing you to become the person you are. And I feel the same about Mark and Maggie."

"Thank you for those kind words, Grandma, but I now know that no matter how hard I try, I will always have some part of Beau Kinsey inside me."

Grandma nodded, "Maybe so, but you'll never convince your Ann and the girls of that."

She smiled and sat up in her seat. "You know, Danny, I don't think your father ever realized just how cruel he could be. With everyone treating him like a king all the time, I think he lost all sense of reality. He felt he could do no wrong. Sometimes I wish we would have lost that game to Tech. Damn that game anyway!"

Danny searched the old lady's kindly face, "Remember those little league games?" He nodded toward the ball field.

The old lady's gray head nodded. "Sure do."

"You came to every game and sat on the end of those bleachers—right over there near the exit." He pointed toward the freshly painted, green bleachers.

"I always loved looking over during the game and seeing you sitting there. It meant so much to me."

Grandma nodded and smiled. "We always had each other, Danny. We always did. And you know what?

Dan's brow lifted.

"We were all pretty tough cookies in our own right. I think we beat that man. I think we showed him, we sure enough did!" she said proudly.

"I think so, I think we did," Dan replied. He squeezed his grandmother's hand and reached for the ignition. "We better get going. They'll think we got lost or something!"

Dan jammed the gearshift into reverse and backed slowly out of the parking area, looking both ways. The rear suspension creaked as he rolled over the raised edge on the quiet country road and then accelerated down the road to his Grandmother's house.

Chapter 31

With the lane to Grandma's house in sight, Dan glanced through the driver's side window at the breathtaking scene outside. The hypnotic field of prairie grass swayed gently in the fall breeze and flowed effortlessly toward a bluish green background of ripening soy beans. Ahead, he was treated to a brilliant stand of crimson and yellow maples towering amidst a canvass of red fire bushes.

"Isn't it breathtaking?" Carrie mused.

"It sure is," Dan sighed. "I truly miss the gorgeous falls in Indiana. The mountains in Colorado are spectacular, but everything just basically turns yellow in the fall. Nothing like this."

"If only it just wasn't followed by winter," Grandma laughed.

Dan smiled and pulled down on the left turn signal. The gravel crunched beneath the tires as he pulled into the drive. After a short and bumpy ride, he slowed noticeably and negotiated his way past a partially opened gate, finally coming to stop on the far side of a circle drive that swung past the front of the rustic old farm house.

He looked with concern at the tall green weeds sprouting from the gray metal gutters and the scaly porch railing that was badly in need of a paint job.

The perceptive old lady shot a quick look at her perusing grandson. Her brow furrowed. "Listen sonny. This old house is solid as a rock and I have those gutters cleaned every year. With all the trees around here, those little helicopter pods fly in there and pop up almost overnight. I take good care of this place, Danny.'

"Oh, I'm sure you do. It's just that it is a lot for . . ."

"An old lady?"

Dan's face turned pink, "Well, uh, no I didn't mean that."

Grandma laughed, "It's okay, Danny, I don't do it alone. I have an old friend who helps me. Do you remember Marvin Fields?"

"Why, uh, yes, I sure do, I worked for him at the schools during the summer," Dan stammered.

"Well, he's gonna have this place painted by winter. He's already started scrapin' on the back."

"I see."

"I'm not a poor lady, Danny. I can afford to take care of my house."

A sheepish grin broke out on her weathered face. "But maybe I did let those gutters go just a little too long this time."

Dan shot her an awkward grin. Independent and self-effacing, his Grandma nonetheless was a woman of some means. Dan's Grandpa Ernie had died of kidney failure at age fifty, leaving his grieving widow a nice little nest egg. "Nearly a million," he bragged just before he died.

Dan also knew how hard his grandpa had worked for that money. A determined sort, he went to work for a small local foundry as a young man. Through hard work and due diligence, and years of long hard days, he ended up owning the business. Over the years, that foundry provided the family with a very good living.

But, when he was diagnosed with lung cancer and faced with a terrible prognosis, he decided to get rid of the foundry. He didn't want to leave his widow facing the pressures of running the rough and tumble foundry. He signed the closing documents from his hospital bed just a few hours before he passed on, leaving everything to Grandma with the understanding that it would go to the kids upon her passing.

Today, Grandma is a well-to-do woman by Maple City standards, but it hasn't changed her much. She is still very frugal and spends very little of her money. Knowing she has money in the bank is good enough for her. The only exception to this rule is the children. She's generous to a fault when it comes to her children and grandchildren.

The three Kinsey kids enjoyed the latest in fashions while growing up. They were each given a late model auto when they turned sixteen. When they went off to college, their tuition, board, and books came out of Grandma's pocketbook—not their father's. A fact that Dan was certain his pretentious father kept under his hat. People in town assumed the children's prosperous lifestyle was the result of their father's well-known auto dealership, Kinsey Chevrolet, but that wasn't the case. A notoriously poor poker player, Beau lost thousands of dollars a year at the local country club playing cards. He gave the kids a little money now and then, but most of their childhood was financed by Grandma.

Dan stepped out of the car and looked around. His grandma's place was nestled in the middle of a beautiful forest of oak, maple, and evergreen trees and located only a few miles outside the city limits. Dan's grandparents had bought the house some fifty years ago in order to take advantage of the low utilities and low taxes of rural living. Over the years, they learned to love their little home, deciding to stay put even after his Grandpa Ernie started making good money.

"I've always loved this place. Mark, Maggie and I had so much fun out here."

"I never said much, unless you got in my garden!"

In her younger days, Grandma always maintained a large garden at the side of the house that was full of tomatoes, green beans, radishes, and squash. She took a lot of pride in that garden, and even after she moved to town to care for the kids, she still came out here and planted her garden every year. Dan looked over at the rusting trellises and grimaced. This was the garden that had provided the tomatoes his mother was preparing to can on the day she took that tragic fall from the ladder.

"Home sweet home," Grandma sighed.

Dan hustled to the back of the car and popped open the trunk. Struggling with Grandma's awkwardly shaped walker, he finally pried it free from the trunk, closed the lid and hurried around to the passenger side.

"Thank you, darling," she said. She stood and slid between the curved handles of the walker and started toward the house. Dan was in close pursuit.

Grandma reached the porch and gave the knocker a quick rub. The faded knocker on the front door was a copy of one of the ingots from Ernie's foundry. She rubbed it in remembrance of her dear departed husband, then she unlocked the front door and pushed it open.

"Won't you come in for a minute? I just made some wonderful sun tea the other day. It's still fresh."

"Sure, I'd love a glass of tea," Dan replied.

Following Grandma through the door, Dan noticed the old yellow telephone sitting on a small round table near the door.

"Can I give Ann a quick call to tell her I'll be a little late?"

"Why certainly, Dan. Help yourself."

Dan lifted the phone and punched in the numbers— the same numbers he had dialed so many times before. Dan listened to the ring and chuckled. It was the same ring pattern he remembered from years ago. *Some things never change,* he thought. After just a couple of rings, Ann picked up,

"Hello?"

"Hi, honey, it's me, you're missing husband."

"Yes, always missing husband, go on."

"Just wanted to give you a quick heads up. Grandma invited me to stay and have a glass of tea."

"No problem, we're all playing Yahtzee. You can join us when you get here."

Ann giggled unexpectedly, "Mark said to take your time. We're having more fun without you."

Dan laughed, "It's nice to be missed."

"Did you say anything yet?" Ann whispered.

"No, dear, not yet. Don't worry, I will."

"Okay, see ya later."

Dan dropped the faded phone back on the base and hurried across the gold shag carpet to her small, well-kept kitchen. Looking around, he was a little surprised by the spiffy condition of the old house. This was the first time he had been inside her house for years and the shabby outside belied the condition of the lovely and neatly appointed interior.

"Excuse the place. It's a little messy."

"Are you kidding? It looks great."

The smiling lady left her walker at the end of the kitchen cabinets, opened a cabinet door and pulled out two glasses that were adorned with etchings of pink roses. Walking her hands across the counter top to keep her balance, she made her way to the refrigerator, opened it and reached in the freezer section for some ice. After shaking the ice container violently, she grabbed a handful of cubes and dropped them in the tall glasses. Lifting the gallon jar of tea, absorbing the sun on a nearby window sill, she carefully filled the glasses. With a firm grip on both glasses, she struggled over to the table. Dan felt concern while watching the old lady pour the tea and then maneuver the short distance to the table.

"Don't you worry, Danny, I do just fine. I've got my way of getting things done."

She smiled and carefully nestled in her chair just as Dan sat down on the other side of the small table.

"There's sweetener and stir sticks in that jar," she pointed toward the center of the table.

"Thank you." Danny dumped a couple of packets of sweetener in his tea and stirred it. He set the wooden stick on the table and looked over at his grandma.

"I'm glad you asked me in. Ann and I have been doing some thinking."

"Oh, is that right?" The old lady's right eyebrow lifted slightly. Her head tilted back a little as she looked at her grandson skeptically.

"Yes," Dan replied. "After my promotion and all, we've decided to build a new, much larger house near Boulder, closer to the mountains. It's such a beautiful area. We're all excited and the house is almost finished."

"Oh, how nice for you."

"While planning our new house, Ann and I decided to build a small apartment on the back for guests or in case one of the girls needs a place to live after college."

"Is that so?" Her tilted brow began to narrow.

"Yes and uh, since the house is almost finished, we both got to thinking that rather than a guest apartment, it would be a great place for . . ."

Grandma interrupted, "I so appreciate what you're about to say, dear, I truly do, but this is my home, honey. I know every nook and cranny of this house."

She turned and pointed through the kitchen window. "I know every tree in that yard out there. I'm familiar with every road around here and every street in Maple City. I've attended the same church for nearly seventy years, and I have shared the same pew with Ed and Janet Miller for over fifty years. And I drive by my old high school every day. It's still there ya know, except it's a middle school now."

Dan implored, "I know, Grandma, but you have

such a long driveway. What are you going to do if one of those big winter storms hits and blows your drive shut for several days in sub-zero weather? And worse yet, what if you would fall or get sick and need medical help way out here. What would you do?" Dan's face filled with concern.

The resourceful old lady sighed. Slightly annoyed, she went on. "Don't you think I've thought of those things, Danny? I didn't get to be eighty-three by being a wimp."

Her grandson chuckled nervously, "Oh, I know. It's just . . ."

She interrupted again, "Forgive me, dear, but let me put your mind at ease."

She scooted up a little closer to the table, leaned forward and planted her bony elbows firmly on the table.

"Right down the road there's a widow man named Charles and he has a John Deere tractor with a big plow on the front."

Dan listened carefully.

"He's only sixty-seven, and he's as strong as a bull. Every time it snows, he comes down here and plows my drive and parking area for me. Then he comes in and asks me if I need anything. If I do, he either takes me to town to get it or he goes and gets it himself. I have several girlfriends who pick me up and take me to the senior center three days a week. At the senior center, we have lunch and play Bid Euchre. Charles and I go to dinner every Friday night, and Maggie picks me up and takes me to church every Sunday. In between times, I'm in a bridge club that meets twice a month and a book club that meets once a month and Pastor Jenkins stops in quite often for unexpected visits." She paused, a sly grin appeared on her face, "My boy, I think that man has the hots for me."

Dan was speechless, an incredulous smile spread across his face.

Grandma was tittering. "There's more, my sensitive boy. If I ever get to the point where I can't stay here any longer—and I know that day will come—I have already made plans to go into assisted living at a local nursing home. I have several girlfriends there already, and they love it. The food is great. They play cards and exercise, take field trips, go to gospel concerts and on many other outings."

"Well, I, uh am sorry, I, uh"

"No, please don't be sorry Danny. What you are suggesting is so very, very kind, my dear, but I would never, *ever* dream of intruding on your life. You and Ann have enough on your plate raising those lovely daughters. And, with your careers and all, you don't need an old lady around to worry about. And as you can see, I'm doing just fine."

"You would never be an imposition, Grandma."

Even though he was disappointed, Dan couldn't help but be impressed with his strong and independent grandmother. She was so typical of the people he had known while growing up in the Midwest. He missed that independence, that pioneer spirit. He missed it a lot.

"I know you mean that, Danny, and tell your wonderful family how very much I appreciate their kind and generous offer, but I decided a long time ago that when the grim reaper comes, I want to be right here in

Maple City. Every time I walk into this house I feel my sweet Ernie's arms around me, caressing me. I want Ernie near me when I die. That means everything to me."

The tough, old lady's eyes began to glisten. Her voice softened as she spoke. "Thanks anyway, darling. Thank you so much for caring!"

"You're really something," Dan smiled warmly.

Satisfied that Grandma would never be moving, he quickly changed the subject. "Tell me about your senior center. Sounds like you spend a lot of time there."

Grandma sat up straight and smiled, "Well, it's the old YMCA building. Remember it?"

"Yeah, I sure do."

"And it's real nice in there now. They've totally remodeled the entire inside. "Do you remember that old . . ."

....

The two family members talked for more than an hour, sharing memories that only the two of them could appreciate. As the conversation and laughter continued, Dan began to feel a burden lifting as he understood that his journey into his past was almost at an end.

When time came for him to leave, they hugged long and hard out on the front porch, knowing that it might be a long time before they would see each other again.

"It was wonderful seeing you, Danny." Grandma said softly.

"God bless you, Grandma, for everything."

Dan kissed her on the forehead and hurried out to

the rental car for his trip back to town.

Driving down the lane past the sagging old gate, he glanced in the rearview mirror at his grandmother, who was still standing with her walker, smiling and waving at him.

A bolt of sadness shot through him and a tear rolled down his cheek. "I owe you my life, sweet lady." He touched his lips and planted a kiss on the rearview mirror.

Chapter 32

The next morning, Dan and Mark were sitting in the family room watching a rerun of the IU and Michigan State game. Everyone else was still in bed getting some much needed rest before their trips home.

"Thanks for staying over another night, Bro, it's been fun," Dan said.

"No problem, we were glad to do it. We don't get to see you guys often enough the way it is." Mark replied. "This game's getting a little boring. The Hoosiers are blowing them out. How 'bout we take a little drive, you and me?"

"Sounds good. I've been wanting to ride in that bad boy new car of yours."

Dan stood and clicked off the TV. The two men hurried from the house and walked through the backyard to the parking area in front of the garage.

"What do ya think?" Mark asked.

"Wow! She's a beauty!" Dan exclaimed.

"New Beemer, five series."

"How'd you get this past Ellen?"

"Take a look at that rock on her finger when we get back. It's three carat. Bought it for her on our last anniversary. She's been pretty open-minded about things ever since."

"Hmm, the recession must not have affected the bond market."

"Yeah, we're different than you bankers."

"I know, the recession really hurt us. Our cost of money has skyrocketed. Our spread has dropped to nothing and the profit squeeze has been hard to manage."

"Sorry to hear that, Bro. Actually, the recession and rising interest rates have helped the bond market. The yields have shot up, and the folks are starting to leave the conventional stuff, like the crap you guys are peddling and jump in with us. As a result, my dear overpaid and underworked brother, I made over a half a mil on the big board in just the last six months of this year."

"Impressive. You must be straight commission."

"Sure enough am."

"Smart ass!"

"Eat your heart out." Mark punched his keychain and the door locks popped up.

Dan glanced down the drive at his rental car. "I better move the rental. It's blocking the drive."

"Don't have to, Bro! Can't believe you forgot," Mark said with a twinkle in his eye.

Dan looked puzzled and then a wide grin spread across his face.

"Oh yeah! The Miller slide. How could I ever forget? Especially since I'm the one who discovered it!" He shook his head.

"Get in, Danny," Mark climbed in and started the engine.

Dan dropped down into the soft bucket seat and shut the door.

Mark propped his right elbow on top of the seat and looked back, carefully eying the narrow escape route. With his left hand firmly gripping the steering wheel, he carefully maneuvered the black BMW between the old white fence post and the cherry tree, just missing Pop Miller's aging birdbath by inches.

"That's tighter than I remember," Mark observed.

He revved the engine slightly and backed over a narrow strip of grass between the two houses landing on Pop Miller's drive next door. He quickly backed down the drive and pulled onto Wesley Avenue. Soon they were whizzing along the busy street, howling like teenagers.

"If Pop ever saw us doing that, he'd kill us."

"Thank God he has a curtain over that side window," Mark howled.

Mark suddenly took an unexpected turn to the left.

"Where are you going?" Dan asked.

"Just sit back," Mark ordered.

He crammed it into second gear and pressed on the accelerator, the powerful auto leaped forward. Soon they were racing toward the edge of town with Mark down-shifting and accelerating quickly around the curves on the narrow city street.

"In a hurry?" Dan asked, gripping the cushy armrest tightly.

"Yes, and I'm driving just fine. This car has the best

suspension in the world. It's made for fast acceleration and tight corners. Just relax."

"I'm trying," his nervous passenger replied. "And if I may ask, where are we going?"

"Just hold on. We're almost there."

Without warning, Mark took a quick turn and the car bounced violently down an obviously seldom-used country road.

"Oh my!" Dan exclaimed. "It's Pony Creek Road. I never came at it from this direction."

Pony Creek Road was a big part of Dan and Mark's growing up years in Maple City. Very secluded, it was a great place to take your favorite girl for a little privacy and long stints of making out. Dan had often wondered why the road had been built in the first place, since the farmers didn't use it, and it didn't lead anywhere in particular. Only a few miles in length, it wove around in the woods next to Pony Creek and then exited on County Road Twelve.

"Never could figure this road. It doesn't go anywhere." Dan threw an inquisitive look toward Mark.

Eyes straight ahead, Mark replied, "Dad told me once that the state built the road years ago as part of an overall plan to develop this area into a state fish and wildlife refuge. It gave the folks a way to get down to the river and do a little fishing, but unfortunately, the funding for the refuge fell through after the road had already been built."

Dan scowled. The seemingly mundane recollection kind of hurt. It was just another example of how much closer his older brother had been with their father. "Oh, I never knew that."

Mark eased down a narrow dirt road into the dusty open area near the creek and came to a stop.

"Lot of memories here."

"Yeah, the pit," Dan chuckled.

During their teenage years, this secluded area was affectionately referred to as the pit, short for passion pit.

"Trees are bigger now, otherwise, things haven't changed much," Mark said.

Mark slid the gearshift into neutral and hit the emergency brake.

"Let's get out and look around."

Sensing the emotion in his brother's voice, Dan nodded his head in the affirmative.

When he stepped out of the car, Dan was greeted with a strong, cool breeze and was showered with bright, red maple leaves that temporarily darkened the sky. It was a beautiful sight, one he had seen many times growing up in Indiana.

Mark walked through the falling leaves to the front of the car and leaned back against the hood facing Pony Creek.

"What was that girl's name, Mark? Erica, uh, something?"

The younger brother gently closed the car door, walked over and fell in next to his brother on the hood.

"Oh, come on!" Mark elbowed his brother, "You know nothing ever happened with her. She was two years older than me. I was clueless."

"Hmmm, I guess you're forgetting about the time I came home early from golf practice and uh, ..."

"Alright, alright, she took advantage of me a couple

of times. What the hell was I supposed to do? She was much older and more sophisticated than I was."

"Poor baby."

Mark smiled at the friendly teasing from his brother.

"You're not going to believe this, Bro, but sometimes I used to come out to his spot as a kid and just meditate. No girls or anything, just little ole me and my thoughts, nothing else."

That comment drew a skeptical look from Dan.

"No, I'm serious," he said sincerely, "I rode my bike all the way out here. After I got my license, I drove out. It was my little refuge from the world, you might say. I would come here during the day when nobody was around. It gave me time to think."

"Hmmm, another thing I never knew. You're just full of surprises today." Dan replied.

Mark's expression didn't change.

"Did it help?"

"A little, I think."

Mark leaned down and scraped a rock off the muddy bank and tossed it sidearm across the creek. The water rippled as the flat rock skipped across the shallow brook and bounced harmlessly on the opposite bank. He swiped his hands clean and leaned back against the hood again.

"Dan, do you think our dad was a good or bad person?"

Dan's eyes shot toward his brother, surprised by the probing question from his usually jocular brother. Wondering where this was leading, he thought for a moment and then replied. "He was involved in quite a bit of charity and community work."

"That's not an answer. Once again, did you think Dad was a good man or a bad man?"

Dan blinked nervously. He took a deep breath and replied, "I don't think our dad was a good man."

"Can you tell me why you feel that way?"

"My, Mark the psychologist all of a sudden."

"Just answer the question, smart ass."

"If you insist." Dan shook his head and paused for a moment before speaking. "I think Dad was somewhat tolerable before Mom died, but after that, he became even more self-centered. People here in Maple City didn't know Dad the way we did."

He glanced at his big brother. "Why do you ask?"

"I guess because I experienced so much fucking grief in my life because of that man, I'd like to think he had some good qualities. I don't want my Dad to be a complete lout."

"I know what you mean," Dan replied. "Are you having any luck?"

"Well, kind of, I guess. Our dad was a very troubled man, but I think that there was some good in him. He bought me that nice bike."

"I know," Dan replied.

"I know it was different for you, Dan."

Dan smiled, "A little bit."

"Do you resent me for that?"

Dan looked at his repentant brother. "No, not at all, Mark. It wasn't your fault, and you were a great big brother to me."

Mark's eyes narrowed and his face turned serious. "Tell me Danny, did Dad ever tell you he loved you?"

Dan got a lump in his throat. He pushed up from

the hood and walked toward the stream. He stopped near the gently flowing brook, staring straight ahead. He spoke softly, "No, not ever. He never once told me that he loved me."

Sensing his brother's distress, a contrite Mark walked over next to his brother and tried to apologize. "I'm sorry, Dan. I didn't mean to . . ."

Dan interrupted, "No, Mark, please don't say you're sorry. This is the first time in our entire life that we've talked about our feelings. It's about time."

Mark kicked another rock loose from the muddy shore with the toe of his shoe and tossed it in the stream.

"I know you thought I was his favorite, because of sports and all; but believe me, that didn't make it any easier. The only time I can ever remember that bastard being nice to me was right after Mom's accident. I think he knew how badly I, uh, . . ." His voice trailed off.

Dan turned toward his brother. Mark's head fell heavy on his chest, a totally unexpected gesture from Mark, still obviously very distressed about his part in his mom's death.

"Did he know what you said to Mom that day?" Dan asked.

Mark looked up. His damp eyes were glistening. "Why, uh, yes. I think he did. I always thought he did anyway. Why else would he be nice to me?"

Dan stepped over and gently laid his hands on his brother's broad shoulders, but before he could speak, the tough-guy, sarcastic Mark turned and fell into his arms, weeping and pressing his face against Dan's shoulder.

"She was such a wonderful mom, Danny, so good and kind. I still so regret what I said!"

"You were fourteen, Mark. There's no reason to feel guilty about it for the rest of your life."

Mark continued to sob, and then, apparently realizing how vulnerable he had become, he quickly stepped back from the embrace without answering the question.

"Sorry," he murmured.

"Look at me, Mark!"

Mark slid his hands in his pockets and turned toward his brother.

"You were just a kid then, and you made a mistake. My God, what kid never made a mistake? You were human, okay? But more importantly, you need to start remembering some of the good things you did as a kid."

"Like picking on you and Maggie?"

"Oh sure, you hassled us a little. What big brother doesn't? But you were always there for us, looking after us and protecting us from the bullies at school."

Somewhat embarrassed, Mark nervously jingled the change in his pocket.

"You were my hero back then, Mark. I hate to admit it, but you still are. And Maggie would be furious if she heard you saying these things. She thinks the world of you."

Mark smiled warmly. "You know bro, I think it's harder when someone like our Dad dies. When you grow up with someone like him, you have this empty feeling inside all the time. You end up spending the rest of your life trying to fill that void, but it never happens. And then he dies, and now there's no hope that he will ever fill that emptiness. As bad as he was, I always loved that son-of-a-bitch, and I wanted him to love me. Now I know I will never have the one thing from my father that I have so desperately wanted all of my life—his love and acceptance of me as a person."

Touched by the heartfelt comments, Dan replied, "I know it's been hard, Mark. It's been hard for all of us. Our dad was such a monster at times, but you've been blessed with a wonderful family who loves you very much."

Mark's pleading eyes looked toward his brother.

"I know, Dan. In spite of it all, we've both been blessed. Ellen and the girls mean the world to me."

Dan laid his hand on his brother's shoulder.

"You and I will always be close Mark. That man pushed us together. I think that's why we stay so close to this day. We all needed each other to survive."

"You're right. I guess he did one thing right, even if it was for all the wrong reasons."

Mark smiled kindly and then his eyes suddenly narrowed. He straightened his shirt sleeves and walked toward the car.

"We better get going," he said abruptly. "I've still got some packing to do."

Whistling happily, he headed for the driver's door, paused and surveyed the open area near his car. "Had some great times here," he said. A big smile broke out on his face. "Some damn good times!"

Bewildered by the sudden mood change, Dan stared incredulously at his brother for a moment and then walked toward the passenger side and leaned forward, pressing his forearms against the top of the car.

The unpredictable Mark, anticipating a sappy comment from his brother, quickly blurted, "Yes Danny, what is it?"

Still brimming with sentimentality, Dan replied, "Well, there's something I've always wanted to say to . . ."

Mark interrupted, "Danny, I really have to get going."

Dan shrugged his shoulders indignantly, "Forget it Mark, just forget it." He dropped in the car and slammed the door.

Mark slipped in the bucket seat, stuck the key in the ignition and the big engine roared to life. He slammed it in reverse and hit the gas. The car jerked and backed out of the parking area.

"Love ya, Bro."

He quickly slid the gearshift into first gear, hit the gas and accelerated down Pony Creek Road.

Dan stared at his confounding brother.

"How do you like that stereo?" Mark twisted the shiny knob louder. "Eight speakers!"

Dan looked with wonderment at his smiling brother. "You're crazy, you know that? You're damned crazy!"

"I know!" Mark's grin broadened.

The tires squealed as he hit second gear. "I'm just a crazy, lovable, son-of-a-bitch!"

Still shaking his head, Dan glanced in the side view mirror and watched as Pony Creek, ripe with so many memories, fade into the lush Indiana countryside.

Chapter 33

Mark's car sat idling in the driveway as the two families enjoyed a few last remarks before the Chicago Kinsey's departed for their four hour drive back to Lake Forest near Chicago. Standing at the passenger side, Ann and the girls were gabbing away with Ellen and her two girls. Dan leaned over and spoke to his brother. "See you at Christmas, I guess?"

"Yeah, guess so. Who's up?" Mark asked.

"We are—another beautiful Christmas in Denver," Dan smiled.

"Don't forget the Coors."

"Not a chance," Dan grinned. "By the way, Maggie called the house today and said to tell you all good-bye. She has missed too many days, so she had to be in school today."

"Oh, I understand, I'll give her a call when I get home. And thanks by the way for taking care of Dad's stuff, his trophies and all."

"No problem. Pop next door offered his truck and his storage locker. The town called and said they really wanted some of Dad's trophies, so I told them we would work that out with them later. We'll sell the rest of that junk at auction and then put the house on the market. Maggie knows a couple of good realtors in the area."

Mark nodded. His pale blue eyes softened. "I could have never made it back then without you and Maggie. I mean that, Bro, I really do." he said sincerely.

Once again, stunned by another totally unexpected comment from his brother, Dan just smiled. "Thanks, Mark." The two of them shared a firm hand clasp.

"Let's do a better job of keeping in touch, Danny, okay?" The older brother tossed his younger brother a 'better not disagree' kind of look.

"That would be great! I would like that." Dan smiled warmly. "Drive carefully."

"Will do!"

Mark patted Dan's hand and then carefully slid the gearshift into reverse.

Ann and the girls made their final farewells to Ellen and the girls. The car windows closed as the Chicago Kinsey's backed down the driveway. Dan, Ann, and the girls watched as the dark sedan accelerated down Wesley Avenue.

Dan felt a longing inside. So much had been said, yet there was so much more he still wanted to say. He wished he could reach down the road with a giant hook and drag them all back to him. He was hurting deep inside. He desperately wanted his tough impulsive brother to come back and be with him, never to leave him again. Other than Ann and Maggie, no one in this world cared more for him than Mark.

He remembered the day when, as a fourteen-year-old boy, Mark stood toe to toe with Dan's massive seventh grade coach, lobbying frantically to get his injured little brother a spot on the team. He recalled the many times Mark had put himself in harm's way to protect him and Maggie from an angry father. Dan knew that during his entire life he would never encounter another human being who would be so willing to make those kinds of sacrifices for him. He felt an inconsolable aching inside as he stood watching the car disappear around a distant corner, taking the best friend he has ever had away from him once again. "Life can be such a bitch!" he whispered.

Dan felt a gentle touch on his arm. "They're great folks," Ann said. "We'll being seeing them again soon."

Dan exhaled, "You're right. We'll be together again before we know it."

He patted his wife on the hand and looked over at the girls, who were giggling and gabbing away on the front lawn.

"You girls go finish packing," Ann ordered. "We have to leave for the early evening, and we still have some cleaning to do."

The laughing stopped and the teenage girls' smiles faded to grimaces. They turned and walked, shoulders slumped, toward the house.

"Honey, why don't you see about taking that stuff in the den to the storage locker?"

"Good idea," Dan replied.

Ann hurried inside, while Dan turned and carefully negotiated the familiar route past the old birdbath and across the crumbling asphalt drive to Pop Miller's place.

Chapter 34

Pop Miller had been their neighbor for as long as Dan could remember. Pop had moved to Maple City from Brooklyn in the mid-forties to run the local chapter of the AFL-CIO. He was a bulldog of a man with a balding, smallish head that seemed to skip the neck and melt into his muscular, broad shoulders. His wife had lost a long battle with polio just before he moved to Maple City. Ten years his father's senior, he was one of the few men in town that Dan's swashbuckling father admired and respected. On the few days that their father wasn't at the club playing poker with the boys, he would often run over to visit Pop.

But Dan barely knew Pop. Smiles and friendly nods were just about the only thing the children ever got from the powerful union man. Once in a great while, when Pop came home from work and Danny was outside, he would stop and ruffle Dan's hair and ask him how school was going. He did the same with Mark and Maggie.

His dad said that Pop was a rich man who lived in a modest house to show the union members that he was an average Joe like them. Dan liked that about Pop and had always been impressed with their mysterious, brawny neighbor.

Dan had been stunned yesterday when the white-haired Pop had shouted at him across the picket fence that divided the two back yards. He said that he would like to offer up his pickup truck and his empty storage locker to Dan if needed. Surprised by the unexpected gesture from the private man, and in need of a truck and a place to store some of his dad's things, Dan took him up on the offer and told him he would be over in the morning. Pop stuck his stubby thumb in the air and quickly returned to trimming bushes.

Arriving at Pop's front door, Dan felt a little anxious as he reached up and pushed the broken button on the faded doorbell. A sharp, grating sound that sounded just like the buzzer in the old gym soon followed. The porch window began to rattle. The big man was evidently moving through the house to answer the door. Danny could hear Pop struggling with the door knob before it finally fell open. He stuck his unshaven face out the door and growled, "Come in, Danny, come in!" with more familiarity than Dan had expected.

"Thank you."

Before stepping in, Dan took a moment to examine the aging man's square, heavily wrinkled face with its deep-set black eyes, framed by bushy gray eyebrows.

"Excuse the doorbell. I've always been a little hard of hearing, and it isn't getting any better. I need something I can hear," he chuckled a nervous, friendly kind of chuckle.

"No problem." Dan smiled.

While Pop was closing the door, he seized upon the opportunity to step over by the living area and take a quick look around. He was surprised by the beautiful furnishings in the spacious room. A large oak dining table surrounded by eight intricately carved oak chairs, and a stunning chandelier filled the center of the smartly decorated room. Behind the long table was an extraordinarily beautiful black maple cabinet filled with very expensive china that was decorated with delicate etchings of various trees indigenous to this part of Indiana. Center stage on the large wall to Dan's left, was a large oil painting of a pretty young woman dressed in an evening gown that overlooked the entire scene.

"That's my Ellie," Pop said, looking longingly at the large oil.

Dan nodded. "She's beautiful. I wish I could have known her."

"You would have loved her. I still miss her." He shook his head. "Something to drink?" he asked.

Dan sensed loneliness in the dark, wrinkled eyes of the former union boss. Although very anxious to get the den emptied and get on with their trip home, Dan's heart told him it was best to stay and share a few minutes with his former neighbor.

"Sure, Mr. Miller, a Diet Coke would be fine."

"Diet Coke it is. And please, call me Pop. Mr. Miller is a little too formal for me."

The big man turned and lumbered toward the nearby kitchen.

Still a little curious about the mysterious house he

had always wanted to see as a child, Dan wandered over to the opening between the main room and nearby family room and surveyed the surroundings. Two large bronze lamps sat atop two oak end tables that bordered a large leather sofa. There was a massive leather recliner to Dan's left with a heavily worn seat and arms, obviously Pop's favorite nesting place.

Continuing to scan the room, Dan noticed a sheer white curtain covering the window that was across from Pop's chair.

A jolt of panic surged through Dan. *Can he see out that window?*

He walked over and leaned forward for a better look. He could see Pop's driveway very plainly. "He has a perfect view," he mumbled. Beads of perspiration popped out on his forehead, his panic grew, just as Pop was arriving with their drinks.

Pop handed him his Coke and then fell quickly into his recliner, claiming his turf before Dan got any ideas. He smiled and waved his thick hand toward the large leather sofa across from him. "Have a seat," he ordered.

Dan stepped away from the window, never taking his eyes off the grinning union boss. He inched over and sat carefully on the edge of the sofa, a perfect spot for an emergency get away if necessary.

"Love this recliner. It's my third one. And they've all been right here in this spot." He winked at Dan.

"Uh, yes . . .yes, it's a nice chair."

"Got a great view of both our driveways from here." His face broke into a sly grin. "I've seen a lot of interesting things out this window over the years."

Dan yanked a handkerchief from his pant pocket

and wiped the growing perspiration from his forehead. He was now regretting his decision to stay and talk. "You have?"

"Oh my, yes," Pop replied, sensing Dan's growing uneasiness. "You wouldn't believe what I saw just this morning."

Dan's back arched, his eyes scanned the interior of the house, further planning his escape route.

Pop went on. "Yeah, I was sittin' here having my morning coffee when I looked out that window and saw this big fancy, black car come out from behind your dad's house and drive right across my little grassy area between the two driveways, then it rolled down my driveway to Wesley Avenue. That car only missed my birdbath by this much." He raised his thick thumb and forefinger, spreading them slightly apart.

"That close, huh?" a mortified Dan murmured.

All of a sudden, a dark shadow fell over Pop's face. A passing cloud had temporarily blocked the sun, darkening the entire room. Dan watched the old-timer lean forward in the shadows, like a wild animal about to pounce on its prey. The large, shadowy figure suddenly raised his huge arms above his head in a terribly menacing manner.

I'm a dead man, Dan thought. *He's going to crush me!*

Pop's hands moved violently downward and slapped against his bulky knees. His big red face broke into a huge smile that soon turned to raucous laughter. He was laughing so hard he could barely get his breath. "So sorry, my boy! I just c-couldn't resist."

Startled by the man's offbeat sense of humor, Dan's stomach was in his throat "Dad's drive is so narrow and all. It's the only way we, uh, could get out. Sorry about that."

"Hell, don't be sorry, Danny. I watched you boys do that when you were teenagers. Never bothered me a bit! I would have done the same thing. Your dad did a half-assed job with that driveway. It's too narrow and it gets clogged up too easily." Still chuckling, the old man wiped the tears from his eyes.

"Mark and I always thought we pulled one over on you," Dan laughed meekly.

"I'll bet you did!" The wrinkly prankster once again roared in laughter, slapping his knees over and over again. The laughing eventually stopped as Pop paused, swiped his eyes dry and looked over at Dan. "I've seen some things out this window over the years that haven't been so funny."

Taken back by Pop's swift change of emotion, a wide-eyed and curious Dan waited for him to continue.

Pop's eye narrowed, "I used to fall asleep every night watching Johnny Carson on television, just a habit of mine, I guess. About two o'clock in the morning your dad would come busting down Wesley Avenue, racking those mufflers like some damned teenager and wake me up. Your dad could be an inconsiderate sort."

"I thought you and Dad were friends," a surprised Dan replied. The curt tone in Pop's voice confused him.

"Oh, your dad was quite the charmer all right. We used to talk quite a bit. He liked me 'cause he knew I didn't buy into all the BS about him being a great basketball player and all. I don't give a damn about basketball, never have. I could see right through your dad and he knew it."

Noticing Dan's concern, he began backtracking and tried to apologize. "I'm sorry, Danny. Please forgive me."

Pop's keen insights into his father's behavior stunned Dan. Wanting more information, he urged Pop to continue, "No please, it's alright. Please go on."

Pop sighed, "Hell, boy, your dad's not even cold in the grave. I shouldn't be talking about him like this."

Dan looked directly at Pop. "I appreciate your concern Pop, I really do, but it wasn't easy being Beau Kinsey's son. For the first time in my life I'm taking a hard look at things. After just a few minutes with you, it's obvious that you had a different relationship with my father than the rest of the folks in this basketball crazy town. For my own healing, sir, I could use your perspective on my father."

Two deeply furrowed lines appeared between the old man's sagging eyebrows. He wrung his hands and spoke softly, so softly that Dan could barely hear him. "I can't imagine what it must have been like for you kids. I should have done more."

"My father was not what he seemed. He fooled a lot of people."

Pop fidgeted with the large gold watch on his arm and stared down at the floor.

"He fooled me for a while. Always coming over and asking my advice on things. But I knew things weren't right over there. I could hear him shouting at you kids late at night, and all the comings and goings couldn't have been good for you youngsters. Thank God for that grandma of yours."

"She was wonderful," replied Dan.

Pop nodded. "How ya fixed on time? There's more I'd like to tell you, if you're sure you want to hear it."

"I'll make time and yes, I want to hear everything."

Pop took a deep breath and leaned up in his chair. "One day I was out in the garage working on that old mower of mine. It was a warm fall day, and I was gettin' plenty hot, so I opened the window next to your drive to try and catch a west wind. Next thing I knew, I could hear your dad's car coming down your drive in the middle of the afternoon. The car skidded to a stop, and I heard the passenger door fly open. Your father was shouting. It was the mean, vicious scream of a damned drunk. I was concerned, so I hid in the shadows of my garage and watched out the side window. You were holding your side as you got out of the car. Your little face was full of pain. Your father was screaming and yelling at you." Pop's angry eyes narrowed. "I knew that bastard had punched you."

"I'll never forget that day," Dan lamented.

Pop paused in an effort to control his growing angst. "I was madder than a hornet. I dropped my wrench and headed for the side door of the garage, but by the time I got there, your father was gone." He sighed and shook his head. "It was probably for the best. I'm not sure what I would have done if I'd have gotten hold of him that day."

Eyes wide, Dan searched the face of the hard man. "I never knew all this Pop. Th-thanks for caring."

The old man smiled, "Sit tight, my boy, I'm not finished, there's more. I wasn't through with your father—not by a long shot! A few days later, I fell asleep in my recliner watching Johnny Carson, just like usual," he laughed nervously. "Then I heard those damned mufflers again. He was revving his engine clear down by Esther Howard's house. I looked at my watch, and it was nearly two o'clock in the morning. It made me madder 'en' hell! It was the last straw. Your father was about to get his comeuppance.

Dan's eyes widened.

"I hurried out back and hid in the shadows next to your back porch. As usual, your dad came racing down your drive and slammed on the brakes. I stood still and watched him crawl out of the car. Even from where I was standing, I could smell him, he was reeking of alcohol. He steadied himself and headed for the house. I waited 'til just the right moment and then I quietly moved out from the shadows." The tough union mogul chuckled, "Boy, was he surprised to see me."

"I'll bet."

I grabbed him by the collar of that fancy golf shirt of his and slammed him up against the car. He shouted, 'Are you crazy Pop? What the hell's going on?' He was shocked and I didn't want to wake you kids and your grandma so I drug him over to my place. And I gotta say, he was plenty strong. I had a hell of a time getting him in this house. He fought like a pit bull. Damned near ripped my front door off. It's hard to believe nobody heard us, but I don't think anyone did."

"Never heard a thing," Dan volunteered.

He just kept saying, 'What the hell ya doin', Pop?' What the hell ya doin'?' I drug him in here and threw him down right there where you're sitting."

Dan looked down at the couch attempting to visualize the dramatic confrontation.

"That's when he started to get indignant. All of a sudden he jumped up and said he was going to kick my ass. Sorry, son, but that was the wrong thing to say to this old boy from Brooklyn. I reared up and punched him hard in the gut." The big man pointed to the center of his still flat stomach. "Right about here. Your old man folded like an accordion and fell back in the chair. I was ready to kill him and I think he knew it. That punch scared him."

"Can't blame him."

"I told him I knew what he did to you that day. His face turned bright red. I crammed my fist up next to his jaw and stuck my chin two inches from his face. I told him if he ever laid a hand on you again, I'd kill him."

Dan was completely mesmerized by the eye-opening proclamations coming from his former neighbor. Never in his wildest dreams would he have ever envisioned Pop Miller taking up for him. It was shocking.

Pop went on, "Your dad just sat there holding his gut. After a minute or so, he looked over at me and gave me a funny grin. Then he said, 'That damned kid just reminds me too much of myself,' and shook his head."

Dan was stunned. He sat in shocked silence at the astonishing revelation. Pop's comments had reinforced everything he had been discovering over the past several days. The only man who could verify his fears, the only person who truly knew, had just spoken from the grave through his former neighbor. Pop had just confirmed to him his deepest fears, that he was, in fact, very much a reflection of his father. He was overcome with shame. He sat in stunned silence, unable to express himself.

Pop looked puzzled, "Does that surprise you,

Danny?"

Dan's head turned quickly toward Pop, "Kinda."

"It surprised me too. I always thought Mark was more like your father. Sometimes I'd catch a glimpse of him walking past my window when you were kids and he looked just like your pa. He was a hell of an athlete too, just like your dad."

"Yes, yes, they were both good athletes," Dan replied so softly it was almost a whisper.

"Sorry if I upset you, son, I was just . . ."

Dan interrupted, struggling to regain his composure, "Oh no, no, Pop, It's okay, I needed to hear that."

The old man struggled up from his chair, stepped over and laid his huge hand on Dan's shoulder. "That's enough talkin'. Why don't we load up that old pickup of mine and take a trip out to my storage locker."

Dan smiled, taking one last opportunity to examine the sympathetic face of his old neighbor before they left the house. "Yes, yes, Pop, why don't we do that."

"My old truck's on 'E'. We'll have to stop and get some gas on the way."

Dan nodded.

Pop took a couple of short steps to steady himself and then walked with shoulders slumped toward the front door.

"It's been great talkin' to you, Dan."

"Great talking to you too, Pop." The corner or Dan's mouth curled up in a weak smile.

The old man waved his arm toward the front door, commanding Dan to leave before him. A few seconds later, the wobbly, old storm door clicked shut behind them as the two men exited the house.

"You must get a lot of snow out there in Denver." Pop implored while wedging his way between the truck and all sorts of boxes and junk against the wall in the garage.

"Well, not as much as you think. We really have pretty mild winters, you know."

Dan had an easier time getting to the truck. He just had to climb over an old push mower and a couple of rusty rakes on his way to the passenger side.

"No, I didn't know that. Isn't that something?"

"It's a high desert climate. We get some big snows, usually in April, but they don't last too long."

Dan got the rusty door open just far enough to slide in the front seat. Pop somehow squeezed in the driver's side and after fumbling around with his huge assortment of keys, he found the right one and stuck it in the ignition.

The old engine belched and stalled out several times before finally grinding to a start. Pop revved the engine a few times to keep it running, filling the small garage with blue smoke. The smell of burnt oil filled Dan's nostrils. Not wanting the ancient vehicle to die out, Pop popped it into gear and jerked out of the garage. As he backed the old Ford truck down the bumpy drive toward Wesley Avenue, Pop was laughing and gesturing with his hands and saying something to Dan. Dan nodded politely, but was not able to hear a word over the ever increasing engine and muffler noises.

Once on Wesley Avenue, he crammed it into first gear and gave it the gas. It jerked down the road, treating the neighbors to an ear-shattering backfire along the way.

Inside the cab, Pop gently patted the dashboard with his giant paw, "She's a beaut, ain't she?"

"She certainly is Pop, she certainly is."

Chapter 35

"Seems weird leaving at night, but the only direct flight leaves at nine o'clock," Ann said.

"Oh well, the girls will enjoy looking at all the lights from the plane," Dan replied.

"Dan, can you please check things out one last time? You know how we're always forgetting something." She smiled warmly at her husband.

"Will do." He felt a moist kiss on his cheek.

"The girls and I will wait in the car."

Dan stood and watched as Ann and the girls left the house. He realized that he was alone with his thoughts in his childhood home for the first time all week. No sounds, no distractions, everything felt different, more intense. Trying to fend off this deepening mood, he quickly scanned the living room for forgotten items and then headed for the back of the house for a final look around.

His first stop was the den where he had removed his dad's memorabilia just a few hours earlier. As much as he tried, he couldn't stop reliving the memories. He recalled the night of the missing track ribbons and the explosive episode between his father and sister Maggie. He could still see the horror in Maggie's eyes when he and Mark rushed to her defense that evening. He shuddered at the thought of that event and the devastating effect it had on her. With a sense of sadness engulfing him, he quickly searched the room, turned off the light and headed for the bedrooms.

He felt scant emotion when he entered his dad's bedroom. But when he headed for his old bedroom, he felt much different. The buzzing tensions that he had often felt as a boy began to once again pulsate through him. The traumatic night when Mark told him about his father's tryst with Timmy's mom burned into his senses. Attempting to relieve his growing anxiety, he breathed deeply and then slowly exhaled, but it didn't help much. Beginning to perspire heavily, he quickly looked around for anything his family may have left behind, clicked off the light and yanked the door shut. Badly shaken, he backed down the hall to the family room without turning around. His shoulder bumped against the doorframe as he entered the family room.

Still reeling inside, he paused in front of his father's old recliner. He could almost see his dad slumped down in the chair, grousing at the small TV about his beloved Hoosiers not getting back on "D". He surveyed the multiple cigarette burns on the arms of the chair and the surrounding carpet—all caused by a drunken father falling asleep with a cigarette still dangling between his fingers.

Just a few days earlier, Dan had been appalled when his brother Mark had sat in the foreboding chair tempting fate, as Dan saw it. Surprised by his brother's actions, he thought he would never, ever be able to sit in that chair, but now just a couple of days later, something seemed to be pushing him to do just that— sit in that chair.

His own journey into self-discovery had given him a new understanding of his father. He thought about what it must have been like to be raised by an unforgiving and terribly demanding father, while at the same time being adulated and given princely status by a basketball-crazy town. The conflict inside his young father must have been overwhelming. Add to this the death of a loving wife early in his marriage and an unhealthy dependence on alcohol, and you have all the ingredients to create a troubled man.

Wanting desperately to completely forgive his father for his reprehensible behavior, Dan suddenly, as if guided by some merciful spirit, turned and stood with this back to his dad's chair. He paused for a moment, took a deep breath, and then fell backwards into the ample recliner. The soft leather pushed in around him. It felt cool and supple.

Eyes wide, he sat waiting for some painful emotional tsunami to occur, but it never happened. Instead, the soft leather became his father's arms around him, caressing him and telling him that he loved him. He felt a kinship, an acceptance of his troubled dad that he would have never believed possible just days earlier. His journey had truly gone full circle now; ending here with him alone in this old leather chair in the family room. He wished he could sit here forever absorbing the positive vibes from his father, but he knew that wasn't possible. He had a plane to catch, and Ann and the girls were waiting outside.

He savored the moment for just a bit longer and then slowly lifted out of the chair and then quickly walked over to the little drawer in the kitchen next to his Dad's old faded wall phone. He looked around in the cluttered drawer for something to write on. He smiled when he found a yellow stick' em pad and pencil. He scribbled a note on the pad, tore it free, hurried over and stuck it on the top of his dad's old recliner. It read: Maggie, Please don't sell or discard! Will make arrangements for delivery to Denver. Love, Dan

Dan heard the toot of a horn outside, Ann and the girls were getting impatient. He reached over and clicked the light off in the family room and hurried through the living room toward the front door. He pulled the door half open, paused and turned around for one last look inside his childhood home. He took a deep breath, exhaled and mumbled, "I forgive you, Dad." He locked the door, put the key under the front doormat and hurried to meet his family.

Ann and the girls were sitting in the car talking and laughing. The gaiety, which was normal fare for his upbeat family, was just what Dan needed right now. Dan hastily opened the door and slid behind the wheel to prepare for their trip to the Indianapolis Airport and their flight back to the Rocky Mountains.

Chapter 36

With the sun falling below the distant landscape, Dan took one last look at his old hometown through the rearview mirror. He could see orange sparks exploding above the giant melting pots at the old foundry on the west side. Bright lights illuminated the sky above the outdoor basketball court, where his hero Eddie had fought the bloody fight with the bigger and stronger Mose Jackson so many years ago. His heart still ached at the thought of that night and the tragic loss of his friend Eddie just a few days later. Not wanting to once again relive those painful remembrances, he looked away from the mirror and back at the road ahead.

Seconds later, he heard the unmistakable snap of a seatbelt opening and felt the armrest brush against his arm. He smiled at Ann, who no longer bound by the constraints of the seatbelt, scooted over and snuggled in next to him.

"What's this?" He grinned broadly and laid his arm gently over her shoulder. "Haven't had this happen since oh, uh high school."

Ann nestled in against his neck. "I know, I'll bet the girls are getting a kick out of this."

"I think they're too busy talking about their boyfriends."

"I think you're right. I just want to be close to you for a minute. I think you're still hooked in a little to Maple City."

Dan sighed, "The scars run deep. It's been a tough few days and I know now that I must forgive my father."

"And have you?"

"Yes, I have Ann, completely."

"I'm so glad, Dan. You've been so preoccupied, I have been worried about you." Her arm fell across his lap.

Dan pulled her closer, gently kissing her forehead.

"Starting to feel better?" Ann said.

"A little bit, better keep it up."

They could hear giggling in the backseat. Dan looked in the mirror and saw Meghan with her hand over her mouth and trying not to laugh.

"The girls have discovered us," he whispered.

Ann kissed Dan's neck, "Better get over." She drug her hand across Dan's lap, scooted back to her seat and snapped her seatbelt.

"Thanks for getting my attention," a big smile spread across Dan's face.

"My pleasure," Ann gave him a little wink and then gently patted his knee and mouthed the words I love you.

"I love you too, Babe, and I can't wait to get you home."

"Me either."

Dan's hometown, full of so many memories, faded into the darkening night as the Kinsey family sped down the narrow country highway toward the airport and their flight back to their home in Denver.

About the Author

In his most recent novel, R B Conroy goes back to his childhood roots to write a compelling tale about the son of a Hoosier legend. His love and understanding of his beloved home state of Indiana is evident throughout this heart wrenching story of a troubled hero and his dark side. As we speak, Conroy is hard at work on his next novel.

R B Conroy's other books are available from:

Amazon.com
and
Barnes & Noble